KENSHŌ
House of Secrets

Rosemary Hamer

Copyright © 2021 Rosemary Hamer

All rights reserved.

ISBN: 9798746671233
Imprint: Independently published

DEDICATION
TO VIV

a reminder of our holiday cottage in North Berwick (2019), where and when I started thinking about this book.

Kenshō
a Japanese term from the Zen tradition meaning 'seeing one's true nature' / 'insight' / 'awakening'.

JAPANESE WORDS / TERMS

Katana-Samurai sword.
Bushidō-Japanese collective term for codes of honour and ideals of samurai.
Kintsugi-Artistic golden repair of a broken ornament.
Dōjō-Space for martial arts/meditation.
Hakama-Skirt like pants, traditional samurai clothing.
Minka-Traditional Japanese house.
Ojii-sama-Formal Japanese word for 'grandfather'.
Tatami mat/Futon-Type of flooring/rollaway mattress.
Geta sandals-Footwear like clogs and flipflops on a wooden base.
Katei-Household, family, home.
Kenshō-Insight, seeing one's true nature.
Arigatō-Thank you (informal).
Sanshō-Japanese pepper.
Sensei-Teacher.
Anussati meditation-Recollective meditative practice.
Bakti-Tibetan for 'obedient boy'.
Reikon-Shinto belief. Reikon leaves body enters purgatory, after funeral joins ancestors or returns to right wrongs or wreak vengeance as yūrei.
Yūrei-Like haunting Western ghosts.
Seiza-Correct sitting position, legs bent, knees forward.
Obon-Festival of the ancestors
Kurisamu-Christmas.
Ōsōji-'Big cleaning' of Japanese house at New Year.
Namaste-Sanskrit 'I bow to you'-greeting guests hands together at heart level.
Watashi ni ie ni yōkoso-Welcome to my house!
Arrigatō gozaimasu-Thank you (polite).
Kampai/Kanpai-Cheers!
San-Added to last name or title as sign of respect.

Gaijin- *Foreigner (negative connotation).*
Gaikokujin- *Neutral way of saying 'foreigner'.*
Chasen- *Tea whisk.*
Matcha- *Powdered green tea.*
Chashaku- *Tea scoop.*
Kendō- *Martial Art, sword fighting.*
Shinai- *Bamboo swords.*
Kacchū- *Protective armour.*
Yoroi- *Breastplate.*
Kote- *Long padded gloves.*
Ohayō gozaimasu- *Good morning (polite).*
Ryokan- *Traditional Japanese inn.*
Ikaga nasaimasuka okyaku-sama?- *Can I help you, sir?*
Hibakusha- *Survivors of the atomic bombs.*
Seppuku- *Ritual honour killing of self.*
Uchikake- *White wedding headdress.*
San-san-ku do- *Three nuptial cups of sake.*
Saiai no magomusume- *Beloved granddaughter.*

KATO FAMILY

Kato, Takeshi m.Sakura (d.1945)

◊

Kato, Riki m.Mariko
(both died 1980)

◊

Kato, Mika b.1980
(Boyfriend Jack Sylvester)

WALLANDER / BLENKINSOP FAMILY

Mr and Mrs Wallander

◊

Violet..........................Baby m.*G.Blenkinsop*
Rose
Tom
Ruby
Pearl
Teddy
Horace
Mortimer
Hubert
(all died 1902)

◊

Colonel Gerald Mortimer Blenkinsop V.C.

◊

Professor Julian Blenkinsop m.Lucy (d.1980)
m.Phoebe 1990

◊

Ptolemy   Sadilla   Kepha

KENSHŌ   House of Secrets
CHAPTER 1
Wajima, Noto Peninsula, Ishikawa, Japan, June 2000

Kato Takeshi raised the katana with both hands. His sword, the soul of bushidō, was the key to heaven and hell. The prisoner, hands tied behind his back, cowered in the kneeling position, neck extended, his whole body racked with rigors of fear as he awaited the strike of cold steel and oblivion. Takeshi leapt high in the air, slicing first left, then right as if slashing at an invisible opponent's head. But it was all illusion, a mere trick of the light. A mirage. There were no prisoners here, only an old man in his dōjo practising the skills of his forebears in an attempt to vent his guilt and shame. His Samurai ancestors would have commended him for continuing the bushidō way of loyalty and honour, but this was a time for peace and reconciliation not war.

Every bit of Takeshi's concentration was immersed in each studied movement. The sun carved sharp pinpoints of brightness through the window, piercing the polished curved blade of the sword as it reflected the light. The silence was all embracing. The last faint echoes of the singing bowls had long died away. Daily, Takeshi fought his own personal battles, not only for fitness but to find his own version of Zen. The discipline had a purity and clarity that calmed his mind. It was a cleansing allowing for forgiveness even if only momentarily.

After hours of practice Takeshi sighed deeply, removed his hakama uniform and re-dressed in his work clothes. It was time to return to the minka, the main house. Before he left his eyes alighted on the bowl; it was a perfect example of kintsugi. His fingers unconsciously traced the path of liquid gold that welded the broken and cracked pieces together. It was all that remained of his beloved wife, Sakura. All those years ago when he'd gone to her parents' home in Nagasaki, there'd been nothing left of her, his beautiful Cherry Blossom. Later it had been a miracle to find

KENSHŌ   House of Secrets

his baby son in one of the orphanages. When he'd uncovered the bowl in the ruins of Sakura's house, he'd always thought about his wife and son, in the same way. Flawless and precious but broken and damaged for ever.

There were always the 'if onlys'. If only he hadn't been called up to fight. If only he hadn't sent his wife and son to her parents. If only his son his beloved son, hadn't had to live with the physical torments of the aftermath of the bomb and die before he could see his baby daughter born. But there was no 'if onlys' for Mika, his granddaughter, the joy of his life, his treasure, his beacon for the future. Being brought up by her old fossil of a grandfather didn't seem to have done her any harm. She was an exquisite orchid about to open to the light. All Takeshi could do was look on in awe at her beauty and spirit. She was the soul of kintsugi, emerging from all that was damaged to represent a work of artistry. If only he could protect her, but how could he when he was the one encouraging her to step out into the world and a foreign one at that? What sort of place would it be? What did he himself know of the modern world? His life was centred in Wajima.

The year 2000 could hardly compare with the horrors and devastation of 1945, but what sort of welcome could a twenty year old Japanese girl expect in the West? Perhaps he'd kept Mika too close, but she meant so much to him. She was all he had left. Maybe he was just a silly old man worrying so much. Mika should live the life he'd never had the chance to experience, but it would be hard to let her go.

He was just sliding the door on the dōjō when he heard Mika's geta sandals click clacking up the path. She was humming a little tune, no doubt some foreign pop song. She sounded excited and happy and called out, 'Ojii-sama (Grandfather), is that you? Shall I serve tea?'

KENSHŌ   House of Secrets

CHAPTER 2
Michaelmas Term
Oxford, September 2000
Arrivals

A hesitant Mika Kato all but fell off the train in Oxford. This was her fairy-tale land of fantasy spires, domes and towers, almost make-believe? A place she'd only ever read about. Would there be anyone to meet her? How would she manage? Her English had been learnt at school and topped up by American TV programmes, mainly cowboy ones. 'Howdy partner' was never going to go down well in the halls of academe. Her grandfather had been so proud when she'd won the scholarship, but Oxford was now a reality not a pipedream. It was up to her to maintain the honour of the Kato ancestors and achieve great things, but nerves were already getting the better of her. Her grandfather had insisted she travel in traditional dress, however as soon as Mika passed through the barrier in Tokyo she'd made for the toilets and dispensed with the kimono in favour of a practical top and jeans.

Unusually tall for a Japanese girl, Mika studied herself in the long mirror. Not sure she liked what she saw, she set about improving her image, proceeding to apply layers of mascara to her almond shaped eyes. Buffing up her gleaming blue black bob, she completed the look by painting her lips with a generous amount of ruby red lipstick. This was what girls in Tokyo did and she'd learnt to copy them by studying the beauty magazines. All Mika wanted was to blend in and be accepted, not stand out like an Oriental misfit. Having led such a sheltered life she was totally unaware of her delicate features and exotic beauty. Takeshi, on the other hand, was only too conscious of his granddaughter's blossoming charms, making him uneasy about what might happen to his 'fragile orchid'.

For Mika, the last year had been crazy. It was as if she was on a roller-coaster. First there'd been the culture shock of travelling from Wajima to Tokyo and the university. No sooner had she

KENSHŌ   House of Secrets

settled into her first year than she'd won the scholarship to Oxford. It had been difficult enough to make friends in Tokyo, so how would she fare in England? Her fellow university students had barely acknowledged her existence, dismissing her as a naïve, shy country bumpkin ill equipped for city life.

However Takeshi was a different proposition altogether and his ambitions for Mika, his only family, knew no bounds. He had been an engineering student at Tokyo Imperial University in the '40s until war intervened, never graduating. He was a driven man determined his grandchild would have the life he and his son had been deprived of.

Once he knew Mika was going to England, Takeshi had engaged an English tutor. Each night after the tutor had left Takeshi would drill Mika on what she'd learnt, although he himself claimed a little knowledge of the language. Mika became more and more resentful. None of this was what she wanted. Would she ever be able to live her own life, or choose for herself?

Despite it all, Mika wished she were closer to her grandfather. He was a disciplined, self-contained man only expressing himself in his daily rituals in his dōjō. She knew he loved her deeply though he never said so. The people in Wajima thought him aloof and hard. Occasionally Mika would glimpse the softer side of him when he looked at her, only for such feelings to be immediately suppressed. Several times she'd attempted to bring up her parents, asking timidly, 'Ojii-sama, please tell me about mother and father.' All he'd replied was, 'They gone, Mika. Past. Future important now.' Mika felt the pain of loss as if he'd stabbed her. She longed for her mother's love, instead there was only a sense of abandonment and loneliness.

Growing up in such an austere environment was never easy, but despite the difficulties the last thing Mika wanted was to leave her home. Moving to Tokyo and the university had been wrench enough, especially being surrounded by thousands of people. All she'd ever really desired was to quietly tend her vegetable patch, buy oysters at the fish market, work in the tourist shop in Wajima

KENSHŌ House of Secrets

selling lacquerware, marry a nice local boy and have lots of smiling babies. But obviously her grandfather had far more grandiose dreams for her.

On her arrival in London, Mika hoped all the American programmes she'd sneaked out to watch at a friend's house would prepare her for what was to come. The journey had been bad enough. Mika, never having never flown before, found she was holding her breath most of the way as if she supposed that would keep the plane in the air.

Heathrow Airport in London was beyond her imaginings. A nightmare. Interpreting signs was impossible. She was always in the wrong queue. When it was her turn to face the passport officer, Mika was so frightened she couldn't speak. The man glared at her as if she were a terrorist and demanded, 'Name? Length of stay?' Mika's command of English nearly failed as she whispered, 'Pleese, student Oxford for year,' pushing across her letter from the University. The official grunted and thrust it back at her, stamping her passport reluctantly. Mika felt triumphant as if she'd passed a test. But what next? Where should she go? Perhaps if she followed the throng they would know where they were going. In the Baggage Hall she spotted her two suitcases and backpack, marked with bright orange tags, spinning past on the carousel. Grabbing them and almost overbalancing, Mika felt relief. At last something familiar. She was more in control as she gathered her belongings together and found a trolley. Wheeling it after the crowds towards the exit, the butterflies in her stomach started again. What would she do if there was no one to meet her?

But she needn't have worried. A smiling woman with a large sign saying 'Kato, Mika' stood in the front row waving. Mika let herself relax and manage a half smile. Thank goodness someone was expecting her. Mika hoped Oxford would be as welcoming.

'Hullo, I'm Brenda,' said the large exuberant lady from the British Council. 'Welcome to England. I'm your greeter. We'll soon have you settled in your hotel for the night, and on your way to Oxford tomorrow.'

KENSHŌ   House of Secrets

Before she had time to collect herself, Mika was unceremoniously deposited in a hotel room in Central London and left to her own devices feeling tearful and lost. The large lady had been kind but officious. Mika had been too fearful to ask any questions before Brenda bid her farewell, assuring Mika she would collect her the next morning. Tunnelling under a mountain of pillows, tightly fitted sheets and some sort of down comforter on the squashy bed, Mika missed her tatami mat and futon. She'd noticed few people took off their shoes before entering their rooms, yet pairs appeared amongst the discarded trays of congealed food left in the corridors. How very strange! There was so much to understand.

Later that night drunken people, back from the clubs, started hammering on doors. At first Mika looked out thinking it might be someone from the hotel, only to be confronted by a group of large, bloated and inebriated young men with enormous Occidental eyes, who on seeing her yelled, 'Come here you Oriental minx. Join the party. We'll show you a good time.' Frightened to death, Mika hurriedly shut and bolted the door propping a chair beneath the handle. She wished she were brave, but at this moment all she wanted to do was go home. Her grandfather would certainly admonish her for lack of courage, but it was as if she'd entered an alien world. The people looked so different and behaved so badly. Fighting her way back through the bedcovers, she lay down and tried to sleep, but blotting out the city noises, the wailing sirens, the blasting car horns and screaming, shouting people was not easy. Her mind was whirling with everything that had happened and what was to come. It was a long night.

The next day when Brenda came to collect her, Mika realised she'd had nothing to eat or drink since the plane. In her room there'd only been a few musty biscuits that looked inedible and a bottle of water. She'd been afraid to venture out of her room, let alone the hotel. Too embarrassed to tell this formidable English lady sprouting the beginnings of a moustache, it appeared Brenda (whose name Mika found difficult to pronounce with the 'b' and

KENSHŌ House of Secrets

the 'r' coming together) had no time for explanations or niceties. She bustled her protégé, bag and baggage into a taxi to Paddington. Buying Mika a one way ticket, she hurried the bemused girl onto the Oxford train and into a seat. Apologising for the rush she wished Mika a hasty goodbye, good luck and sped off to her next assignment.

During the journey no one spoke to Mika except the ticket collector. She sat stiffly upright hugging her rucksack like precious cargo. Brenda had carefully stacked all Mika's luggage in the rack at the far end of the carriage. Feeling anxious that someone might abscond with her luggage, Mika moved to sit closer. No sooner had she moved than an announcement was made they were pulling into Oxford. There was a tremendous scrum to get off. Delicate, insubstantial Mika was all but trampled in the stampede. Pushing and struggling to manage her two cases and rucksack Mika stumbled off the train, her luggage flying all over the platform.

Crouching down trying to collect together her belongings, Mika became aware of someone standing over her. Blinded by the sun, Mika could just make out a tall slender shadowlike like figure who spoke in a soft, tentative voice, 'Excuse me, are you Mika Kato? I'm Phoebe.' Mika sprang to her feet and bowed deeply, 'Yes I Mika, solly excuse.' and looked enquiringly at the woman.

'I'm Phoebe,' the apparition repeated. Noting Mika's mystified expression she added, 'Professor Blenkinsop's wife. Let me help you with your bags.'

'Arigatō, thank you,' Mika stammered, embarrassed not to have realised who Phoebe was. People in England were known to be informal, but it was disconcerting when people didn't introduce themselves correctly. She supposed it was something she would have to get used to. Truthfully, she knew little of the family she was going to live with for the next year. Her tutor had told her the bare minimum as if it was of little account. All he'd said was that Professor Julian Blenkinsop held a prestigious position in the Nissan Institute of Japanese Studies at St. Anthony's.

KENSHŌ House of Secrets

Mika's first impressions of Phoebe were of a dishevelled, waiflike creature towering over her. The faded long pinafore dress sprigged with tiny flowers, ugly sandals (which Mika later found out were called Birkenstocks) and ankle socks did her no favours. Phoebe's dirty blonde hair was gathered up in a half-hearted ponytail from which long strands were already making their escape. She had obviously been in a hurry to apply makeup as a quantity of peach pink lipstick had migrated to her teeth.

Phoebe herself was confronted with an overly made up delicate little waif of a girl with bobbed hair that shone a lustrous blue black in the sunlight, porcelain skin set off by dark, enigmatic, and sad almond shaped eyes and overpainted rich ruby lips. How would such a fragile, flawless creature survive the travails of student life in Oxford, let alone their boisterous household? Mika looked more like an eminently breakable china doll than a living breathing person.

Rousing herself to action, Phoebe gathered up and took charge of the luggage. Handing the rucksack to Mika, she said, 'Welcome to Oxford, Mika. The old jalopy's out front. We'll be home in Wolvercote in no time. I expect you could do with a cuppa. Not Japanese style I'm afraid, just the usual old builder's brown stuff.'

Mika was utterly confused but was too polite to ask. What was 'a cuppa and brown stuff'? Maybe it was food. She could certainly do with something to eat. Obediently she followed Phoebe towards a rusty station wagon that had seen better days. It was parked in front of the station in a skew-whiff fashion as if the driver had arrived in a hurry. Phoebe opened the back door, thrusting in the cases and said, 'Watch out for the dogs, Mika. They tend to be over friendly in the beginning,' adding as an afterthought 'do hope you like dogs.'

Two over excited dalmatians threw themselves at Mika who could barely keep on her feet. With no experience of dogs, Mika wasn't at all sure she was going to like them.

KENSHŌ   House of Secrets

'Don't worry,' Phoebe said airily, 'Dot and Dash are harmless. They'll get used to you.' But would Mika get used to them? Was this how English people behaved? It was so offhand and casual.

There was worse to come. Phoebe was a terrible driver and tore through the narrow streets of Oxford at breakneck speed, weaving her way through cyclists and oncoming traffic with several near misses. All the time she rattled on, 'Thought I would give you a whistle stop tour of the colleges on the way home.' Clinging to her seatbelt and the door handle, Mika sent up a quick prayer to the Shinto gods.

Finally and virtually intact, they arrived at the end of a driveway, screaming to a halt in clouds of dust. Phoebe announced, 'Here we are, Kenshō House.' Seeing Mika's bewilderment, she added, 'I'll explain about the name later.' Collecting the dogs and weighed down with Mika's luggage, she disappeared through the open doorway, leaving a shaking Mika standing staring at her first sight of an English house.

KENSHŌ   House of Secrets

CHAPTER 3
Introductions

The house, a sprawling mismatch of Victorian Gothic architecture interspersed with eclectic add-ons, was almost hidden amongst lush overgrown trees and bushes that enveloped the building in a strange greenish light. It appeared Phoebe had forgotten all about Mika who, unnerved by it all, didn't know whether to enter the house or not. Although the stone arched front door had been left wide open, Mika noticed there was no sign of people's shoes in the porch. The English obviously weren't that fussy about floors, or even about their guests honouring their homes.

Mika stepped into the gloom of a large foyer resplendent with paintings, skeletal animal heads and marble busts. It resembled a museum. A strange musky smell pervaded the space as if a hundred years of dust had been stockpiled in the crevices. Running her hand over the deep grain of the dark console table which took centre place in the hallway, Mika felt an electric shock run up her arm. There was a dark sinister quality about the interior as if something were lurking in the background. Without warning Mika felt herself gripped by the throat, nearly choking to death. In a second it was over. She felt she'd been given a warning. Mika shuddered and thought of her ancestors' beliefs that everything, even houses, have souls. Perhaps this house had a 'reikon' and she wasn't welcome. A terrible anxiety overwhelmed her. She would have turned and fled if Phoebe hadn't bustled back into the hall at that moment, 'Sorry Mika. I'm all over the place today. Here, give me your rucksack. I'll settle you into your room.'

As they proceeded up the main staircase, there was the sound of a lift creaking its way down to the floor below, 'That's my father-in-law,' Phoebe said 'he lives in the other part of the house and we rarely see him. We're putting you up at the top of the house on the old nursery floor. It used to be the servants' quarters. It's a bit of a climb but it'll be quieter for you and well away from the

KENSHŌ House of Secrets

children. Just beyond your bedroom there's a playroom we've converted into a study for you. There are some other rooms on the floor but they're not in use and locked up.' Three flights up, Phoebe opened a door which overlooked the back of the house. The external greenery must have been edging its way up the walls and across the windows as there was little external light. Once again, a strange murky greenish light pervaded the room giving the cream wallpaper a sallow appearance. There wasn't a vestige of colour in the whole room. Mika shivered involuntarily.

Phoebe took one look and sighed in exasperation, 'Honestly, I hadn't realised it was as bad as this. I must get Julian to do something about all that undergrowth or one day we'll find ourselves entombed.'

The bedroom was vast but sparsely furnished with a solitary wooden bedstead, dressing table and wardrobe taking up one wall. The sprigged muslin bedding had seen better days and now lay limp, lifeless and yellowing covering a wilting duvet and pillows. To give extra light an ancient Anglo poised lamp had been positioned on a wooden crate next to the bed. A second door opened on to an even larger room equipped with a rustic wooden table, rickety chairs and metal bookcases. Piles of toys were piled up in one corner of the room together with an ancient rocking horse, as if a half-hearted attempt had been made to sort things out and then abandoned.

'We want you to feel at home,' Phoebe declared, 'I know everything must feel strange to you but you'll soon acclimatise.' She hesitated, 'Sorry, you know what I mean 'adjust', 'get used to everything.'

She mumbled the last words. Mika, recognising the sentiment, smiled and nodded. This was hardly the home from home she'd envisaged. Weren't English homes meant to be warm, cosy, and inviting like the picturesque thatched cottages Mika had seen in books. These rooms felt cold and sterile as if they'd not been used

KENSHŌ   House of Secrets

in years. The coldness seemed to pervade her bones. She shivered again.

This time Phoebe noticed and said apologetically, 'I'm so sorry Mika, there's little heating on this floor. The boiler doesn't seem to permeate up here, so the radiators are always lukewarm. I'll find you a couple of electric fires. I should have thought of that. Honestly, I don't know where my head is sometimes.' Dumping the rucksack and gesturing to the two suitcases standing side by side, 'Why don't I leave you to unpack. I'll collect you in an hour and take you on a tour of the house. By the way, you have your own bathroom at the end of the corridor, so you won't have to fight it out with my children.' She laughed and ran out of the room, intent on her next task.

Mika hadn't realised there would be children, dogs and an aged parent to contend with. It was going to be a complete change from the peace and tranquillity of hers and her grandfather's katei. How would she be able to study with all these people milling around, and could she settle in these rooms? There was such a sense of foreboding about this part of the house that Mika wished she'd found out more about where she'd be living. Maybe it was just her imagination and the stress of the upheaval. Things would look better after a good night's sleep.

Later, looking round the house with Phoebe, Mika was amazed to see how enormous it was. There were rooms and rooms with various staircases ascending to goodness knows where. It was a wonder the family didn't get lost. As they approached the other wing of the house, Phoebe whispered, 'You better come in and meet the Colonel. He won't be pleased if he's not the first to be introduced. After all it's his house really. We're mere squatters.' Mika looked perplexed as Phoebe rabbited on, 'About the Colonel. In fact he's Colonel Gerald Mortimer Blenkinsop V.C., but everyone just calls him 'the Colonel'. He inherited the house just after the war when he returned to England.' She forbore to add 'after years as a Japanese prisoner of war.' All that was history

KENSHŌ   House of Secrets

now, best forgotten. Surprisingly, despite his suffering at the hands of the Japanese, the Colonel had insisted on calling his home 'Kenshō House'. Phoebe shrugged and raised an eyebrow at Mika as if to say I have no idea what 'Kenshō' means.

Delighted to be able to contribute, Mika said, 'Ken' 'see', 'shō' 'nature'. Perhaps 'see one's nature'. Strange name, why pleese?' Mika asked politely.

Phoebe shrugged, 'Who knows? Even Julian, his son, has no idea. Must be something in the old man's past. Personally, I think he's far too arrogant and pleased with himself to be self-aware. He's a mysterious old bird. We don't have a lot to do with him except on special occasions like Christmas or birthdays. An ancient old batman, Sanshō, does everything for him.'

Mika giggled, 'Sanshō' - Japanese pepper?'

'That's him alright,' Phoebe retorted, 'a spicy old pepper that's seen better days.' By now they'd ascended yet more stairs. Phoebe apologised, 'Sorry about the stairs but only the Colonel and Sanshō use the lift. We're like poor relations. Not allowed.'

Arriving at last before a heavy oak door decorated with gargoyles, Phoebe knocked quietly. The door creaked open to reveal a tall, thin, elderly man dressed in a Buddhist monk's saffron robe. The man palmed his hands and bowed from the waist, saying, 'Namaste.' Mika returned the bow and the greeting, but an exasperated Phoebe strode past ignoring the monk who was obviously the infamous 'Sanshō'. Mika gave the monk a weak smile and followed Phoebe into a large sunlit room overlooking a balcony at the front of the house. At the far end of a wood panelled room an old man in a wheelchair sat at a desk studying ancient manuscripts. At his feet lay an aging greyhound, its once dark fur smudged with grey. It raised its head with curiosity when he saw them, but soon losing interest placed his head back on his paws and closed his eyes. Most of the walls of the room were lined with

KENSHŌ   House of Secrets

glass fronted cases exhibiting Japanese militaria and artifacts. Mika immediately recognised the katana swords her grandfather used in his practice.

Phoebe stood expectantly in the middle of one of the exotic, plush Turkish carpets and waited. Mika realised Phoebe was in awe of the Colonel, however much she criticised him behind his back. Mika felt herself becoming more and more agitated as the silence continued. Eventually the old man condescended to acknowledge them. Looking up from his studies and over his glasses he said, 'And to what do I owe this signal honour, Phoebe? And who is this?' (as he noticed Mika lurking in the background).

'Colonel, this is Mika. Remember, I told you months ago Julian and I were having an exchange student from Japan to stay for a year.' Phoebe was gabbling by now. The Colonel took little notice. He beckoned Mika forward and raising his still very black bushy eyebrows said, 'Well Mika. What part of Japan do you come from?' The old man's lined face had the same yellowish hue and wrinkled appearance as the parchments he was reading. In contrast his distinctive shock of thick white hair stood up proudly like a coxcomb. Mika could barely take her eyes off it.

Bowing deeply she replied, 'Colonel Blenkinsop san. I from Wajima on Noto Peninsula.' Trying to be helpful she added 'North West Honshu Island.'

The Colonel scowled, 'Yes, I know. What on earth are you doing in Oxford?'

'Plees Colonel san, I come to study English language and literature.' Hoping to say the right thing, Mika swallowed and mumbled, 'Love read Shakespeare.'

'Don't we all,' the Colonel quipped dryly. 'I think the bard would be turning in his grave the way they produce these modern versions of him today. Anyway, I daresay you and I won't be seeing much of one another.' There was a definite undertone of warning in the sentence, which Mika had no problem interpreting. He dismissed them both with a wave of the hand and returned to his papers. Mika bowed deeply and wondered if she should walk backwards as in the presence of Royalty but thought better of it.

Once outside the door Phoebe breathed a sigh of relief, 'Well that's done,' (as if she'd ticked another item off her unending list). 'You won't have to deal with him again. Of course, he's a great scholar. Not like Julian of course, but self-taught. However, he has an impressive reputation here in Oxford. Probably because of his eccentricity I suppose. He and that so-called Buddhist monk mate of his practise something called 'anussati' meditation every day, whatever that is. Goodness knows what else they get up to.' She hurried Mika back to the other side of the house, 'The children will be home soon with Daisy, and they are nowhere near as formidable as the Colonel. Shall we have a cuppa before the rabble arrive?'

Mika was guided back down to the kitchen, still pondering why the English seemed to have this need for a 'cuppa' whatever the occasion. Taking tea at home was such a sacred ritual for Mika and her grandfather, it was hard to fathom why tea drinking here was regarded as a habitual way to fill in gaps between activities.

KENSHŌ   House of Secrets

CHAPTER 4
The rest of the household arrives

Later that afternoon a screaming hubbub of children and dogs descended on Kenshō House, making Mika feel she'd entered bedlam. The two older children, Ptolemy and Sadilla, swooped on her as if she were a new toy and Kepha, the youngest, made every attempt to climb into her lap.

Daisy, the equable young cleaner and sometime nanny, seeing Mika's discomfiture, explained, 'They don't mean any harm. They're excited to see you, someone from so far away.' Turning to the children she warned, 'Be careful, kids. Mika's probably not used to such pandemonium. Honestly, Mika, they're loving children, you'll find out for yourself. I see you're puzzled by the names. It's Phoebe's doing of course. She studies Egyptology, Greek and Hebrew and so on and so on, hence the mix of names. We generally shorten the names to suit ourselves. Feel free to do the same.'

Mika was dazed. Getting to grips with a new house was bad enough. Now she had to cope with children as well and such young ones. Japanese children were brought up to follow the rules and not run amok in public. However, after a time she began to calm down. Daisy exerted her skills of persuasion to corral both dogs and children. She got them sitting quietly at Mika's feet explaining that Mika was a guest from Japan and had to adjust to English ways. The two older children nodded their heads sagely, but four year old Kepha's mind was elsewhere. He kept hold of Mika's hand tightly as if she were all he had left to cling to in this terrifying world. Mika began to soften and, drawing the little boy close to her, allowed him to sit on the seat next to her. He laid his head on her arm and she felt the first maternal stirrings she'd ever felt in her life.

Daisy nodded and smiled. Kepha could melt the coldest of hearts. He was such a sweetheart. It was a pity his mother wasn't more

KENSHŌ House of Secrets

interested in him. Phoebe did her best, but she was often floating off into the distance thinking about her Egyptology studies and making a hash of running the house. The children were the last thing on her mind and just as they all settled Phoebe ran into the room, at her usual breakneck pace, saying, 'Come on, Daisy. The children must have their tea. Please don't inflict them on poor Mika any longer. She's barely arrived. You know we must get them fed, watered and to bed before Julian comes home. Otherwise it'll disturb his equilibrium and he'll be tetchy all night.'

Daisy made a face at Mika behind Phoebe's back as if to say look what I have to put up with. Reluctantly she collected Kepha and threw him over her shoulder, bidding the other two to follow with the two dogs, Dot and Dash, bringing up the rear.

All apologies, Phoebe practically threw herself on Mika's neck, 'I'm sorry, Mika. You must think we're barbarians. Don't judge the English by what you've seen today. The Colonel is one of a kind and there aren't many of those old codgers left, thank goodness. As for the children, they're thrilled to see someone new and foreign. Please don't tell Julian. He'll be home soon and will be eager to hear your first impressions, and I don't want them to be bad ones. Tell me we haven't upset you before you've had a chance to settle in.'

Mika smiled weakly, attempting to reassure Phoebe, who obviously held her husband in high esteem as head of the household, saying politely, 'Children delightful. I know them soon. Not used busy house. Lead quiet life with grandfather. He dedicated Samurai, meditate and keep silent sometimes for days.'

Phoebe looked aghast, 'Do you mean he doesn't speak to you?'

'He believe people talk too much, much noise. We gain nirvana through quiet. Understand self.'

KENSHŌ   House of Secrets

Eyes widening, Phoebe said, 'Goodness, I'd never cope. I have so much on my mind and so much to do. I have no time to sit and be quiet and contemplate my life.' She added tactlessly, 'Perhaps it's because your grandfather's old and done everything he needs to, but it's hardly right for a young girl with her future before her. Anyway, we'll do our best to introduce you to life whilst you are here in Oxford.' Giving Mika no chance to reply, she hurried out of the room saying, 'Now the children's tea. What have I got in the freezer? I suppose it'll have to be fish fingers again, or those horrible chicken nuggets they adore so much. I must get them fed and out of the way before Julian gets home or there'll be hell to pay.'

Once again Mika was left to her own devices. She supposed she would get used to all this coming and going and started wondering what Professor Blenkinsop would be like. He was the last piece in the puzzle. Where would he fit? As it happened, she didn't have long to wait. Sitting in one of the two front sitting rooms mulling over her impressions of the day in relative calm, she was startled by the sound of loudly squealing brakes and the blast of Beethoven's Fifth on a car horn. Peering through the casement window's grimy panes shrouded in foliage, Mika could just about make out a flashy sporty scarlet Ferrari. Surely this couldn't be Professor Blenkinsop, could it? Mika had pictured a studious elderly academic with white hair, bifocals and perhaps a neat goatee beard.

Shyly, Mika prepared herself to move towards the foyer ready to meet the master of the house if this was him, but to her dismay and without warning, the household seemed to suddenly descend into chaos. She found herself surrounded by half fed children running wild. Kepha, his face plastered with tomato sauce and without any idea what the fuss was all about plonked himself down in the middle of the furore and set up a series of bellowing wails. Phoebe and Daisy ran around madly collecting up children and dogs and herding them back through the foyer and down a narrow passageway to the kitchen, where the door was shut

KENSHŌ House of Secrets

firmly on the hullabaloo. Phoebe returned and much to Mika's bemusement proceeded to attempt to retouch her errant lipstick in one of the foyer's less dusty mirrors. Glancing down at her pinafore dress which now showed signs of smeared red sauce and congealing egg yolk, Phoebe grimaced and shrugged. Seeing Mika hesitating in the doorway, Phoebe beckoned her forward, 'Julian's arrived, as you might have guessed. Never without his usual fanfare of course. It always sets the children off.'

Mika looked expectantly towards the closed front door, but Phoebe said, 'Don't worry he'll be awhile yet. He always examines that red beast of his minutely to make sure there's no scratches. It's his pride and joy.' Grinding her teeth, she murmured practically under her breath, 'I just wish I received that much attention.'

No sooner had she finished speaking than the door was flung open. A tall figure stood on the threshold. Julian Blenkinsop liked to make an entrance. As he stepped into the foyer, Mika saw a striking man with dark hair. Touches of silver at the temples gave him a distinguished air. His deep set sharp penetrating dark eyes accentuated his aquiline features. It was as if he was constantly appraising people to see if they matched up to his expectations, however on this occasion his face broke into a charming charismatic smile as he advanced towards Mika and bowing said in perfect Japanese followed by English, 'Watashi ni ie ni yōkoso, Kato Mika san. Welcome to my house, Mika Kato.'

Mika, warmed by his attention, bowed deeply saying, 'Arigatō-gozaimasu.'

During this exchange Phoebe stood on the sidelines waiting to be noticed. Finally, Julian acknowledged her and drew her into his charmed circle, 'Oh there you are, Phoebe.' He inspected her as if she were on parade, sighing deeply, 'You seem to be covered in red liquid, and what's that yellow? Is it egg?' His face contorted in disgust, 'It might be an idea to change, don't you think? In the

KENSHŌ House of Secrets

meantime, I'll entertain our guest. Perhaps (looking enquiringly at Mika) she might like a little sweet sherry and get used to our more depraved English ways when it comes to alcohol consumption.'

A flustered, tearful Phoebe scuttled off up the main staircase, whilst the urbane Julian escorted Mika into his panelled study. 'I'm sorry my dear, we don't have any sake or beer at the moment, would you like to try this Oloroso?' and poured Mika a thimbleful.

Mika was hesitant and would have liked to decline, but such was the force of Julian's personality it seemed impossible to refuse him. 'Arigatō gozaimasu, Professor san,' she mumbled.

Julian raised his glass of whiskey to her and said, 'Kampai. Good Health. The next thing we must do,' he said as if to himself, 'is to get you settled at the University and find you a mentor, a confidante of your own age.' He was all business now. Oblivious to her presence, he placed his drink on the side table and sat back in one of his formidable leather chairs, fingers tented whilst he thoughtfully contemplated Mika's future.

Trying not to disturb him and remain unobtrusive, Mika continued to perch on one of the leather stools and sip the amber liquid she'd been given. It tasted like medicine, but she could hardly spit it out in front of the Professor. She was very much afraid she might be sick due to her empty stomach. It wouldn't stop rumbling, and Mika began to wonder if they ever ate in England. Since she'd arrived, she'd been offered nothing to eat. All she'd had was a cup of brown stuff purporting to be tea. Now hunger pangs were well and truly taking over, but the Professor appeared abstracted as if he were resolving some complex theory. After a time he came back to himself and announced, 'Dinner should be just about ready,' and rang an old bell pull that hung from the ceiling.

KENSHŌ House of Secrets

He kept ringing it until a frazzled Phoebe ran into the room in yet another faded flower sprigged pinafore dress. 'Will I do?' she asked Julian charily.

'At least it's clean this time,' was the reply. 'Now what about dinner. This poor girl must be starving. I hope you gave her something to eat when she arrived.'

Phoebe bit her lip, 'No, only a cup of tea. I didn't think.'

'That's the trouble my dear, you rarely think. Now is dinner ready or not, otherwise I'll have to get the car out again and take this poor girl to the pub?'

'It's ready but I'm afraid it's only cold meat and salad, with new potatoes.'

'Honestly Phoebe, I don't know what you do all day. Surely you could have come up with something better on Mika's first night. A roast at least.'

Phoebe practically grovelled, '... it's the children... a handful tonight.'

'Isn't that what you've got Daisy for. I don't know. Anyway, Mika my dear, let's avail ourselves of what poor fare my aberrant wife has deigned to serve up.' He took Mika's arm and pushed past Phoebe, who was left licking her wounds. Mika was dumbfounded. She would never dream of talking to her grandfather like that, or even anyone in their local village. Was this how all English people behaved? What sort of family had she joined? Although not able to pick up every nuance of the language, she could read faces, body gestures and behaviour well enough. There was something wrong with this family and this house. Having studied psychology at school, she wondered if this was what her teacher might call a 'dysfunctional' family?

CHAPTER 5
Homelife at Kenshō House

Breakfast was sacrosanct for Professor Julian Blenkinsop - a ritual of orange juice, coddled eggs, wholemeal toast and black coffee accompanied by the morning newspaper and his mail - an inviolable ritual not to be shared with three obstreperous children, dogs or his wife. Every day Phoebe would preside over the scrum in the kitchen, whilst Julian sat in splendid isolation in the ornate dining room. On the first morning Mika didn't know where she belonged, but it appeared that she was expected to join the razzmatazz in the kitchen. Daisy arrived early and helped get the children up, washed and dressed. After that Phoebe divided her time between catering for Julian's every whim and the demands of the children. This was never a healthy compromise as an over-exercised and absent minded Phoebe generally forgot something or someone, so complaints were rife in both the kitchen and the dining room.

Whilst she was pouring her husband yet another of his cherished coffees, Julian remarked from behind the Telegraph, 'Phoebe, I was thinking of Primrose Houndsworth-Gore, what do you think?'

A bemused Phoebe nearly dropped the ancient silver coffee pot, 'Who, what? Sorry Julian, I've no idea what you're talking about.'

'No need to be snappy, my dear. I was thinking of Mika and how she'd need some sort of companion/confidante to steer her through her first few months here.'

Flustered, Phoebe replied, 'Sorry Julian, not sure I know Primrose. Has she just started at Oxford?'

'Of course you know her, old thing. Do you remember the garden party for the dons last summer? She was with her grandfather, Lord Houndsworth, wearing if I remember rightly a very fetching

KENSHŌ House of Secrets

white sundress with black stripes and a large cartwheel hat that wouldn't have looked out of place at Ascot. You remarked on it at the time.'

'Yes, I remember now. I thought her somewhat overdressed for the occasion.'

'That's just because you have no regard for clothes, my poor love.'

Phoebe was not thrilled to be addressed as 'my poor love' and said tartly, 'I hardly think that snooty Primrose will prove to be the best of companions for Mika. She's far too up herself.'

Julian, unused to hearing his wife express herself so vehemently, put down his paper and asked mildly, 'Have I upset you, my dear? You don't seem to be your amiable self today. Anyway, I'll ask Primrose. She's reading English too and I think at Balliol. Next on the agenda is a bicycle. Do you know if Mika rides?'

Completely beaten down by everything that was going on, Phoebe threw her hands up in despair, 'How would I know? I've barely had a minute to have a proper conversation with Mika let alone find out if she's a cyclist.'

A frowning Julian reiterated, 'What's got into you today, Phoebe? You've lost the plot. Perhaps you need a holiday?'

Grateful, a relieved Phoebe leapt at the idea, 'I'd love that. Where shall we go?'

'I didn't mean now, my dear. The Michaelmas term is just beginning. I was thinking about next summer.' Phoebe's face dropped. Her shoulders sagged as she started back to the kitchen.

Uncharacteristically alert to his wife's disappointment, Julian shouted after her, 'Why don't you give yourself a treat. A day in London at the shops or the Egyptian section at the British

KENSHŌ House of Secrets

Museum or the Petrie. I'm sure Daisy can manage the kids for a day.'

Returning to a kitchen overrun with heat, noise and chatter, Phoebe mumbled a stream of expletives under her breath. Julian had a bad habit of handling her as if she were a recalcitrant child, one you could palm off with a lolly or a little present to keep happy. Was this due to the age gap? In their early days together, when she'd been besotted with him, twenty years or so had been nothing but now Julian in his fifties appeared to be going through a middle age crisis what with his scarlet sports car and his obsession with the gym. Maybe the age gap was more evident now.

Attempting to distract herself and focus on other things, Phoebe turned to Mika who was stoically working her way through a dish of steaming lumpy porridge swimming in milk and syrup. 'Mika my dear, please don't eat that if you don't like it. I'm sure you must find it stodgy. I can make you some eggs. What would you eat at home?' Longingly Mika thought of the rice and miso soup she would have had, followed maybe by some spinach and egg. All so light and nutritious, not like this type of concrete mush, but she said politely, 'Arigatō, must try English way when here.'

Daisy looked across at Mika pityingly as she absentmindedly wiped Kepha's overfull mouth. The poor girl thrust into this crazy household when her home was so far away. The Prof, Daisy could never bring herself to call Julian by his first name, meant well of course giving Mika this opportunity. He could never do wrong in her eyes but obviously he hadn't thought through the practicalities. Nobody in Kenshō House would have time to help Mika. There was so much for the girl to learn. Daisy's compassion was stirred and she determined to become Mika's protector and look after her; it was the least she could do. Of course, there might be some unintentional payback. No doubt Julian would be grateful. He might even show her some attention, which perhaps in the long run develop into something physical. Daisy knew if

KENSHŌ House of Secrets

Phoebe wasn't around Julian would be hers. Fond though she was of Phoebe, in Daisy's estimation, Phoebe was not the right match for her beloved Julian. He was the main reason Daisy stayed, him and the children of course. It certainly wasn't for the embarrassingly low wages. There were no perks in this job except Julian.

By now Julian was shouting from the dining room, 'Phoebe, please tell Mika to be ready. I'm off to college in another ten minutes. I need to settle her in with Primrose if I can contact her. It's bound to be busy as it's Freshers' Week, but I want Mika to experience everything to do with the University.' Phoebe hastily attempted to explain to a dazed Mika what Freshers' Week was and packed her off to her room to collect what she needed for the day.
Packing the children's sandwiches, Daisy said, 'Look Phoebe, I can find time to take Mika round Oxford if that helps.'

'That would be wonderful, Daisy, I'd be grateful. I've so much on today. There's an OU programme on Egyptian antiquities I'd like to watch this afternoon. Talk to Julian, I don't know what he's planned for her.'

A smug Daisy practically danced into the dining room to offer her assistance to Julian, who knitted his brows and glowered at being disturbed, 'I don't know…'er…Daisy. I'll have to see. Thank you for the offer though. I'll let you know later when I've had the chance to meet a possible companion for Mika.' He hesitated, 'On second thoughts though, perhaps you'd be willing to come and collect Mika from college today and bring her home. I don't know when I'll be back tonight,' he smiled winningly at her, looking deeply into her eyes. Daisy melted, as if she were a fondant filled soft centre, willing to agree to anything.

'That's settled then. Thank you. I'm in your debt, my dear.' Julian let loose the full force of his charm. Daisy, almost fainting, clung to the back of one of the dining chairs.

CHAPTER 6
The university

Driving with Julian into the heart of the colleges, Mika was overcome with the mellow golden beauty of the buildings and the architecture. Although Phoebe had driven her through the centre of Oxford when she'd arrived, Phoebe's lack of driving skills had frightened Mika so much she'd spent most of the journey with her eyes shut. It was different in Julian's red Ferrari. Despite the powerful motor straining at the leash, Julian liked to drive at a slow pace. Needing to be star of the show and attract attention, he took his time. Passers-by turned their heads to gawk at both him and his beautiful car. Julian, loving the interest, raised a desultory hand and flashed a magnetic smile, particularly at some of the beautiful young girls.

Mika had no idea where they were going. Julian had said something about Balliol. When she'd tried to ask what that was, he'd muttered there were a number of colleges belonging to Oxford University at different places with different names. 'You'll soon get the hang of it. It'll all become clear in time. I need to find Primrose Houndsworth-Gore as soon as.' Mika sat back and awaited her fate. Who was this person he was looking for, and what did she have to do with Mika?

Julian parked the car haphazardly. He and his wife seemed to have that in common. Julian enquired at the Porter's Lodge for Primrose and was told she was in her room. Walking across the quadrangle Mika was enchanted with the building. It was like a series of fairy palaces with turrets and towers. They climbed the narrow steep stairs to Primrose's room, whilst Julian explained this was one of the oldest colleges. He knocked sharply on a door and a slender willowy blonde answered. She seemed sleepy; eyes half closed. Later Mika realised this was her style. Primrose drawled, 'My goodness Prof, to what do I owe the honour? Please come in. Sorry about the mess. I've only just arrived. The place is full of boxes.'

KENSHŌ   House of Secrets

Julian had the grace to look discomfited, 'I do apologise about disturbing you. I need a massive favour.'

'Whatever I can do, Prof. Name it.'

'This is Mika Kato from Japan. She's here on a special scholarship for a year to read English Language and Literature.' He paused and, unleashing the full force of his mesmerising personality, added, 'I wondered, as you are on that course too, if you would be inordinately helpful and take Mika under your so enchanting wing. You know the drill. Show her round and accompany her to tutorials and lectures until she finds her feet. I realise this is an imposition but it's a personal kindness to me, and one I'll be eager to return in due course.'

Primrose's face said it all, however she maintained her composure. There was a distinct silence whilst she weighed up the pros and cons. Having Prof Blenkinsop on side might not be such a bad thing. After all, she hadn't come to Oxford to work but to husband hunt. It would be a pain to be burdened with this beautiful, delicate Japanese girl, a weight round her neck and definite competition. However, on balance it might have its advantages. The Prof would certainly owe her and he might just come in handy when or if she failed any of her courses. She might as well do it and then dump the girl at the earliest possibility. 'Of course, I'll do it, Prof. Shall we start tomorrow? I have the Freshers' programme for the week. If you drop Mika off here first thing tomorrow that will be fine.'

'Good of you, Primrose, good of you,' Julian blurted out, too taken with Primrose's willowy legs that went on forever, rather than Mika's welfare. 'I'll take her back with me now to the Institute and be back in the morning. I'm exceedingly grateful.' He bundled Mika out without introducing her or letting her utter a word. Mika felt like an unwanted package to be dropped off at the earliest convenience.

KENSHŌ House of Secrets

On the way to the Nissan Institute, Julian pointed out different colleges and landmarks. He said, 'Balliol, where Primrose is studying is central for lectures and the Bodleian Library. You should be able to walk everywhere but we could rent you a bicycle, what do you think?'

Mika shook her head, 'I not ride. Walk everywhere, no problem. But how return Kenshō House?'

'Don't worry about that for now. Daisy will come and pick you up today. After that we'll sort out lifts or buses for you.

No sooner had they pulled into the Institute car park than a blonde tearstained girl came running up and started banging on Julian's door. Mika heard Julian curse under his breath. In a second he'd pasted on one of his more dazzling smiles as he opened the door and greeted the distraught girl, 'Rhianna, my dear, whatever is the matter? Surely nothing can be this bad.' As soon as he made to get out of the car, Rhianna grabbed his sleeve with a tenacious grip, 'Julian, Julian darling, what am I to do? I'm in a mess. I need help.'

Only too aware of Mika's presence, Julian abruptly disengaged himself from the girl's grip, smoothing down the creases in his Armani jacket, 'Now my dear, you can see I have a guest with me. Can we talk about this problem of yours later? I need to show Mika around.'

Rhianna burst into floods of tears, 'There's no time Professor, there's no time.'

'There's all the time in the world,' Julian said forcefully as he handed the weeping girl a pristine white handkerchief. 'Come to my room at two. We'll discuss your concerns then.' Turning, he dismissed the sobbing Rhianna and beat a hasty retreat. Mika, loath to leave the distraught girl, followed reluctantly. By now Julian was practically at reception and Mika had to run to catch

KENSHŌ House of Secrets

up with him. Before he entered the building she put her hand on his arm and speaking softly said, 'Professor san. I wait. You help girl plees.'

Julian shook his head, 'Don't worry your little head, Mika. Rhianna's life is always in chaos. Who knows what it is this time, an essay she hasn't finished on time, an aberrant boyfriend? I can barely keep up. The first years are all the same, missing their families, the comforts of home and looking for a father figure to latch on to.' He sighed impatiently, 'Let's go to my office. My secretary will find you some tea whilst I go over the day's mail.' Mika acquiesced but wondered why the poor girl had addressed the Professor by his first name and called him 'darling'? Mika would never have dreamed of being so familiar or calling her sensei by his first name. Mika sat quietly for the next hour as the Professor rifled through his post. She observed how sharp he was when he spoke to Janice, his secretary. Perhaps he had something on his mind. Of course, he was an important man, a person of status, head of his department.

After a few hours Julian remembered Mika and exerting himself took her round the building, introducing her to his colleagues and showing her the Bodleian Japanese Library. Everyone was friendly and welcoming but many of the people flinched at the Professor's superior manner as he introduced them as his 'staff' rather than his 'colleagues'. Obviously, the Professor was a person to be revered rather than befriended. This behaviour, of course, would be the norm for a person of status in Japan. Yet Mika was disconcerted, did the English behave like this as well? As the day wore on and lunch was served, the Professor became more irascible. By two o'clock he was markedly waspish, shouting to Janice, 'Ring Daisy for me. Ask her to come and collect Mika.' Addressing Mika, he said, 'I'm sorry, my dear, can you wait in the outer office with Janice? Daisy will be here shortly to take you home.' Banging his door loudly, he strode back into his room.

KENSHŌ House of Secrets

Janice raised her eyebrows and offered Mika a magazine. Mika politely accepted and, as she leafed through the celebrity laden pages, the outer door flew open and Rhianna stood on the threshold. Her eyes were red and blotchy, her whole demeanour forlorn and wretched as she drooped over Janice's desk and whispered, 'Is he in?'

Janice nodded and buzzed through, 'Rhianna's here, Prof.'

The girl barely acknowledged Mika but sped straight to Julian's door, her hands shaking as she attempted to turn the handle. Once she'd finally managed to open it, Mika caught a brief glimpse of Julian standing the other side of his desk with a face like thunder. The door was swiftly shut. Within seconds there was the sound of raised voices and sobbing, then all went silent. Janice and Mika looked at one another but neither said anything. As the silence continued the outer door to Janice's room opened. A smiling Daisy put her head in and said, 'Ready to go, Mika? I'm parked in someone's space, so we better put a move on.' Mika wasn't sure she was ready to go. By now she was agog to know what was going on in the Professor's room but, as her grandfather would have said, salacious curiosity was not something to be proud of, so she meekly followed Daisy down the corridor.

Daisy was jubilant, laughing, joking and talking non-stop about Julian. 'How's the Prof today? Did he mention me? He's such a wonderful man. He gave me money this morning for our expenses. We can spoil ourselves on the way home. Shall we stop for a cream tea? It's unlike him to be so generous. Perhaps that's a good sign, do you think? Maybe he's finally 'seeing' me at last. Anyway, we can stuff ourselves like pigs.' Mika had trouble following this frenetic conversation. Something about money from the Professor and maybe Daisy's hopes and expectations, but then what about 'pigs'? Did that mean they were going to eat 'pork' – surely not with cream? Not only the language but the English themselves were a complete mystery to her. Would she ever understand them or their ways?

CHAPTER 7
Settling in

The first nights at Kenshō House were scary. Mika felt alone and deserted on the third floor. It was as if ghosts of children past flitted across her bedroom from the playroom beyond. She must be dreaming. On the second or third night she was woken by a bright light shining directly onto her face. Terrified, Mika jumped out of bed and peered through the windows only to see the Professor's car arriving home. The strong halogen headlights reflected into her room. Why was he coming home at three o'clock in the morning? It was even stranger that his car lights had penetrated the dark greenery that shrouded her windows. Of course, she realised she hadn't bothered to close the thin curtains that Phoebe had put up at the last minute.

Now wide awake, Mika put on the light and decided to read. 'Oxford and its Colleges' should help put her to sleep. It was then she heard a distinct slithering noise from the playroom. Maybe the Blenkinsop children had sneaked up from their floor and were playing some sort of trick on her. Irritated and cross, Mika jumped out of bed and threw open the playroom door. There was no one there. With the light from her room she could just about make out the various heaps of ancient toys, games and an old rocking horse. It was the rocking horse making the noise, swaying gently back and fore on its rockers, white mane softly flowing in rhythm. As if aware of Mika's intrusion, it stopped, one blue beady glass eye staring straight at her.

Mika shivered as she felt a blast of cold air run through her. Could the children have set the horse rocking? Yet there was no entry to this room except through hers. Ghosts? Never. Her grandfather would not have sanctioned a thought like that. In the morning she must ask Phoebe about the likelihood of draughts up here. Tentatively Mika moved forward and put her hand on the old steed. It was still. Despite pushing against it there was no movement. Looking closer Mika could see the springs were well

KENSHŌ   House of Secrets

and truly rusted. Shivering as if someone had walked over her grave, Mika shut the door firmly and went back to bed. A restless night left her dreaming of hordes of wild white horses with flying manes.

The next morning at breakfast as Phoebe flitted in and out of the dining room seeing to Julian's needs, Mika asked, 'Daisy, you long time here?'

Daisy nodded as she tried to aeroplane porridge into Kepha's unwilling mouth, 'Since the kids were born, why do you ask?'

Mika told her what had occurred the night before. Daisy frowned, 'Seems odd. Never heard tell of ghosts in the old house. I know the kids were in bed. I put them there myself early in the evening. Maybe the dogs – but they usually are only too keen to bed down by the Aga in the kitchen. They rarely wander around in the night once they're fed. It could have been the wind of course. This old place is draughty. None of the windows fit.'

Mika nodded, quick to concur, 'Yes, understand,' but was not convinced. She could still remember the upsetting experience she'd had when she arrived and ran her hand over the hall table. There was something sinister about the house. Never having thought that inanimate objects had a life of their own, Mika began to wonder if old houses could harbour malevolent spirits. She was busy rejecting this idea when she realised the eldest Blenkinsop child, Ptolemy, was staring at her as if he could read her thoughts. Mika smiled and he immediately bent his head over his boiled egg. Wishing she knew how to communicate with children, Mika asked, 'School, you like?' and then stuttered over his name 'Ptolemy' to shrieks of laughter from the two younger children.

Daisy giggled, 'Don't worry Mika, everyone finds his name difficult. We call him 'Tolly.' Addressing the child directly she said, 'Answer Mika. Where are your manners?'

KENSHŌ House of Secrets

Sullenly, Tolly mumbled, 'S'pose, it's boring most of the time. I like finding things out though 'specially secrets.'

'He's a clever boy,' Daisy said fondly, patting his blonde curls, 'much too bright for his class. He's got his father's brains.'

Tolly squirmed and tried to escape Daisy's stroking hand, 'Not clever. I only came second in my class last term.'

'See what I mean,' chortled Daisy, 'intelligent and humble with it. Crumbs, I would have given anything to come second in my class. I was bottom in everything,' adding ruefully, 'not that it matters now does it, kids?'

The two youngest looked up at her adoringly, 'We love you, Daisy.'

'That's all I need even if my darling Tolly hasn't time for his old Daisy anymore.'

Grimacing and growling, Tolly got down from his chair and made for the dining room.

'Don't,' Daisy said sharply, 'on any account disturb your father at breakfast. You know the rules. If you've finished go and collect your satchel and blazer. We'll set off once the other two are ready.'

Mika could see Tolly was in a sulk but did as he was told and disappeared. Mika finished her breakfast and left to take the stairs to her room. She found Tolly sitting on the top stair with the two dogs, Dot and Dash, on either side. They looked like a set of china figurines. Tolly looked up and smiled and Mika realised what an enchanting child he was despite his moods. 'You want?' she asked tentatively, not knowing what to expect.

'Yep.' he said, 'Sorry I was rude.'

KENSHŌ House of Secrets

Mika was relieved that it wasn't anything else and smiled back, 'Is fine. I like know you if want.'

'I like,' Tolly replied, 'you wanna be my friend? Conspiratorially he beckoned her down to his level, 'Can you keep a secret. Don't tell anyone, swear.' He spat on his grimy paw and held it out. Inwardly amused, Mika realised he meant her to do the same so unenthusiastically spat on her own palm, and they clenched hands.

'Now we blood brothers, friends for life 'til we die,' Tolly announced dramatically and, taking to his heels, he hopped over the bannister and slid all the way down, shouting out, 'Sees you later, Mika.'

Mika didn't know whether to be flattered or offended. For some inexplicable reason Tolly had taken a fancy to her. She'd been selected to be his friend. It was touching to be asked to become this child's 'secret friend' when he hardly knew her. She speculated on why he'd decided on her when he must have lots of friends at school plus his family. Mika wondered what next? Were there to be more surprises in store for her at the University, and with the rather superior Primrose?

KENSHŌ   House of Secrets
CHAPTER 8
Oxford

Freshers' Week shot by in the blink of an eye. Primrose Houndsworth-Gore unenthusiastically paraded Mika around the colleges, introducing her to the clubs and activities on offer and providing her with a map of the layout. Petulantly, Primrose complained, 'I don't know why you don't join the Japanese Society, Mika. At least you would be with your own kind and chat away to your heart's content.'

'No,' Mika said obstinately, 'I come England to learn better English. That what want.'

'Please yourself,' Primrose drawled. 'Anyway you'll have to entertain yourself for the next few days. I'm busy with friends.' This became the pattern of their relationship. Primrose would show up for a few days, make indifferent efforts to show interest and then vanish. Mika didn't mind. She'd become more comfortable as the weeks moved on and was now only too happy wandering round the colleges, the library and the town centre as the shops prepared for Christmas. Once the proper lectures started, Primrose and Mika's enforced liaison continued in much the same way. Primrose would sit with Mika for a few days, then disappear off to join her posh friends or not attend college at all. Her excuses were of the same ilk, 'I had such a lovely weekend in Hampshire with the Bagley-Carstairs I couldn't bring myself to leave' or 'I just had to join the gang for a quick trip to Cannes. It might be the last bit of sun I get.'

One morning sitting in a lecture on Victorian literature, Mika was laboriously taking notes, when one of her fellow students leaned over, 'You don't have to write every single thing down, you know. Just the main points.'

'But language difficult,' Mika protested, 'not sure main points.'

KENSHŌ   House of Secrets

'Look, meet me in the library after lunch, I'll go through everything from this morning.'

'Thank you,' Mika said gratefully.

The helpful student turned out to be Jack Sylvester Jnr from Boston. 'We 'foreigners' must stick together,' he joked.

'But you perfect English. Not 'gaikokujin' like me.'

'If that means 'foreigner' the English wouldn't agree. They think we Americans are descended from gangs of criminals and ruffians who were deported to the colonies.'

Mika looked confused, 'I solly, know little American history.'

'It's just that these public school types in Oxford are snobbish, (Mika had a sudden vision of Primrose and her rich cronies) and look down their noses at us American roughnecks. As to American history, I'll fill you in when we become better acquainted,' Jack chuckled, 'see I'm doing it now. 'Better acquainted' is so formal and British. I don't know what my dear departed Mom would say.' Mika was enraptured by Jack's devil may care attitude and cheerful candour but could barely keep up with his trains of thought. He was a breath of fresh air after the supercilious Primrose and the inscrutable inhabitants of Kenshō House - a world away from the formality of her upbringing. This was someone she hoped would become her friend. Following Tolly's example, she decided she would choose her own friends and not have someone inflicted upon her.

Life began to fall into a routine for Mika. The Professor would deliver her to lectures each morning. Mika would follow this up with a trip to the Bodleian unless she had a tutorial and then onto lunch with Jack. The lunches had started with a sandwich in the park and then as the weather got colder had moved to the refectory. Both were on strict budgets and had to watch their money. Mika never mentioned Jack to anyone at Kenshō House. She decided if she and Tolly could be secret friends then so could she and Jack. As Mika's command of English improved day by day, so did her awareness of the goings on in the house and the family. The Professor would occasionally ask about Primrose but Mika would evade his questions and Julian soon lost interest. She got used to making her own way home at the end of the day on the bus. Whenever she got back to Kenshō House at teatime there was always Daisy or the children to talk to and have a meal with. Phoebe was rarely present, making only brief appearances to hastily boil up pasta or prepare a casserole for Julian's dinner.

As Mika and Jack's relationship developed, he began to say, 'Stay on tomorrow, Mika. Wait for me in the library. I've got a late tutorial. We could go for a pizza afterwards. My father has sent me some money. We could splurge for a change.' The next morning Mika would offer a carefully constructed lie to Phoebe and Daisy, who were only too accepting, assuming Mika was making her own friends. Jack, who lodged with one of the lecturers, had a motorbike and would give her a lift home. Mika loved the freedom of it and would urge him,' Go fast, Jack. Fast.' As the wind whipped through her hair Mika felt sheer joy, as if she'd been released from a cage.

'I didn't see you as such a daredevil,' Jack teased. 'Whatever would your grandfather think or my father for that matter?' Jack lived in Boston with his father, an austere controlling lawyer, who had much in common with Mika's grandfather. 'Since my mother died all my old man does is work. He had little time for me when Mom was alive and even less now,' Jack said ruefully. 'I don't know what he'd make of my wanting to become a writer. He expects me to go to law school in the States once I've graduated, then join his firm.' Jack made a face, 'I'm hardly my father's son, certainly no chip off the old block, and he'll have to get used to it. But what about you? What will you do at the end of the year, Mika? Could you stay on and take your degree?'

KENSHŌ House of Secrets

'I don't know.' Mika had never considered the future. She'd been too busy living in the present enjoying her course and having her first boyfriend, though it was strange to call Jack 'a boyfriend'. He was such a good companion it often felt like having a girlfriend to chat to. But she could see in his eyes that he felt more for her than a friend, perhaps, although she didn't recognise it yet, she did too.

The one day the capricious Primrose showed her face at a lecture, plonking herself down next to Mika and focussing her full attention on her, 'I hear from chums you've bagged yourself a boyfriend. An American at that. You sly little thing. I think I should have kept a better eye on you. So, who is this chap? Who's his family? Do they have money?'

Mika was incensed. How dare Primrose just turn up and start questioning her. They were hardly friends. Trying to avoid the barrage of questions, Mika said coldly, 'Jack and I just friends.'

But Primrose, not deterred by Mika's icy exterior, said, 'What about Prof Julian? Does he know about this? Maybe I should keep him informed. After all, he put you in my charge. I've a duty to tell him, don't you think?'

Mika shrugged, 'Do what like, but I tell him how abandon me, go off with friends, not attend lectures.'

Primrose's eyes widened, 'My, the cat has claws. What happened to that sweet green little Japanese girl I was introduced to at the beginning of term? You've certainly grown up. I daresay Jack has had a hand in that. Well played. We'll call it even. I'll let you get on with your Asian American romance. Good luck to you. If you think some wealthy American is going to marry you and take home some slitty eyed Japanese to his apple pie mom, you've got another thing coming.' Mika was so angry she could have slapped Primrose. Trying to keep her temper under control, she thought about what her grandfather would say. He would caution self-control and calmness. Though that was easier said than done.

KENSHŌ House of Secrets

Jack, leaning across the aisle, could see by the rigidity of Mika's body and her expression there was something wrong. Glancing towards the malevolent Primrose, he whispered, 'What did she say, Mika?'

'Is nothing, stupid remark. I take no notice. I fine, no problem.'

Jack ground his teeth. He was sure that there'd been an insult involved but following Mika's example decided to keep his own counsel. Later that day he said, 'Best keep away from that Primrose and her cronies. Sit next to me from now on. We'll make sure we sit in the front at the end of a row, as no doubt those dudes wouldn't like to be called on to answer questions.' Mika for the first time in her life felt she was not alone. Her confidence was increasing all the time and she was starting to discover her own personality. It was as if she'd been underground for years and suddenly emerged into the light.

KENSHŌ   House of Secrets

CHAPTER 9
Wajima, Noto Peninsula, Ishikawa, Japan, Autumn 2000
Communications

It had been weeks since Takeshi had heard from Mika. As the days passed, he felt a growing anxiety. Even his daily bushidō practices couldn't relieve his mind. The last contact he'd had from Mika was when she'd arrived in London and that had only been a terse postcard depicting the Houses of Parliament, saying, 'Arrived UK. Love Mika.' Obviously, this was indicative of today's young people, brusque and to the point, with little regard for the person at the other end.

Takeshi knew only too well that over the years he'd kept himself aloof from other people, even Mika. He wondered was it because he was afraid to let go and show his feelings, or had he trained himself too well in keeping his emotions at a distance. After the war, he'd learnt to disengage himself from the overwhelming grief he'd felt at the loss of his wife Sakura and her family whilst searching for his baby son. The guilt of what he'd seen and done clung to him. War brutalised men, turning them into killing machines and torturers and he was certainly no exception.

How could he have ever imagined that serious moral young engineering student of 1943 would end up as one of the Japanese's most successful and feared interrogators? It had been a time in his life he wanted to block out, so immersing himself in the Samurai disciplines and ways had helped. Of course, none of the practices were demanding enough to blot out the past but the exacting self-control and restraint allowed him moments of respite.

The years he'd devoted to his sick son Riki had blunted some of the memories, and once Riki had found happiness with Mariko life had taken a turn for the better. There was even to be a child. But it was not to be. Riki had finally succumbed to the effects of

KENSHŌ   House of Secrets

the radiation, and the operations he'd endured. Shortly after, Mariko died in childbirth. When a healthy Mika was born, Takeshi had no choice but to put everything aside to concentrate on bringing up his granddaughter. Caring for a young baby had been a discipline in itself and, with that and his daily rituals, Takeshi had little time to reflect on the past. Mika grew into a beautiful child, adaptable and easy to mould. Occasionally he glimpsed the carefully concealed sparks of a rebellious spirit. He wondered now if he'd quenched the fire in her with his rigid discipline and long periods of taciturn contemplation. Now she was so far away, would sweet Mika unleash that wayward side of her? Had he truly known her or had he just allowed himself to see her as he wanted her to be? There was every reason to be concerned.

Halfway through the first term his anxiety was eased when Mika rang. She began in Japanese, 'Honourable grandfather, please to forgive my silence. So many new things to learn. Life is crazy.'

'No Japanese,' Takeshi replied. 'English, plees.'

'But Ojii-sama, you struggle with English.'

'No matter. Now you in England. That what we speak. Tell all.' Takeshi had never admitted how good his grasp of English really was. Since the war he'd done his best to forget that language. It was a reminder of horrific times.

'It take long time,' Mika said excitedly. 'I love Oxford. Like picture books. The Blenkinsops big family. Three generations live in house, parents, children, dogs, grandfather. Difficult people to understand.'

'You mean – language?' Takeshi asked.

'No. Customs different. Free, easy. Not formal. Sometime treat one another badly.'

KENSHŌ   House of Secrets

Takeshi was not pleased to hear this, wishing he'd been able to vet the family first. He'd hoped that as this was a Professor's house it would be run along traditional English lines with the formality due a high status academic.

'What about University?' he asked.

'That good,' Mika answered as if that was the last thing on her mind. 'Students and tutors friendly.'

'Your work, your work?' Takeshi asked impatiently.

'Oh, work. English improve but need study hard with literature. No understand English history or books.'

'Perhaps tutor?' Takeshi offered hesitantly.

Mika thought for a moment. Jack was proving to be the best tutor for her but she could hardly tell her grandfather that. Jack had introduced her to the books she needed to read and given her brief summaries of English and American history.

'No, OK,' Mika said. The last thing she wanted was her grandfather writing to Professor Julian and asking him to provide a tutor for her. She'd have no spare time to spend with Jack.

Takeshi winced at the 'OK', 'Hope you not learn American slang – not good, not good,' he grumbled.

Mika scowled at the other end of the phone. She would have to be careful. Being with Jack every day, her precise English had begun to drop and now she drawled the occasional Americanism.

Takeshi continued, 'Study hard. Year soon finish. Make most. Behave.'

KENSHŌ House of Secrets

Indignant, Mika said sweetly, 'Of course Ojii-sama, work hard and behave.' The thought of going back to Japan at the end of the year had begun to prey on her mind, but it was no good thinking about that now. For the present she intended to enjoy Oxford and her liberty. They finished their conversation with brief salutations. Takeshi was not satisfied and speculated whether his sweet tempered compliant Mika had changed, maybe not for the better, and Mika realising she didn't want to return to that rigorous monastic-style life in Wajima.

KENSHŌ   House of Secrets

CHAPTER 10
Concealment

Professor Julian Blenkinsop was not a happy man. His day had consisted of one problem on top of another. Now he was taking his bad temper home. His family, though not yet aware of it, were in the direct line of fire.

Phoebe received the first blast. As was her custom she was waiting for him in the foyer, dressed in a neatly pressed white cheesecloth peasant blouse, corduroy dirndl skirt and Doc Martens. Julian violently kicked open the front door and confronted by his wife spat out, 'What is this? Fancy dress. I don't know why you have to dress like somebody from the 70s! You were barely out of nappies then. Why persist in dressing as if you were part of that decade. Can't you at least make it to the 2000s. Remember, I have a position to maintain. Having my wife looking like an alternative hippy won't do, won't do at all.'

Phoebe shivered as if a cold wind had shot through her. Her shoulders dropped and she wilted. There was more to come. 'Perhaps you need to take a leaf out of Daisy's book,' Julian suggested, carrying on relentlessly, 'at least her rolled up jeans and crop tops are modern and sexy. Not that I really want you in that sort of thing either.' As a malicious afterthought he added, 'I'll get one of the Fellows' wives to take you shopping. Perhaps they'll give you some pointers, and at least help you dress for your age and my position.'

At that very moment Dot and Dash escaped the kitchen and launched themselves at him. 'Phoebe, can't you keep these dogs under control, they'll have to be put down if you can't.' Attempting to fend the dogs off, Julian spun round too quickly and turned his ankle on Kepha's wooden pull-along wagon. 'What in heaven's name is this doing here? Surely the boy's too old for this type of toy, and why has he left it in the middle of the floor? I've told you time and time again to get the children to tidy

KENSHŌ House of Secrets

up their toys after they've used them.' Tossing the toy to one side he limped his way to the kitchen shouting, 'Daisy, Daisy, where's Kepha? Get that child here this minute.'

A shocked Daisy protested, 'Prof, he's in bed. What do you want with him?'

By now Julian had worked himself into a monumental rage and though obviously suffering from the effects of the wrenched ankle managed to take the stairs two at a time. Staggering along to Kepha's room, he yanked the small boy out of bed, thrust him over his knee and began to paddle his backside. A shocked Kepha started yelling and screaming as Phoebe and Daisy raced up the stairs. 'You stupid careless child,' Julian screeched at the top of his lungs, 'don't ever leave your toys where I can fall over them, do you hear?' But Kepha didn't hear. He had no idea what was going on and was now red in the face and hysterical from howling. Daisy and Phoebe between them manhandled Julian aside, pulling Kepha upright.

'He's only four, for goodness sake,' Phoebe shrieked, 'he doesn't know what he's done wrong.' For once her maternal instincts kicked in and she pulled Kepha to her bosom, rocking him gently as he continued to whimper. Once the sobbing had eased, she wiped his blotchy face and lifted him into bed. Daisy straightened the covers, tucked the boy in and stroked his head.

'See, see what I mean.' Julian barked. 'You two are mollycoddling that little boy to death. He'll end up a Nancy boy, mark my words. My God, I need a drink after all this.' Beginning to calm down he added, 'All a chap wants when he gets home after a particularly hard day is a bit of peace and quiet, and a beautiful attentive well-dressed wife to hand him an aperitif.'

Phoebe jumped up, leaving the distraught child to Daisy and said, 'I'm sorry, Julian. Go down to your study. I'll bring you a G&T. How's your ankle?'

KENSHŌ   House of Secrets

'It'll do.' Julian said, somewhat pacified. 'Very well then, we'll say no more about it. Make sure the children clean and tidy up after themselves in future.' He vanished downstairs and Phoebe, heaving a huge sigh of relief, followed intent on maintaining the status quo. Soon a becalmed Julian sat in his study sipping his drink in splendid solitude whilst Phoebe and Daisy withdrew to the kitchen.

'I've never seen him in such a paddy before,' Daisy remarked.

Scurrying round the pantry, Phoebe muttered, 'Something's upset him badly. I expect it's college. I better find an alternative to the chops I had for his dinner. Frenziedly ferreting though the freezer, she called out, 'Wasn't there some venison steaks in here somewhere? Here they are. They'll do and perhaps smoked salmon to start and crème caramel for after. I think there's another bottle of that claret we had for his birthday in the wine rack. That'll put him in a better mood, what do you think, Daisy?'

Daisy was not inclined to discuss food. Her adored Julian had shown a side to him she didn't like. There was no doubt he was worried to death about the 'something' at college, and Phoebe chose a time like this to fuss about food. If only she could help Julian, he might start to see her differently as something other than Daisy the child minder and sometime housekeeper. His violent temper of the night had brought back unpleasant memories of her alcoholic father. Daisy and her mother could never do anything right when her Da was in one of his drunken rages. It had been a relief when he'd died of cirrhosis, though her mother had never been the same since.

The next morning after Julian had gone to college, the kids to school and Phoebe out shopping, Daisy decided to investigate for herself and find out why Julian had been so upset. Mika was around somewhere but she hardly counted. Surreptitiously Daisy made for Julian's study. Usually it was out of bounds to the rest

KENSHŌ House of Secrets

of the household, especially her and the kids, but this was an emergency.

Leaving the door ajar, Daisy began rifling through Julian's papers in one of his drawers. He always kept the top of his desk pristine, shoving all his current work out of sight. It wasn't long before she unearthed a letter from the Dean requesting Julian to call in for a meeting the following week 'in regard to an important matter that had come to his attention'. It sounded and looked serious and hardly in Julian's favour, so it wasn't too surprising he'd been in such a mood the night before. As she carefully replaced it, her eye fell on a wooden box pushed to the back.

Indulging her curiosity, Daisy eased open the box's rusty lock. It seemed to only contain a bunch of dusty papers, yet slid down one side was a photograph. Lifting it out Daisy could see it was a photo of a much younger Julian with his arm round an attractive blonde woman. Aware that Phoebe was Julian's second wife, Daisy wondered if this was wife number one. She was impatient to know more but the sound of screeching tyres on the gravel announced Phoebe's return. Only Phoebe drove like that. Replacing the photo and the box, Daisy hurried out. The last thing she wanted was to be caught prying. Convinced there was more to find out about her beloved Julian, she knew she was exactly the right person to do it.

KENSHŌ   House of Secrets

CHAPTER 11
Confidences

Tolly had become part of Mika's daily routine. When she arrived home from college he would sit at the bottom of her flight of stairs waiting for her. Usually he'd already had tea with the two younger children but would join her in the kitchen whilst she went through her ritual tea making. The only thing Mika had brought from Wajima was a set of tea making equipment. She would carefully set out the tea whisk(chasen), the powdered green tea(matcha), the tea scoop(chashaku), the tea bowl, a plate for some sweets she had bought on her way home and, of course in this instance, the electric kettle.

During her brief time in Oxford, Mika had found a shop that sold Japanese imports and purchased a tatami mat. In the months she'd been living at Kenshō House she'd taught Tolly all about the tea ceremony. Each evening they would lay out the tatami mat in the conservatory just beyond the kitchen, eat their sweets and solemnly Mika would prepare the tea and place the tea bowl in front of Tolly. He would manipulate the bowl as she'd taught him, and they would drink. He would bow and express his thanks. All this would take place whilst Daisy was bathing the two youngest, Phoebe was embroiled in one of her endless OU programmes and the dogs were banned to the garden. Mika loved this time. It was the only true link she had with home, just like making tea for her grandfather at the end of a day. Tolly was a delight and took it all very earnestly as if he'd been born to it.

'So how was your day?' Tolly would ask in his most grown up voice.

Trying not to laugh Mika would respond, 'Velly good, as usual. I learn about mystical poets.'

'What's them?' Tolly asked pretending to show interest.

KENSHŌ House of Secrets

'Browning, Wordsworth who wrote Daffodils and Blake. Poetry of mystical things.'

'Pah, poetry,' said Tolly. 'We had to learn that there Daffodil poem by heart at school. It was rubbish, a lot of fuss about them dancing in the breeze. Anyone can see flowers get blown about in the wind. Fancy putting that junk in a poem. Now mysteries I knows about. My grandfather is one of them.'

'One of what?' Mika asked, concentrating on the tea.

'Why mystics I s'pose. Him and that there Sanshō carries on odd ceremonies. I wants to know but Mum won't let me ask them.'

'Ceremonies?'

'Oh, I don't know, sitting bent over on mats. Making funny 'ooh and aah' noises and ringing a bell. 'Meditating' Mum calls it.'

'How you know what they do?' Mika asked intrigued.

'Why I sees them through my spyhole. There's lots of secret rooms and passages in this house. I might shows you sometime.'

'I like, but not spy on grandfather. Not polite.'

'I don't care. They's don't know and can't see me. Daisy says, 'What people don't know can't hurt them.'

'But it's their privacy,' Mika protested.

'They's don't need privacy.' Tolly remarked, 'They's just old men. We never sees Grandpa anyway. He's a hermit or summat, that what Mum says.'

'Recluse.' Mika contradicted. 'He retired Colonel. Must respect.'

KENSHŌ House of Secrets

'Well,' said Tolly, 'that don't matter to me. He never sees me, or the other kids. His Christmas presents are lousy. Last year he got me a wooden fat man with a big belly and said I could rub it for good luck. What good is that to play with? Then he gaves Sadilla a pink rock for her birthday, says it was some sort of precious stone. It was rubbish. I's could have got her one of them from the garden.'

'He mean well,' Mika said in a soothing voice.

'I dunno about that. I think he and that there Sanshō is up to something. Summat real bad I expect,' Tolly added in an ominous tone. 'That's why it's my job to keep an eye on 'em and protect everyone here. If you likes, I'll shows you my spyhole.'

Mika carefully took another sip of her tea, 'Arigatō Tolly, not today. Other time.'

KENSHŌ   House of Secrets

CHAPTER 12
Old mens' meditations

It was five o'clock in the morning with no likelihood of Tolly being at his spyhole. The Colonel and Sanshō were up and ready to carry out their morning rituals. Sanshō carefully lifted the Colonel on to a low specially made leather seat with a back, placed on the meditation mat. There had been arguments over the years about the Colonel's discomfort. Sanshō would try to insist the Colonel sat in a comfortable chair or even stay in his wheelchair. The Colonel was having none of it. He claimed the pain and discomfort was part of the practice, something the Anussati meditation helped him endure.

Sanshō himself, already in his late seventies, painfully lowered his lean frame to the floor and sitting cross-legged on the mat proceeded to play the water filled Tibetan singing bowls. The Colonel clasped his two hands together, bowed his head and closed his eyes. Before long, with Sanshō emitting the 'Om' sound from deep in his chest, both were totally immersed in their meditations. This process occupied the first hour of every day followed by a meagre breakfast of flatbread, one piece of fresh fruit and Oolong tea, all prepared by Sanshō in the tiny galley kitchen. The Colonel spoke little but indicated when he wanted something. Sanshō, hobbling back and fore, would do his best to provide it.

Having been together during and since the last war, they were like an old married couple. On this particular morning, the Colonel was more talkative than usual, 'Perhaps a walk today, Sanshō. What do you think? It's a fine autumn day and there may not be many more before winter.'

Sanshō nodded, 'Whatever you wish, Colonel. If we wait till after the household has departed for the day you won't be bothered by small children and dogs.'

KENSHŌ House of Secrets

'I like dogs,' the Colonel declared out of the blue. 'Look at your old greyhound, Bakti, just like his name 'an obedient boy'. He's no bother.'

'But he's ancient like us.' Sanshō remarked. 'It's those excitable dalmatians that are a nuisance. What with them and the children. I can't think why Mrs Phoebe can't control them.'

Snarling, the Colonel said, 'That woman my son married is useless and far too involved in her studies to run the house properly. In my day women knew their place. My late wife, bless her heart, when we were first stationed in Singapore before she went back to Blighty, wouldn't have dreamed of carrying on like Phoebe. She was always there to support me, rallying the wives and organising cocktail parties for the officers. It's a pity Julian ever took on this dippy creature. His first wife Lucy was a lady. What a pity she died so young.'

Sanshō, never a devotee of Mr Julian's first wife who'd been an incorrigible snob, managed a weak,…'Um.' These days the old man, as he called the Colonel, was showing early signs of senility and displaying more sentimentality than he used to, although only a few weeks ago he'd arrogantly sent Phoebe and that Japanese girl away 'with a flea in their ears'. It was odd the Colonel hadn't been more interested in Mika in view of his great admiration for Japanese artifacts. Why he'd developed such a collection was hard to fathom, considering his experiences after the fall of Singapore. However, it was never a good idea to remind the old man of that period of his life. Generally he dismissed it as 'just one of those things', becoming surly and evasive if questioned further. Sanshō was of the opinion that there was a secret surrounding that time, but having his own secrets he was in no position to delve into the Colonel's.

At eight thirty on the dot, the household broadcast their departure for the day. There was a loud blast of Julian's musical horn, the screeching of Phoebe's brakes, the barking of dogs and the yelling

KENSHŌ House of Secrets

of the various children as they exited with Daisy in her scruffy little Mini. Then peace.

'This is our chance,' Sanshō whispered in the Colonel's ear. 'Let me wrap this tartan rug round your legs and we'll be off.'

'Don't fuss,' the Colonel grumbled but acquiesced and, accompanied by a languid Bakti, they headed for the lift.

It was a confined space. Sanshō huffed and puffed as he manoeuvred the dog, the wheelchair and himself in. Descending into the foyer they made their way out by a side door into the back garden. As ever, the Colonel complained bitterly, 'Just look, Sanshō, at the state of the place. It's so overgrown you can barely see the house. I wish I were more mobile, I'd show that Julian a thing or two. He's neglected everything. Goodness knows what he finds to do at that college, always coming home in the early hours of the morning. Doubtless he has a bit of fluff on the side. Sanshō, you'll have to get out here with a scythe and cut it all back.'

'I'll do my best Colonel, but I'm not getting any younger. I haven't the energy I used to.'

'Oh nonsense,' the Colonel retorted. 'You're a mere whippersnapper compared with me. On the other hand, perhaps you're right. I'll get that silly Phoebe to engage a gardener, though she'd be better off doing it herself rather than spending her days studying Egyptian hieroglyphs.'

Sanshō sighed. At times he thought all this was getting too much for him. The Colonel, at eighty six, seemed to regard Sanshō, at seventy eight, as a mere youngster but Sanshō could feel the years catching up with him too. There were more aches and pains now when he sat on the floor cross-legged for their morning mediations.

KENSHŌ House of Secrets

After the Colonel had finished his usual harangue, they sat in silence for the next hours. The sun shone down, the birds sang and Sanshō drifted back to his time in India during the war. He quietly thanked the Buddha for the ashram that had rescued him from being a soldier. It had been a safe haven and he often wished these days that he'd stayed there. Of course, the authorities had finally caught up with him. It had been a choice of an Indian prison, which he'd had a taste of, or becoming the Colonel's driver and batman. When they'd moved to Singapore and the Japs had taken them prisoner, he'd still stayed close to the Colonel. The camps had been hellholes yet the men, despite the hardships, the beatings and the other deprivations, looked up to the Colonel. He was their leader. An example of British standards, morals and fair play. Whatever he'd done to betray them, it was Sanshō who stayed loyal. There was no one else. Sanshō had been sick and half out of his mind with dysentery at the time. Once he'd recovered, the camp was close-lipped about what had happened, and never acknowledged or spoke to the Colonel again.

As the years passed, the Colonel suffered both mentally and physically. Sanshō knew, in his heart of hearts, that every day the Colonel lived with some sort of guilt and yearned for redemption. Perhaps it was this that made Sanshō stay. Was it compassion for the man, or because he himself had nowhere else to go?

The Colonel roused himself from his nap and said roughly, 'C'mon man, let's make our way to your place for a spot of luncheon. I'm hungry.'

Sanshō lived in an old coach house at the bottom of the drive. It was a crumbling edifice, but the Colonel loved to visit because the garden was a sight to behold. Sanshō had spent decades making the Japanese style garden with its miniature temple, bridges and scaled down tinkling waterfalls. The coach house itself was a late Georgian converted cottage with a sagging roof and little to commend it. There was one large room downstairs, with a small bedroom and shower room upstairs and little in the way of

KENSHŌ House of Secrets

furniture. Sanshō and Bakti shared a pallet on the floor in the bedroom, huddling together each night for comfort, and falling asleep to the melodic strains of sitar music played on an ancient spool tape recorder.

Like Sanshō the Colonel had little interest in the house itself but, generating a surprising show of vigour, staggered from the wheelchair to a bench in the garden. He let out a great gasp of pleasure saying, 'This is what the grounds of Kenshō should look like, not that bushy scrub Julian neglects.' Like a rajah in residence, he sat and waited whilst Sanshō brought out chilled Singapore Slings and Indian delicacies in authentic tiffin boxes.

'I'll say this for you,' the Colonel said appreciatively, 'you make a spiffing lunch. Quite takes me back to Raffles. Did you ever lunch with me there before the Japs came?'

Sanshō shook his head, 'Hardly, Colonel, I was only your driver remember, not officer class. They'd never have let me in.'

'What rubbish,' the Colonel declared, 'all that colonial snobbery. It had its place I suppose but look at you and I now. We're equals.'

Sanshō smiled sardonically. There was nothing equal about their arrangement. Certainly, he lived in the coach house rent free but for all practical purposes he was a glorified servant and carer. The Colonel at times liked to call him his 'guru'. However, from Sanshō's knowledge of 'gurus', they didn't have to wash the Colonel's underpants or change his bed in the night when he had his frequent little accidents. The ashram looked more and more inviting these days. Sanshō wished he'd decided to return there years ago. It was too late now of course, far too late. He and the Colonel would have to wend their way to Nirvana together and hope they wouldn't be sharing the same accommodation for eternity.

KENSHŌ   House of Secrets

CHAPTER 13
Shopping

Phoebe had taken Julian's words about her appearance to heart, realising she should smarten herself up. Her looks had never been of particular interest to her. It was the mind that was important. However, this very morning she'd received a letter from America. Geoffrey was an old friend she'd not seen in years. Now he was a visiting Professor at a California University. In the letter he apologised for his long silence and not keeping in touch. He was about to embark on a sabbatical year in Oxford and wondered if there was a chance they could meet up and relive old times. Phoebe was flustered. What did Geoffrey want with her after all these years? They'd been close in their first year together at Oxford - well more than close - but she didn't want to think about that now. After all, it had been ten years. It was at the time Julian had begun to take an interest in her.

She studied her reflection in the bathroom mirror. As Julian pointed out on a regular basis, she was nothing to write home about. However, a different hairstyle and new clothes could make all the difference. Geoffrey's letter seemed to have provided the impetus she needed, far more than Julian's words.

Determined not to be taken under the wing of one of the Fellows' wives, Phoebe decided to invite Daisy and Mika on her shopping expedition. Mika would represent convention and sense and Daisy, well what could you say about Daisy? She had a definitive style of her own. Perhaps too 'out there' but certainly memorable. Surely between the three of them they could transform an ageing, faded hippy and harassed mother into an up-to-date sophisticated thirty year old.

Mika and Daisy were all for it. Daisy suggested, 'What about early in the week. It won't be so busy in the town centre.'

KENSHŌ   House of Secrets

Mika agreed, saying she'd only planned to go to the library and would much prefer to go shopping. This would be a chance to get to know Phoebe better, Mika thought. They'd hardly spent any time together. All Mika ever saw of Phoebe was the back of her head rushing through the house.

For Phoebe, any form of shopping was a revelation, and not a pleasant one. She hardly ever thought about herself, as there was always Julian, the children, the house and her Egyptian studies. As Mika and Daisy put their heads together, chortling like schoolgirls, Phoebe felt she ought to enter into the spirit of the thing. 'Where shall we start? How do you think I should look?'

Without a moment's hesitation, Mika said, 'Must be true to self. Elegant but comfortable.'

Daisy, always wanting to be the centre of attention, said, 'No, you must stand out, make a statement, get people to notice you. After all, you are the Professor's wife. It reflects on him. You must do Julian proud.'

Phoebe rolled her eyes; this was going to be some shopping trip. She just hoped her two companions would agree when they got to the shops.

They started in Westgate. Phoebe, to her consternation, was soon outfitted in dresses, suits, leggings, jackets, cargo pants and every imaginable outfit in-between. 'Girls, girls, stop, please stop,' Phoebe begged. 'I can't take any more. I'm gasping for a drink and a snack.' They sat down at a tiny café serving lemon drizzle cake, homemade scones and Earl Grey tea. Phoebe and Daisy chatted ten to the dozen, but Mika, finding it difficult to keep up with their swift changes of topic, studied their surroundings noticing a stylish boutique nearby. Tentatively, she broke into the conversation, 'Phoebe, shop interesting,' enthusiastically pointing to a shop across the road. 'Can we look?' It was virtually impossible to hold Daisy back when there were more clothes

KENSHŌ House of Secrets

shops to view. Dragging the exhausted Phoebe in their wake, they inspected the windows. Before Phoebe had a chance to protest, they were riffling through rails but coming up with nothing suitable. Looking at one another in despair, they heard a polite cough and a voice enquired, 'Can I help?' The owner, a soignée lady in her fifties with silver hair, looked at them expectantly.

'Our friend here needs a new wardrobe, a new look, a makeover,' Daisy piped up and thrust an embarrassed Phoebe forward. Before she had a minute to catch her breath, Phoebe was guided to a changing room. The owner proceeded to bring out ranges of outfits, assuring a red faced, perspiring Phoebe that, 'What you need is a staple wardrobe of separates you can build on. I see you're an average size. Let's start by trying you in this skirt and top and layering it with this jacket. This will co-ordinate and then I can find trousers and shoes as well.'

Three hours passed and Phoebe blasted her way through the credit card Julian had unwillingly given her that morning. Manhandling the bags between them, they were about to return to the car park when Daisy hauled the by now shattered Phoebe into a nearby hairdressers and asked, 'Any chance you can fit this lady in? She's badly in need of a haircut.' The hairdresser took one look at Phoebe's bedraggled blonde locks and winced, 'I see what you mean. I'm sure we can do something.' He plonked the unwilling Phoebe in a chair and shrouded her in a cape, with Phoebe pleading, 'Please don't cut my hair short. My husband will never approve.'

Daisy, however, stood her ground and said, 'Give her a cut to suit her face, maybe something elfin or a bob.' The hairdresser grinned, 'Leave it to me,' and turning to a squirming Phoebe said, 'You won't know yourself soon.'

An hour and a half later, a defeated Phoebe was finally allowed to see the results in the mirror. In place of her long tangled ponytail tied in a mess of rubber bands was a gleaming mass of softly curled blonde hair in a short cut that framed her face. Phoebe could barely breathe. Turning her head this way and that, it was hard to believe it was actually her. She looked so young. What would Julian think? This was scarcely the matronly look he'd had in mind when he'd wanted to smarten her up, and what about all the money she'd spent.

Daisy, generous when she wanted to be, said, 'You look fabulous, Phoebe. Julian will be proud,' though, as she said the words, she felt a sharp pang of jealousy. If only it had been her Julian had spent his money on. Phoebe was sweet but not the right wife for an important ambitious man.

They were finally on their way back to the car when Phoebe spotted an elegant dark red silk cheongsam embroidered with green dragons in a shop window, 'Look Mika, I know it's Chinese but you'd look wonderful in that.' It was if something reckless had come over Phoebe since the haircut and, without listening to Mika's objections, she pulled her into the shop, 'Try it on, do.'

Mika declared, 'Is too expensive. I not afford.'

'Don't worry, Mika, Julian can pay, it will do him good,' a truculent Phoebe announced.

The dress highlighted Mika's delicate beauty. 'You must have it,' chorused Phoebe and Daisy, 'it's made for you.'

'But the Professor, what he say?'

'Don't worry,' Phoebe said, now drunk on euphoria and totally out of control. 'I can handle him.'

Mika suddenly had a picture of Jack's face seeing her for the first time in this dress in a smart restaurant. If only they had the money for such things. When would she ever wear such a dress, but she let herself be persuaded.

KENSHŌ House of Secrets

Later that afternoon after arriving home, an out of character Phoebe said, 'Let's finish off the day with a bang and open one of Julian's prized wines and have a drink to celebrate.'

'What about the children?' Daisy said, 'It's nearly time to collect them.'

'Oh bosh, just one drink. Then we'll all go and get them in the old banger and take them out for fish and chips. They'll love that.'

The children were thrilled to have so much adult attention, especially as their mother was in such a good mood. It was after six thirty by the time they returned home. Julian's Ferrari stood in the driveway. Before they had a chance to get out of the car, Julian thundered out the front door, 'What's happening here? Where've you all been? Why aren't these children bathed and in bed?' Glaring directly at Phoebe, he demanded, 'Where's my dinner?'

Phoebe nonchalantly waved him away, 'Don't worry, we've brought you back scampi and chips. All I have to do is warm it up in the microwave.'

Julian was too flabbergasted to speak. What had happened to malleable timid little Phoebe who wouldn't normally say 'boo to a goose'? It was then he spotted the haircut, …'your hair, your hair... .'Eyes bulging and shaking his head as if he were having a convulsion, he stumbled back into the house and slammed the study door.

Phoebe, Daisy and Mika burst out laughing. The children, copying them, rolled about the floor giggling. Dot and Dash, who didn't want to be left out, leapt on top of them all.

CHAPTER 14
Julian faces the music

Julian knocked on the Dean's door. He was not feeling on the best of form. Having been subjected to Phoebe's transformation and all her spending, he was a sad and sorry shadow of his former self. What had come over his wife? Even his breakfast today hadn't been the same. Instead of waiting on him hand and foot in her usual faded flowered pinafore dress, Phoebe had sent Daisy in with the eggs, toast and coffee. She'd arrived later and sat down at the other end of the table after helping herself to a coffee from his cafetière. Dressed in a smart grey check suit she'd asked in a conciliatory tone, 'Doing anything special today, dear?' as if she'd forgotten all about his important interview with the Dean although he'd told her several times in the last few days. This was all very peculiar as he'd never known her initiate a conversation at breakfast, or in fact at any time, in all the years they'd been married. No wonder he felt off balance.

But he must pull himself together. He would need his wits about him now. There was a sharp, 'Come' from the Dean's room. Julian opened the door, went in and waited to be asked to sit down. However, the Dean, an easy going avuncular man in his sixties, carried on writing, leaving Julian standing as if he was a naughty boy reporting to the headmaster. Eventually he looked up, 'Well Julian, this is not something I ever expected to have to talk to you about - a man of your standing.' He didn't ask Julian to sit down. 'This is a formal matter I'm afraid. Of course, at this juncture it's between you and me. If I get a reasonable explanation then it can all go away, but otherwise I would have to take it to the Chancellor and the College Board.'

Julian was shaken. What was this about? Hadn't he had enough shocks at home in the last few days without being subjected to more.

KENSHŌ   House of Secrets

Taking a letter from one of the folders on his desk, the Dean said, 'Oh sit down, man. You look on the verge of collapse.' He studied the letter for a minute or two as if reminding himself of its contents, 'One of the students has made a serious complaint about you. We have to look into it, of course.' Julian's mind immediately flew to Rhianna. What had she said? He thought he'd made it clear that they should keep everything between themselves and she'd promised she would. Why had he got involved with such a highly strung girl, and a first year at that? He could certainly pick them.

The Dean carried on, 'I'm sure there's nothing in it, however the girl in question did say you were overly familiar, had a bad habit of putting your arm round her shoulders and stroking her neck when you were explaining something. I know we are in 'loco parentis' with these young people but that doesn't mean we can be intimate. As an institution we have a strict policy on sexual harassment. That means being ultra-careful with these impressionable youngsters particularly first years desperate for father substitutes.' Softening his tone, he said, 'If there was anything, I expect that's what it was. Giving a young student a few encouraging pats. Though that won't do either,' and half talking to himself murmured, 'often open to misinterpretation. To be avoided at all costs.' He looked questioningly at Julian.

Disorientated, Julian's mind kept reverting to Rhianna. Their relationship was hardly about a few 'encouraging pats'. 'Sorry Dean, I'm not sure what or who you're talking about. Can you give me more details, please?'

The Dean nodded, 'It was one of your students from last year, who's now opted to move to another college. She said that during one to one tutorials you were overly tactile and kept sitting next to her though there were other seats in the room. You constantly looped your arm round her shoulders, stroked her neck and patted her back.'

KENSHŌ House of Secrets

'What's her name?' Julian asked, feeling a great sense of relief. At least there'd been no mention of Rhianna.

'I'd prefer not to give you that yet. Is there any truth in what she claims?'

Julian thought for a moment, 'I only had two female students last year. One of them was quiet and hardly said much and is moving on with my year group this year so it can't be her. The other one was vocal, bright and a beauty. She was a bit of a feminist I think. I certainly don't remember stroking her back or putting my arm round her shoulders, though of course it could have been inadvertent. Surely she would have said something to me at the time.'

'One would have thought so,' the Dean said. 'This does sound like the girl in question. She might be looking for trouble, I suppose. She does add that you had a bit of a reputation for spending more time with the pretty ones and paying them a lot of attention. I don't know why you would. After all, you're a happily married man with a young attractive wife. Wasn't your wife one of your students before you married?'

Grimacing Julien said, 'I admit I have an eye for a pretty girl. Who doesn't? I would never dream of doing anything about it though,' he crossed his fingers as he sat on his hand. 'Yes, Phoebe, my wife, was one of my students but that was a good ten years ago. As you say, we're happily married now and have three young children.' He began to calm down. It looked as if he was off the hook. Just a case of a rap on the knuckles and he would be free and clear.

The Dean looked thoughtful, 'I'll write an appropriate response I think. That should be the end of the matter, unless of course this girl does want to cause a fuss. However, Julian, I feel I must give you a warning on behalf of the college. Be more careful with your behaviour to the female students in future. It's not a formal warning on this occasion, but we can't be too careful. Just make sure you treat the female population with due respect and deference and we needn't speak of this again.'

'Thank you, Dean,' Julian said, 'I'll do as you say.' Once out of the room he practically skipped down the corridor but then had second thoughts. He must sort out the Rhianna mess or next time he might not get off so easily. Rhianna was proving difficult to contact despite the countless messages he left. When at last Julian did get a reply, she was aloof and seemingly disinterested in meeting.

'I thought you said it was an emergency last time we met,' Julian said huffily.

'No, I'm busy at the moment. I've a lot on my mind. I'll see you next week some time.'

'What about the…,' Julian asked warily, reluctant to actually name the trouble, 'surely that can't wait?'

'You'd be surprised. You've messed me about long enough. I'm going to do what suits me. Now you'll see. I did warn you.' An ominous clunk confirmed Rhianna had ended the call.

Julian didn't know what to think. His earlier jaunty mood descended into gloom. What if his wife or even the Dean found out what he'd been up to? His future at Oxford would be kaput. He'd have to take action but what and how?

KENSHŌ   House of Secrets

CHAPTER 15
The House

As the noisy inhabitants of Kenshō House went about their business living out their personal dramas, the house stood sentinel over its own mysterious history. Built in the late nineteenth century, it had all the lugubrious and gothic characteristics of a late Victorian abode. It was only the red brickwork of the Edwardian extension that lightened it, adding a touch of irreverence to the ornate heaviness of the main building. During the day, the house stood square and solid not encouraging visitors or sightseers. Night-time was a different matter. Groaning and creaking, the house came alive recollecting past occupants, the scenes and sagas that had taken place.

A wakeful Mika, ensconced in splendid isolation at the top of the house, constantly saw shadows racing through her rooms. The muted sounds of children's laughter and scurrying feet alarmed her. Burying herself further under the coverlet, she would appeal to the Shinto gods and even Buddha in the hope there was nothing evil lurking in the darkness, convinced by now it wasn't the mice Phoebe had talked of. There was something sinister here, yet no one in the house ever mentioned the word 'ghosts' not even Tolly who knew everything there was to know.

Mika's grandfather didn't know the meaning of fear, and he would expect her to be just as brave and bold and investigate further. Never a man to accept things on face value, Takeshi believed there were many things in this world beyond our understanding, however Mika knew she must check out practical explanations first. When she was a child, other children would tell Mika about the yūrei and how they came back from the dead to wreak revenge on the living. Takeshi dismissed these ideas as Japanese folklore, but Mika was not convinced. She began to wonder if Kenshō House was haunted. Did the yūrei have unfinished business with her? Had they returned to demand a reckoning? But for what?

KENSHŌ   House of Secrets

Tolly was the person to help. He appeared to have an open mind and a taste for adventure. One particular afternoon when Phoebe, Daisy and the two youngest had gone out shoe shopping, Mika spotted Tolly sitting disconsolately at the bottom of her stairs. Once she explained the situation, Tolly accepted everything she said and was eager to start exploring the house. 'Wonder what it or they is. Let's look everywhere,' he exclaimed with gusto.

There was nothing to be seen in Mika's bedroom, despite Tolly knocking on walls and banging floorboards. They moved to the playroom. The room appeared darker and colder than usual. There was an unpleasant smell Mika had never noticed before. Tolly wrinkled his nose, 'Smells like a dead body. D'ya know Mika, they used to boards up mad people up in them Victorian days in attics and cellars, and never lets them out?'

Mika laughed merrily, 'Much imagination, Tolly.'

Tolly rubbed his grimy hand over his face, 'There's something though, ain't there. You can feel it too. I know you can. You's just trying to be grown up but I knows.'

Hesitantly, Mika nodded, 'Feel cold, bad feeling. House not like me from start.' She moved towards the old rocking horse and, like last time, gave it a good push but it was rock solid with rust and didn't budge an inch.

Tolly, impatient for action, jumped on the horse's back but there was still no movement. He stalked off to the pile of toys and started sorting through them in a desultory manner, 'Rubbish, just rubbish,' he mumbled to himself,' nothing here the kids and I can play with.' But then his hand fell on an old silver rattle and he started shaking it back and fore. The rattle seemed to get louder and louder. Mika, looking through the other piles, became irritated and annoyed. Before she could say anything, an icy shiver ran up her spine. Urgently she said, 'Tolly plees to give me.' The instant she held it she could hear the muted tones of a woman

KENSHŌ   House of Secrets

crying piteously. It was nerve wracking. The rattle had an engraving on one side. Mika bent over trying to decipher it. As she did so the rattle burned red hot in her hand, and she dropped it with a squeal.

'What is it? What is it?' Tolly asked eagerly, 'Did you feel something? Tell me, tell me.'

Mika shook her head as if to clear it, 'Nothing, Tolly, nothing. Imagination only.' Not wanting to frighten the boy, she added, 'I think we pack now. Ask mother to get rid of toys.' As they sorted the toys into lots, it was as if the piles grew larger and larger. Tolly, tired of the whole thing, said, 'Black bags is what we need. We stuffs everything in and takes them down to the outside sheds,' but even the appearance of the bags barely made a dent. Eventually, determined not to be beaten, they hurriedly bagged up everything except the horse. Gingerly, Mika threw the old silver rattle on the top, and they lugged the bags down the three flights to the hall.

Phoebe, in her usual manner, was racing into the house with the children, 'What have you been doing? You really don't have to do housework, Mika. We have old Mrs Briggs for that. She comes in twice a week. She could have sorted that lot.'

Mika explained they were the old toys from the playroom and she'd just wanted to clear the nursery. The three of them dragged the bags to the nearest shed and dumped them. 'I'll get someone from one of the charities to collect them tomorrow, Phoebe said. 'It's another thing for my list.'

Mika and Tolly returned to the playroom. The back of the room was empty except for the rocking horse whose one remaining eye stared at them threateningly. Mika carefully turned the old horse to the wall and they continued their search.

KENSHŌ   House of Secrets

'There's nothing,' Tolly announced dispiritedly, 'no ghosts after all. I'm starving Mika, let's get something to eat.'

Mika agreed. Perhaps it was all in her mind after all. Everything in this country was so new to her. Maybe she was dreaming up spirits in the dark but that night she was woken again by the sound of laughter, little feet and a young child crying. Furious, she put on all the lights, determined to end this. Stalking into the playroom, she was stunned to find all the toys and games they'd cleared away earlier piled up again in the corner. To top it all, the old rocking horse was quietly swaying on its springs looking at her with its beady eye. She was sure it gave her a wink. Closing her eyes Mika opened them again quickly, not believing what she saw. There must be yūrei here. Resolving not to be bested by ghosts, Mika advanced on the rocking horse and physically pushed and pulled him to face the wall again.

Panic stricken and more afraid than she was prepared to let on, she returned to bed leaving the lights on. First thing in the morning as soon as it was daylight, feeling tired, grumpy and convinced she'd been hallucinating the night before, Mika dragged herself out of bed. She was sure she'd left the lights on. Maybe it had been a dream after all. Making for the playroom she found everything as she and Tolly had left it the day before. The games and toys were gone but the old horse she'd turned to the wall was now parked defiantly in the centre of the room, looking at Mika malevolently.

That was it, she'd reached her limit. If she were to stay she must find out who'd occupied these rooms previously. The only person who'd know was the Colonel. Would he see her, let alone talk to her, and tell her about the house?

KENSHŌ   House of Secrets

CHAPTER 16
Bribery and corruption

Phoebe was in such a good mood these days that Mika had no difficulty in approaching her for help, 'I like speak with Colonel. Possible?'

Phoebe frowned, 'Why on earth would you want to do that? You know he's not keen on visitors. Most of the time he's cantankerous. He and Sanshō keep to themselves, thank goodness.'

Mika had obviously touched a raw nerve as Phoebe let loose a stream of resentments, 'I'm always worried about his frightening the children. He can be such a malicious old man sometimes. He and Sanshō perform all those mystical rites. Who knows what they're all about? It seems pagan to me, though Julian says it's to do with Eastern religions. Honestly, I don't know why they can't behave like God fearing Christians, I'd understand that.' Aware of Mika at last, she said vehemently, 'It's not possible, Mika. Anything else but not that,' and she bustled off to the dining room.

Mika decided to try the Professor next as he might be more amenable, but all he would say was, 'I'm sorry, my dear. My father's a bit of a hermit. He likes to be left alone with Sanshō, his studies and that manky old greyhound. I must say I'm glad of it.'

Not deterred, Mika took a few days to think, then remembering the Colonel's love of Japanese regalia, dragged a reluctant Jack round the Oxford antique shops searching for the perfect gift. Bribery might be the answer. Jack protested vehemently, 'Seriously Mika, the way you describe him I can't see the old chap being willing to see you, and certainly not to open up and talk to you about the house. You'll end up getting 'your ear bitten off'. I warn you, he'll upset you.'

KENSHŌ House of Secrets

'No, Jack,' Mika was adamant. 'I not care about 'ear' or upset. There is reikon now yūrei in house. Afraid come for me. Maybe to do with ancestors or grandfather. He never talk about war. Maybe do bad things. I not sleep peaceful until find out.'

'I never thought you superstitious, Mika. All this talk about souls turning into yūrei who walk the earth until they sort out their pain. It's unreal.' Privately he thought it nonsense but, caring for Mika as he did, he desperately wanted her to be comfortable in that strange house. After all, she might take it into her head to pack her bags and leave, and then what would he do?

'Jack, you say to me Boston and New England Puritan, see death different to Japanese, so you not understand.'

Laughingly Jack tried to make light of Mika's seriousness and joked, 'Why should your ancestors return more than anyone else's? I expect mine were convicts sent from England or even Red Indian scalp hunters. Take your pick.'

Mika was offended by Jack's indifference to his ancestors. 'In Japan ancestors important. Even grandfather who see few people celebrates Obon in summertime when ancestor spirits return to world to visit. His life spent making amends for shaming ancestors in war.'

'But Mika, your grandfather was forced to go to war. He should face the consequences of his actions, not you.'

Mika shook her head, 'Not work like that, Jack. We must comfort and honour ancestral spirits. Is part of our Eastern culture. I may look Western to you, like Western life, but traditional.'

'If it's that important to you then we must keep looking,' Jack replied stoically. 'Perhaps we should check out eBay. There's bound to be Japanese militaria for sale.'

KENSHŌ   House of Secrets

Seeing Jack was flagging and realising she herself had no idea what form any gift should take, Mika capitulated. Maybe they would be better looking on the Internet. Was she too obsessed with finding the right gift? Yet her intuition was telling her that Kenshō House was her nemesis. For some reason, the house recognised her as the catalyst who might unlock its secrets. Secrets it was loath to part with.

Days later in the middle of a lecture on the Romantic poets, Jack whispered excitedly in Mika's ear, 'I think I've found the very thing. It's expensive but I'll raid next term's allowance. It'll be worth it to give you peace of mind up there,' tapping the worry lines on Mika's forehead.

'What is it?' she asked tremulously.

'A sword. Not just any old sword but a Muramasa. It's being sold from some dead G.I., estate for one hundred and thirty dollars. What do you think?'

Mika's eyes lit up, 'Perfect. Is original?'

'Of course, antique at least. Should I go ahead and bid for it?'

'Plees. I talk to Sanshō make meeting.'

It took all Mika's courage to venture up to the second floor in the house and knock on the oak door. The gargoyles stared at her menacingly. When the door creaked open, Sanshō stood there in all his magnificence and bowed. He made no attempt to invite Mika in but waited, blocking the doorway.

Mika stammered, 'Plees I like appointment with Colonel san.' Sanshō barely cracked a smile, 'Colonel is busy, Miss. No time for visitors.'

KENSHŌ   House of Secrets

'Not now plees, next week,' Mika looked imploringly at Sanshō, 'I have gift.'

A bemused Sanshō shrugged and said, 'Leave it with me. I'll pass it on to the Colonel, Miss.'

Mika shook her head, 'I not have yet but it special.' Determined to stand her ground, Mika could feel her knees knocking, but she persevered, 'I present to Colonel san in person only.'

Sanshō frowned, 'Not sure Miss. I'll enquire.'

He shut the door firmly in Mika's face. Minutes elapsed and finally he returned. Bowing again, he said, 'The Colonel is intrigued. He will grant you an audience this time next week,' and, not waiting for a reply, shut the door again.

Now all Mika had to do was take possession of the sword, but how could she accept money from Jack when she had no idea how she felt about him? They hadn't even kissed, although she fantasised about it. She was still shy with him even if his extrovert personality and confidence swept her along. He was tall, blonde, handsome and larger than life and talked ten to the dozen, constantly encouraging her to express herself. Mika couldn't understand what he saw in her. Yet he was always there, helping, supporting and laughing at her struggles with the language. Nothing phased him. It was as if he'd arrived fully formed in the world, bubbling over with self-belief.

Days later Jack presented her with the sword well wrapped in some sort of cloth and brown paper. Mika was so excited and eager to see it, she practically snatched it from Jack's hand. 'Take it easy, Mika, it's a weapon not a toy. You could cut yourself. Let me open it up.' Once exposed to daylight, the sword glowed as if it was alive and ready for action, its curved blade shimmering. A stunned Mika stepped back and gasped, 'It magnificent...but the cost...how to pay? Maybe too much for gift...I had no idea.'

KENSHŌ House of Secrets

Jack was silent which was unlike him, 'It's worth it. It's like you, unique, exquisite, honed to perfection.' Mika blushed and bowed deeply, too overcome to show her face. Jack continued, 'Believe me, the Colonel will take one look and covet it. As for me, I want nothing in return but a promise.'

'Promise?' Mika was aghast. 'What promise. I make no promise. I return home end of year.'

'I meant an understanding between you and me, Mika and Jack, Japan and America.'

Mika was confused. What sort of 'understanding' could they have? Did Jack mean marriage? If not, what other sort of 'understanding' could he mean? And why did he bring their countries into it and make it sound like some sort of treaty? Her English wasn't up to unravelling all this and she found herself unwilling to say so in case she lost Jack. That was the last thing she wanted.

Hesitantly, she accepted and rewrapped the sword. What would the Colonel think? Would he be prepared to talk to her? Could the gift of the sword be seen as an insult? The Colonel was so much like her grandfather. These stern, hostile, disciplined men frightened her. Yet she was more frightened of the yūrei. Would the yūrei leave her alone if she discovered the house's secrets?

KENSHŌ   House of Secrets

CHAPTER 17
An interview with the Colonel

It was a cold wintry morning when Sanchō broached the subject of Mika's request. It was never a good idea to warn the Colonel in advance. Sanshō had taken it upon himself the week before to make the arrangements with the girl without the Colonel's say so. Old people could be ornery, particularly the Colonel who went out of his way to be belligerent over the least little thing these days. The Colonel's pallor looked greyer than usual. Draped in an old sheepskin cardigan, he held his gnarled hands over a small two bar electric fire. Bakti curled round his feet sniffing at the Colonel's ancient leather slippers. Sanshō, primed for the worst, had prepared the Colonel's favourite breakfast, - scrambled eggs and smoked salmon accompanied the usual flatbread and Oolong tea. This was followed by a generous piece of mango.

'And to what do I owe the honour of such a repast?' the Colonel demanded sarcastically. 'I suppose there's a favour coming. Do you want a day off or a holiday or something?'

Sanshō shrugged, ignoring the sarcasm. There were no such thing as days off or holidays in this job. 'No, I have someone in the house who's asked for a meeting with you. They want to give you something.'

'Who? Who? Speak up man, I can barely hear you. There's no one in this household who has any need to see me, let alone give me something. Explain properly. I've no time for this.'

'It's Mika, Colonel. Mika.'

'Who? Never heard of her,' the Colonel said grimly.

'Don't you remember? She's the little Japanese girl Phoebe brought to meet you last month. She's staying with the family for the year, studying at the university.'

KENSHŌ House of Secrets

'Oh, that chit of a girl who tried to impress me by throwing Shakespeare into the conversation. Absolutely not. Why would I want to see her? You know I rarely see anyone even Julian.'

'But that's it, Colonel. For some reason she's incredibly determined and has a special gift for you.'

'Tell her to leave it with you whatever it is. Why should she give me anything? I hardly know her and don't want to.'

'I've no idea, Colonel. Aren't you curious? Shouldn't you find out what this is all about?'

'I don't know. I don't know,' the old man grumbled. 'Why can't people leave me alone. I'm too old for socialising.'

'Hardly socialising, Colonel, just a young girl in awe of you who wants to take advantage of your great wisdom.' Sanshō knew flattery would make all the difference.

'Very well, Sanshō, my friend. As usual, you've talked me round. Make it a short meeting. My arthritis is playing up today. I'm not in the mood for long talks.'

'Of course, Colonel. I told her to come later this afternoon after your nap.'

'You old rogue, I suppose you've set this up already.' The Colonel managed to crack a smile, 'Just like you. No wonder I have no control over my own life with you around. Very well then, if I must, I must. Let's get it over with.'

Later that afternoon Mika arrived laden down with a well wrapped parcel nearly as big as herself, which she carried gingerly in front of her.

KENSHŌ House of Secrets

Bowing deeply, Mika held out the parcel to the Colonel saying, 'You would do me much honour, Colonel san, if you would accept gift for your collection.'

The Colonel looking down at his twisted hands nodded to Sanshō who came forward and took the parcel, placing it on a nearby table. The Colonel, never a man to be easily won over, mumbled, 'Beware of Greeks bearing gifts or in this case Japanese. Well child, I don't what this is about. You better explain.'

A nervous Mika, deciding to be as wily as the old man, said, 'I tell all. You open present first and decide if want.'

The Colonel pursed his lips but had to admit he was interested. It was the word 'collection' that had done it. He'd spent years amassing Japanese paraphernalia. The swords in particular were his obsession. He didn't know why, when he'd endured years of torture at the hands of the Japanese, yet their culture and attitudes to life, honour and death absorbed him. He often compared them to the Egyptian civilisation he studied in his old manuscripts. The Egyptian sphinx with its human head and lion body (power controlled by human reason and justice) was comparable with the Samurai and their codes of discipline and bushidō.

Sanshō could see the old man's mind wandering. He was probably harking back to his ancient manuscripts. Intervening, he said, 'Colonel, would you like me to unpack the parcel then you can see for yourself?'

Mika was all for it and eagerly moved nearer but the Colonel, fractious to the last, put up a hand and stopped her, 'Hang on Missy. Not sure I want to accept a gift if I don't know what you want in exchange. People always want something.' A nervy Mika stuttered out the words before she had time to think, 'It's the yūrei, they haunt me in house.'

KENSHŌ   House of Secrets

Sanshō and the Colonel were struck dumb. Eventually, the Colonel recovered and said, 'I remember now. The yūrei are the returning souls of the dead. I can't see how they would affect you here. We've nothing to do with your ancestors, Missy.' But no sooner had he said it than without warning he felt the heavy hand of his own dead ancestors pressing down on his heart. Were they coming for him too, claiming vengeance for what he'd done? He shivered inadvertently, but declared, 'That's poppycock, Missy. There's nothing here to be afraid of. Why would you think so?'

A stammering Mika told her story of interrupted nights, the cries, the toys, the silver rattle and the rocking horse. Neither the Colonel nor Sanshō uttered a word. Finally, the Colonel said, 'I've never heard of any haunting here before. Are you sure it's not your imagination playing tricks? After all, you're far from home and must be lonely up there on the top floor.'

'No, Colonel san. Something bad happen up there. Must find history of house.' Mika was now so adamant that the Colonel actually began to nod in agreement with her. Sanshō was amazed to see the Colonel slowly coming back to life right before his eyes. The girl seemed to have caught his attention. The old man's vigorous mind was recharging at a rate of knots. Delving back into his memories, the Colonel said, 'All I know about the house is, I inherited it from an elderly aunt in 1946 after I came back from Japan. She and her family moved into the house in 1901 and the old lady refused to move out ever after. I was the only living relative, so the house came to me. There are a lot of old papers in the attics, perhaps we should take a look.' The Colonel looked at Sanshō questioningly, but the old retainer said gloomily, 'Leave it to Mika, Colonel. I think a stint in those damp attics would do for you.'

'I suppose so,' the Colonel said unwillingly. 'Very well, Mika, it's up to you. I'll need a full report, d'ya hear?' He was back on the parade ground, commanding and giving orders now, but Mika

KENSHŌ House of Secrets

felt nothing but relief. Things were going better than she'd expected. At last, the Colonel was calling her by name.

'Arigatō Colonel san, I will.' Tentatively she asked, 'Plees you want to open parcel now?'

'No need to bring me a gift. You could have come and spoken to me,' the Colonel said robustly. Feeling in a better frame of mind, he said pleasantly to Sanshō, 'Bring the table a little closer, my friend. Let's see what Mika has brought.'

Sanshō moved the table and began to unwrap the parcel. 'No, my friend, I can manage.' The Colonel carefully untied the string with his crippled hands, unfolding the sheets of paper one by one until there was only the material left. 'You've certainly wrapped this well, Mika. Must be something precious.'

As the last piece of material fell away, the sword was revealed. The late afternoon sun caught the gilded glitter of the curved blade setting the room aglow with golden light. Sanshō and the Colonel caught their breath. Time stood still. Mika breathed unevenly. Sanshō glanced at the Colonel. Despite being mesmerised by the sword, the old man was pale as a ghost, his lips turning blue.

'Colonel, Colonel,' Sanshō reacted urgently, 'You need to lie down. Let me get you a brandy.'

Mika was shocked. What had she done? She hadn't expected this, 'Doctor?' she asked looking questioningly at Sanshō.

He shook his head, 'Just one of his turns. I'll get him a drink. He'll be alright in a minute.'

Revived by the brandy, the Colonel said, 'Don't fuss, you two. It was the sword. I could have lived my whole life and never seen

KENSHŌ   House of Secrets

another Muramasa sword. What a beauty. I can't believe it.' He touched the blade reverently.

'But Colonel, I insist you lie down. It's been too much for you.'

'Don't be an old woman, Sanshō. You're frightening Mika.' Turning to Mika the Colonel said, 'I'm overcome, I don't know what to say. I can't accept the sword, though I want to. It's too expensive and too valuable.'

Mika shook her head, 'Colonel san. It yours. Plees to take. Accept with honour, respect. My grandfather would want.'

'Do you mean your grandfather sent this from Japan?'

'No Colonel san, but grandfather Samurai disciple. He want you have as admirer of Japanese militaria.'

'In that case, I can't refuse. I would like to meet your grandfather someday,' the Colonel said disarmingly. Having made a speedy recovery from his shock, he announced to a stupefied Sanshō, 'I think we can take tea now, Sanshō,' adding 'Mika will stay won't you, my dear.' It was clear he could exert as much charm as his son when he wanted to.

Sanshō bustled off to the little kitchen sighing. What a turn-up for the book. One minute the old man was about to collapse, the next he was ordering tea and preparing to captivate Mika. What was going on and why had the sight of the sword given the Colonel such a shock?

CHAPTER 18
Reunion with an old friend

Since her shopping trip and the makeover, Phoebe had taken on a new lease of life and become a force to be reckoned with. Her vagueness and passivity had vanished, and Julian found that he had not only a much better turned out wife but also one that was prepared to be assertive and question his judgement. There was many a day now when he wished he'd never mentioned the idea of Phoebe going shopping and improving herself. After her late return on that fatal day of her transformation, Phoebe had begun to remodel the old house as well as take the children in hand. These days, Daisy was firmly but kindly put in her place, and the children now gathered round their mother at the end of a day. The Open University course and Phoebe's studies had been packed away and consigned to the storeroom. Phoebe was energised and ready to face life.

The long awaited phone call from Geoffrey came. Phoebe couldn't believe how excited she was when he rang and announced in an American drawl, 'I'm in Oxford, Phoebe. I've got a suite at the Old Bank Hotel. Do you know it?'

Phoebe's eyes nearly popped out of her head. Of course, she knew of it but had never experienced it at those prices. Trying to show a level of sophistication, she answered nonchalantly, 'Of course, it's so central for the colleges.'

'How about lunch? Any chance you're free today, one o'clock in the Quod Restaurant? I hear the food's spectacular. What do you say?'

This was hardly the same Geoffrey Phoebe had known ten years before. He sounded mature, decisive, and completely in control of the situation. Her mind started flitting around arrangements for the children and Daisy and, more importantly, what to wear.

KENSHŌ   House of Secrets

Coolly she responded, 'I'd love that. As it happens, I've nothing important on today. Shall I meet you there?'

'Wonderful,' Geoffrey said. 'It'll be fabulous to see you again. I'll reserve us a table. Au revoir for now, darling.'

Geoffrey appeared to have acquired the American style of overenthusiastic hyperbole quite unlike his youthful self. When they'd been students together in their first year, he and Phoebe had been painfully shy and clung together. They were both totally inhibited by the cohorts of overconfident ex public school types that surrounded them. Both hailed from rural working class homes in deepest Dorset, and constantly struggled to find their place in the groves of academe.

Phoebe was in a complete dither about what to wear. As Daisy was out shopping, she decided to enlist Mika's help. Struggling up the three flights to the third floor, she found Mika studying in her bedroom rather than the playroom. Mika had moved the desk and chair through to sit by the window. Phoebe frowned, 'Are you comfortable in here? I'd have thought you'd have had more room next door.'

Mika winced, 'No, good. Feel at home here.' She was not going to admit to Phoebe how much the playroom scared her. It was as if there was something waiting for her in there. Normally she tried to do all her work in the Bodleian, but as today was free she'd been reluctant to trek into college in the wintry weather. The tiny electric fire Phoebe had provided was of little benefit. However, Jack had given her some fleecy lined slippers so at least her feet were warm.

Hesitantly, Phoebe said, 'I wondered if you could help me. I'm going to lunch with an old friend, someone I haven't seen for ten years. I don't know what to wear. Could you come down and help me choose an outfit?'

KENSHŌ   House of Secrets

Mika beamed, surprised at being asked. Her relationship with Phoebe was uneasy and Mika was never sure how to change that. The three of them had got on so well when they went shopping but since then Phoebe had gone back to being remote, distrait and preoccupied. Daisy was easier to understand as she always said what she thought. Phoebe was quite a different matter. Cheerfully, Mika said, 'If can will help.'

The pair of them slipped back down to the front of the house to Phoebe and Julian's master bedroom. It was a sizable room with substantial oak fitted wardrobes down one side and an enormous brass bed in the centre. The furnishings were heavy and over-elaborate and the wallpaper, curtains and carpet had seen better days. Phoebe apologised, 'It's a bit of a mausoleum in here but Julian's first wife, Lucy, designed it, and Julian won't have anything changed.' She opened one of the further cupboards, so Mika could see all the newly bought clothes they'd shopped for a few weeks ago.

'What do you think? A suit, matching coordinates or a dress?'

Mika thought for a moment, 'Is informal?'

'Definitely informal. Geoffrey and I are old friends, but I do want to impress him as he hasn't seen me for years.'

Mika pulled out a green wool dress, 'Look good with hair and eyes. Modern.'

Phoebe's face lit up,' The very thing. How clever you are, Mika. I can wear my new camel coat and the gold loops Julian gave me last Christmas. Thank you so much,' and hugged Mika tightly and with warmth.

Mika wondered why there was such a fuss about a lunch meeting? Was there more to this rendezvous? Did Julian know? The English appeared extremely casual about their marriages. In her

KENSHŌ House of Secrets

hometown no woman would disrespect her husband by eating out with another man. Tokyo, of course was different, being a city and more Westernised.

On her arrival at the Quod, Phoebe speculated whether she would recognise Geoffrey. When she'd known him last he'd had a shock of blonde curls, but the man who came forward to greet her no longer had curls but blonde thinning hair. He was as tall as she remembered. His deep set blue eyes were still the same, though faintly lined, but the smile, the smile was as tender and affectionate as ever. 'My dearest Phoebe, you look not a year older than when I saw you last. To think you've three children, I can hardly believe it.' To her consternation he turned her this way and that, commenting quietly, 'What a beauty you've turned into, and so elegant. That green dress compliments your eyes to perfection,' and, before she had time to respond, he enveloped her in a warm close hug.

Phoebe was flustered. Julian rarely said anything flattering these days not even about her new clothes. To be admired and held so close was almost more than she could bear. She pulled herself out of his arms, determined to get the reunion on an even keel. 'Geoffrey, it's good to see you. Did you manage to book us a table?'

'Of course, my dear.' He took her arm and led her to a table in the furthest corner. 'I think it might be a bit too busy in here for my taste,' he commented in his slight American drawl, 'but I'm sure we can find something more private next time.'

It took Phoebe a moment to realise Geoffrey had every intention of seeing her again. Was this a good idea? Before she could collect herself, he'd taken her coat, and they were soon immersed in the menu and wine list. This was a vastly different Geoffrey to the young, school boyish student she remembered. Now he was a man of the world completely focused on her. Phoebe could feel herself squirming as he looked deep into her eyes. Without any

KENSHŌ   House of Secrets

preamble he said, 'Tell me everything about your life and what you've been doing for the last ten years. I want to hear everything. I've never stopped thinking about you and what might have been.'

Phoebe found herself blushing. He would surely not want to hear 'everything'. Of course, there was something he should hear but now was not the right time. Possibly there would never be a right time. Instead she said, 'Honestly Geoffrey, my life's been pretty boring. Just children and struggling with an old house that Julian's father owns and we all live in. Nothing else.'

'And how is dear Julian these days?' Geoffrey said drily, 'Running the college I expect by now.'

'Not exactly. He's head of the Nissan Institute of Japanese Studies. It's a new set-up at St Anthony's College. I don't suppose you've heard of it.'

'No, but I'm sure he revels in being head of an Institute,' Geoffrey said sarcastically. There'd never been much love lost between him and Julian even when Julian was their personal tutor. 'How old is he now? He must be getting on a bit?'

'He's in his fifties,' Phoebe said frostily. She didn't want the age subject rearing its ugly head again.

'And are you happy with him?' Geoffrey asked probingly.

There was a deafening silence whilst Phoebe tried to concentrate on eating her profiteroles. Finally, she said, 'Of course, why wouldn't I be?' realising too late that throwing out that last defensive question meant asking for trouble.

Geoffrey sat back in his chair and smiled triumphantly, 'Yes, why wouldn't you be? I think we've got a lot to talk about and catch up on. Why don't we do this again next week? I'll find us a quieter

KENSHŌ   House of Secrets

place.' Phoebe, relieved to be off the hook so easily, nodded passively. She wasn't at all sure she wanted to see him again. He unsettled her, yet she couldn't bring herself to refuse.

Geoffrey paid the bill and wrapped Phoebe in her camel coat as if she were a precious possession. 'I'm sorry, dearest Phoebe, that this has been a bit of a rush but I've yet to get settled in. I start lectures next week and must earn my bread as a visiting professor. I'm staying here in the hotel for the duration until I find an apartment or house to rent. Can I ring you and arrange our next assignation?' Weakly, Phoebe agreed, mesmerised by the strength of Geoffrey's personality. 'Assignation' sounded distinctly dubious, having definite undertones of an affair. What did Geoffrey want with her, an old married woman with three children?

Geoffrey hustled her out the door and escorted her to her car. Just as she was about to open the driver's door, he spun her round and kissed her thoroughly on the lips, then went loping off calling behind him 'A Bientôt.' Phoebe was almost too shocked to drive home. Once she pulled into the drive of Kenshō House she found she was shaking and sat for a time with her head in her hands. When Geoffrey had kissed her like that it was as if the years had fallen away and they were back to being young lovers. She must pull herself together, compose herself. She was a married woman with responsibilities, and those responsibilities would be arriving home from school at any minute.

KENSHŌ   House of Secrets

CHAPTER 19
Kendō, the way of the sword

In the weeks that followed Mika's meeting with the Colonel, she had little time to think about the papers in the attic or the yūrei. She had deadlines to meet, essays to write and meetings with her tutor. It was difficult to get together with Jack who was anxious to know what had happened about the sword. Making light of the meeting with the Colonel, all Mika would say was that 'Colonel san accept sword. Overcome, need brandy, but friendly, take tea with him.'

Jack was frustrated, 'But what about the house? Have you found out about the house?'

'He say papers in attic, but no time now. Much work,' was the only response he could get.

At times, Mika could be closed, silent, and tight lipped. Jack would feel there was a barrier between them that he'd never break down. Was it cultural or personal, he didn't know? Every time he thought he'd made progress in their relationship, the shutters descended and he'd be forced to start again. Of course, Mika had spent the majority of her life living with an old man who rarely spoke and was a disciple of the Samurai. Perhaps the answer was to get better acquainted with the Samurai way of thinking.

Jack, finding the college work relatively easy, made enquiries and discovered the Kendō Association. It might be worth a shot Jack thought. At least it was a martial art and might lead him to a better understanding of Mika's grandfather's practices. After all, 'Kendō' appeared to be a modern version of traditional Japanese sword fighting with a rigid, disciplined code.

Excited with the challenge of learning something new, Jack longed to talk to Mika but these days Mika had withdrawn completely. Totally preoccupied she spent most of her time in the

KENSHŌ   House of Secrets

Bodleian. Attempting to distract her Jack suggested, 'Perhaps a ride on the bike today - it's such a lovely afternoon.' But despite Mika's love of his motorbike, she shook her head, 'Must study, Jack. Not easy for me. Find language difficult. Read books again and again for understanding.'

'I could help,' Jack offered.

'No, must do self, as not learn,' Mika said doggedly but, realising he was doing his best to support her, said, 'You take ride in countryside. Do good. I see you later.'

Jack felt hurt, trying not to take it personally. Perhaps if he went ahead with learning Kendō it might give him a sense of the Japanese mind and, of course, impress Mika.

On his first evening at the dōjo, Jack was awe-struck. The head sensei gave the starters a potted history, followed by a demonstration. Two Kendōka dressed in hakama (uniform) with stylised helmets and grilles, a breastplate (yoroi), leather and fabric body flaps, long padded gloves (kote) and bamboo swords (shinai) took their places barefoot. They bowed, eyeballed their opponent and starting with a shout (kaiai) thrust and fought with their shinai. Jack, at first alarmed by the sinister character of the black uniforms and helmets, the shouting, the armour and the ferocity of the shinais, was soon transfixed by the rites and techniques. When he'd been at boarding school he'd learnt to fence, but there was much more to Kendō. He was thoroughly fascinated.

The sensei, recognising his enthusiasm, warned, 'It takes time and effort, Jack, to learn such a physical and mental discipline. You'd have to start with the foot-work before you could progress to the wooden swords, and then more time before you could move on to the shinai or think about meeting an opponent. There's no room for impatience. Kendō requires rigor and self-control but is

KENSHŌ House of Secrets

character building. Come next week and see for yourself if it's for you.'

An eager Jack returned to his lodgings. He knew he needed to be stretched. The English course was hardly demanding. What would Mika think? He decided not to tell her until he'd gone to a few more sessions at the dōjo. One thing he knew about her was that she wouldn't approve if he only went a few times and dropped out. He suspected there was a lot of her grandfather's intransigence in her.

It was a shame he hadn't someone to confide in. Although he was exuberant and outgoing it had been difficult to make friends at Oxford. His classmates had already formed friendships at public school before they came and it was impossible to break into any of the cliques. Mika was his one and only friend, well more than a friend he hoped.

Since they'd met he'd realised how his homelife paralleled Mika's, despite coming from different parts of the world. Like her grandfather, his father was a reserved man wrapped up in his law practice and clients barely acknowledging his son. The pair of them rolled around in an enormous ornate mansion outside Boston with a handful of ancient retainers to keep the place in order, but it was a lonely life for Jack. Whenever he came home from boarding school or college it was if he and his father were strangers, barely conversing at mealtimes and then only exchanging trivialities. Jack was not encouraged to invite friends to stay and had been urged to build a life outside the home. Even when his mother had been alive there'd been a distinct uneasiness between the three of them. His Mom was a glamorous socialite running his father's life like clockwork, making sure he was introduced to the right people and the right contacts. Jack was an inconvenient adjunct to their lives, abandoned to a succession of nannies and au pairs. Despite constantly asking about other relatives, it was as if any forebears had been erased. His mother never talked about her family, as if she were ashamed of them. All Jack had gleaned from something he'd heard her mention was

KENSHŌ House of Secrets

that his grandfather had been a German immigrant who'd escaped to England before the war. As he grew up, Jack began to realise that his parents had transformed themselves into pillars of Boston society. As long as he performed with propriety they were prepared to accept him, preferring to play no part in his life. It was a bleak existence; one he didn't want for his children.

Kendō might be the making of him, give him structure and purpose, and turn him into his own man as well as helping build bridges with Mika and perhaps her grandfather.

KENSHŌ   House of Secrets

CHAPTER 20
Sleuthing

During their late afternoon tea making rituals, Mika decided to co-opt Tolly's help in searching the attics for the papers the Colonel had mentioned. The little boy asked, 'Should we ask Mum?'

'No, have Colonel's san's permission. Your mother not be pleased. Better leave. She busy.'

They chose a Saturday when the household was occupied elsewhere. Mika was more nervous than Tolly who'd come well prepared with a torch and black bags. He manfully led the way up the steep rickety stairs just above Mika's floor to the attic in the eaves of the house. Mika had never realised there was another floor as the entrance was behind a carefully concealed loose panel at the top of her stairs. Tolly, racing ahead, whistled, 'Wow, I didn't know this place existed. Hurry up, Mika. It's a treasure trove.' There was little room in the roof space. By the time a breathless Mika reached the top of the stairs, she had to be careful not to hit her head. The attic smelt of damp and rat droppings. Cobwebs hung like lace curtains. Mika squeaked in horror as they tore across her face and hair.

Tolly giggled, 'Don't be such a girl, Mika.' There was one bare electric light bulb hanging dejectedly from the ceiling. Carefully making his way round the walls with the aid of his torch, Tolly located a switch and, to their amazement, it lit up with a pale greenish glow. Mika began to feel anxious as they slowly made their way across the floor. Most of the boards were rotten and felt as if they would give way at any moment. What if something happened to either of them? No one knew they were up there. The attic spanned the old part of the house. Everywhere there were piles of trunks, suitcases, discarded furniture, old paintings, mirrors, lamps, even parts of an old tandem, and generations

KENSHŌ   House of Secrets

worth of detritus. Panicking Mika said, 'Tolly, Tolly never find papers. Where start?'

But Tolly, not a boy to be thwarted, immediately made for the trunks and cases, 'See Mika. I betcha there's summat in here. People always puts valuables in these. 'Spose they won't rot or something.' He was like a ferret amongst the cases. Before long, whilst a disconsolate Mika looked on, he unearthed a small blue leather bound book and holding it up triumphantly said, 'A find. Grandpa's old diary. 'Spect it's from the war. Shall we take a peek? Bet there's summat really shocking.'

Moving quickly, Mika snatched it out of his hand before he could flick through it, 'Private, Tolly. Respect elders. I keep for safety.'

Tolly sulked but soon turned his attention to another trunk and digging into the bottom began to pull at something else, 'What 'bout this then, Mika. Looks important.' It was a black moth-eaten Moroccan bound folder, full of dog eared handwritten pages.

Scanning it, Mika could see it contained a collection of old invoices about the building of the extension in 1901; perhaps it was worth a more detailed look. Mika began to feel encouraged and joined Tolly in delving through boxes and tin trunks. Eventually she uncovered an old photo album with sepia pictures of the original house and its inhabitants. With the aid of the torch they stared at the photos, though it was difficult to make out much in the poor light.

'Take with us,' Mika whispered.

'Why are you whispering?'

'Maybe spirits here. Not want us to see.' She shivered, thinking of the yūrei.'

KENSHŌ   House of Secrets

'Tosh,' said Tolly, 'there's nothing up here but a load of old junk. No one cares what we see or take from here. Mum hasn't been up here in years.'

They continued their sifting, Tolly humming under his breath. He was a stalwart boy, resilient and helpful. Nothing phases him, Mika thought. The family don't appreciate what a treasure they have. While she was considering his virtues, Tolly shouted out in glee, 'Hey Mika what's this?' He held a small case in the air. 'Think this might be something but it's locked. Shall I bash it open?'

'Plees no, Tolly. We take to my rooms. Maybe important.'

'Oh, let's go now,' Tolly said eagerly, 'I can't wait to see what's in it.'

They gathered up the folder, the album, the Colonel's diary and the case and carefully renegotiated the stairs down to Mika's rooms. Putting the other articles to one side, she and Tolly struggled to open the small case. It wouldn't budge despite its age.

'I knows a way,' Tolly said importantly, 'I watches all these crime shows on the telly. I just needs a hairgrip and some wire. That'll do it.' It was easier said than done, and although the little boy struggled for a while, there was no movement in the lock. 'I'll get a hammer and screwdriver,' he said, weary with his efforts, 'and give it a good bash.' Within minutes he was off and racing downstairs to the outside tool shed. Mika sighed. Had it been such a good idea to get Tolly involved in this? Would he get into trouble? She went back to fiddling with the lock. To her surprise, it slid open as it if had been waiting for her to try it all along. Inside was a disappointment. There were just files and files of household invoices and receipts. Most were discoloured and falling apart, but at the bottom of the case was a thin folder called 'The House'. It was as if someone in the past had sat down and

KENSHŌ   House of Secrets

written a history of the house. It was no more than twenty or thirty pages of foolscap tied together with pink tape. The handwriting was small and neat but easy to read. Mika was intrigued. Was this what she was looking for? Hearing Tolly thundering back up the stairs, Mika took the folder and thrust it under her mattress for later.

A crestfallen Tolly was left looking at an opened case stuffed full of ancient bills and household accounts. 'There's nothing here Mika. We might as well give up and make tea.'

Seeing his pained expression, Mika softened, 'I buy English crumpets yesterday. We try. You make tea. I toast. We bring West and East together, yes?'

Taking hold of Tolly's grubby hand she raced down the first set of stairs with him. Then as he broke his grip on her hand she watched him slide down the bannisters of the next two floors shouting, 'Come on, slowcoach. I'll get there before you.' At the bottom he fell on the hall floor dramatically and lay there. Mika, concerned he might have hurt himself, ran down the rest of the stairs and knelt over him. No sooner had she done so than he sprang up saying 'Gotcha', running into the kitchen chuckling. The two younger children joined him screaming and laughing and tumbling on top of Dot and Dash, as the dogs scrabbled to find their footing on the newly polished floor. A smiling Mika followed at a more leisurely pace thinking about what they'd found. If the yūrei kept her awake again tonight at least she could read about the house's history.

Later that night, as she'd expected, Mika couldn't sleep. Tossing and turning, she replayed the day's activities. There were no signs of the yūrei, children running about or a baby crying yet sleep eluded her. Turning on the light she reached for the folder on 'The House' and began reading. Part One started in 1890...

'At the time the house was called 'Greensleeves'...

KENSHŌ   House of Secrets
CHAPTER 21
Part One: 'The House' begins its story
'Greensleeves', 1890

...'Take the tea up to the Missus, she should be up from her afternoon nap by now. Though what makes her so tired is beyond me. Most of the day she just lies on that there chaise longue.'

Nelly snatched up the tray, glad to be out of Mrs Price's sight. It was an easy enough job if she could put up with the housekeeper's sharp tongue - certainly a lot easier than looking after her six younger siblings whilst her mother was laid up with another baby on the way. The money wasn't bad either, although she had to give over half of it to her family.

Mrs Price tutted you couldn't get the help these days, so many of the young single girls were moving out of domestic service to work in factories or as 'typewriters'. 'Service' was becoming a dirty word. Of course, she wasn't really a 'Mrs', it was purely a courtesy title, but she wasn't about to tell young Nell that. Her one and only beau had been killed in the First Boer War, when the bullet he took in the groin turned septic. Every night after kneeling for her prayers she would get into her single iron bed on the top floor. Before sleeping, she would kiss the framed studio photograph of Private Harold Deakins standing proudly in his scarlet uniform soundly on the lips.

Mrs Price knew she was on a good wicket here. The running of the house was left to her. Mr Cornelius Moore, the young master, an architect, was out all day. He'd bought this newly built house in 1880 at a knockdown price from a bankrupt builder and moved straight in with his bride when they returned from the Grand Tour. His wife had named the house 'Greensleeves' after her favourite folk song. Mr Cornelius was a gentleman which was more than one could say for his wife. It was claimed he had distant kinship with Queen Victoria herself. Mrs Agatha,

KENSHŌ House of Secrets

however, was a poor specimen. A wan, pale wraith of a woman, the daughter of a cotton mill owner, who'd come with a substantial dowry though little else.

Nelly returned, 'Looks like a death's head does the Missus. Refused the tea and turned to the wall. That poor husband of hers. Doesn't look like she's coming down for dinner either. What's wrong with her?'

'Nothing to do with you, young miss. Minds your business and let them minds theirs. Posh folks have their ways. We's not paid to heed. Now get on with that washing up. There's pans to be scrubbed, and after that you can start peeling potatoes for dinner.'

Nelly put out her tongue behind Mrs Price's back. It was going to be one of those days was it? They were the only two below stairs these days, except for old Ada who came in twice a week to do the heavy work, but they were never on friendly terms. Mrs P was only too aware of her position in the house making sure Nelly knew it too.

As the clock struck six, Mr Cornelius came bounding through the front door. He was a good looking athletic young man, full of life, vigour and well moustachioed. Without even glancing in the drawing room he tossed his street clothes on the settle in the hall, and ran up the stairs calling 'Aggie, Aggie, I've news.'

Mrs P, laying the table for dinner, could hear the murmur of raised voices. Suddenly Mr Cornelius began shouting at the top of his voice, 'This can't go on. We've seen all the doctors we can. They say there's nothing wrong. I can't see why you don't get up and come downstairs. I can't take anymore.' There was a lot of banging and crashing of furniture, followed by a red faced and flustered Mr Cornelius running back down the stairs and shouting to Mrs Price, 'Forget dinner tonight, I'm off to the club. Just see to Agatha.' Grabbing his coat and silk hat, he banged the door behind him.

KENSHŌ   House of Secrets

Mrs Price returned to the kitchen, rubbing her hands in glee, 'Looks like we're going to have ourselves a feast tonight, young Nelly. I bought some lambs' kidneys special for Mr C, as I know how he likes a devilled kidney. We'll have to eat 'em or they'll go off, and there's that sherry trifle we've made. Go and fetch it from the pantry and a drop of madeira from Mr C's wine cellar.'

'What about the Missus? Should I go up and see if she wants something?'

'No, best leave her for now. We'll check on her before we go to bed and perhaps take up some hot milk.'

Taking advantage of Mrs Price's amenable mood, Nellie asked, 'What's it all about then? What's wrong with the Missus?'

Mrs Price tapped her nose, 'Children I expects. As far's I know, they's been married ten year. She lost a lot of babies. Any amount of doctors have seen her. There's naught to be done. In the first year they even turned the connecting room next door to mine on the third floor into a nursery, so's a wet nurse could have the room I'm in. That was long before I came as housekeeper. The child was still born. They'd bought all these toys including a rocking horse. Even had a silver rattle engraved with the child's name 'Edward', as Mrs Agatha was convinced it was a boy. Since then it's been one miscarriage after another. Of course, the toys is packed away now and left to rot in the nursery. The Missus never sets foot up there. She's either lying down in that boudoir, as she calls it, or on that sofa thing in the morning room.'

As they tucked into their supper, Nellie said, 'Don't you feel sorry for her? She must be suffering.'

Mrs Price sniffed, 'Why should I feel sorry for her? Look at this place. She's got it all. The master adores her. You go down the slums in Church Street in St Ebbe's. You'll sees women much worse off, ragged, barefoot children pulling at their skirts, babies

KENSHŌ   House of Secrets

on the breast and not a penny or a crust of bread between 'em. That's real suffering.' Turning to Nellie she added, 'Just likes your mam. Too many mouths to feed, dragging about in filth and muck and always in the pudding club. I don' suppose they've the luxury of taking to their beds and crying their hearts out if they loses a baby. No, they carry on scrubbing floors, boiling laundry, and trying to feeds their families.'

'That's harsh,' Nellie retorted and added brazenly, 'anyway you've no children of your own, so you dunno what it's like to lose one.'

Mrs Price flicked her across the head with the dishcloth, 'Don't be cheeky to your elders and betters. We've a prime billet here. I don't intend to change that. If you've any sense you'll learn to keep your mouth shut. That's a warning.' Never sure of Mrs Price's moods, Nellie decided to take the advice and kept her thoughts to herself, but she couldn't help feeling sorry for the poor Missus waning away upstairs.

Over the next month there were a lot of comings and goings. Important bearded gentlemen in frock coats and silk hats arrived. Nelly was kept busy answering the door, whilst Mr Cornelius was on hand to escort them to his wife's room. Nelly would look at him in awe. He was a fine figure of a man with a ready smile for her. If she had a husband like that she wouldn't spend her life lying down with the vapours. In the past Mr Cornelius would often give her a knowing wink when she was struggling with a heavy silver tray at teatime. These days he looked grim. His face was drawn with worry, and he stumbled up and down stairs with his illustrious visitors as if he was an old man. Nelly longed to comfort him. She might feel pity for the Missus but her little heart was beating with an aching desire to comfort the master and hold him to her immature bosom. It was love, pure love and adoration. The one thing she mustn't let Mrs Price know. Not being stupid Mrs Price could see young Nelly's infatuation but said nothing. The silly girl would soon get over it and find a more suitable beau

KENSHŌ   House of Secrets

to take her out on her afternoons off. In fact, the coalman's lad had been eyeing Nelly up for some time, lurking around the back scullery hoping for a glimpse of her. When Mrs Price mentioned him, young Nelly turned her nose up, saying, 'I can do better than that, thank you very much.'

One evening when Mrs Price was carefully laying out the master's drinks on the dining room sideboard, she caught a glimpse of Mr Cornelius striding up and down his study, head in hands. Softly knocking on the half open door, she enquired, 'Can I get you a drink before dinner, sir?'

Startled, he looked up with a weary smile saying, 'That would be kind, Mrs Price. A whisky and soda if you please.'

Bringing the drink through on a silver salver the housekeeper enquired diffidently, 'And how is Mrs Agatha, sir?

'Not good Mrs Price, not good at all. The doctors are at their wits' end and talking about the Warneford Asylum at Headington. They take private patients there, but I can't bear the thought of my sweet Aggie in with a lot of lunatics. Perhaps we could manage if I engaged a private nurse for her. Would you be able to continue running the house ,Mrs Price, what do you think?'

'I'll do anything, sir. Anything to help,' Mrs Price said hastily. What a bonus, she thought smugly. I'll soon has this house working just the ways I wants it.

'Let me think some more. I'll let you know,' Cornelius said with a deep sigh.

That night it was if a strange air of doom hung over the house. Even Mrs Price, who was rarely influenced by anything of a sensitive nature, remarked to Nelly, 'I have the strangest feeling tonight, as if something is about to happen.'

KENSHŌ   House of Secrets

Nelly paid little attention, absorbed in the Missus' copy of 'The Ladies Companion' and fantasising about fashions and a life with Mr Cornelius, but managed to mumble, 'It's your imagination, Mrs Price. There's a storm coming. I'm sure I can hear rumblings of thunder. It always gives me a bad head.'

Mrs Price, not pleased at having her feelings dismissed so summarily, snapped, 'Well whatever it is, I think a drop of the hard stuff will do us both good,' and she poured them each a generous nip of gin. Nelly was all for that and after a few more nips they settled in their two rockers in front of the range and were soon fast asleep and snoring loudly.

An almighty bang and clatter woke them both. Mrs Price looked at Nelly, 'Was that thunder or upstairs? Run up and see if anything's amiss. Your young legs can make it faster than mine.'

Nelly shot up the stairs just as Mr Cornelius emerged from his study. 'What was that?' he enquired to thin air as he saw the back of Nelly speeding up the stairs to the first floor bedrooms. Following her, he took the stairs two at a time.

Nelly by now was running towards the Missus' room but there was no sign of her, either in the bedroom, the boudoir or the closet. Not waiting for Mr Cornelius, Nelly continued on to the second floor. Again, there was no sign of the Missus. Beginning to panic, a breathless Nelly soldiered on up to Mrs Price's room and the old nursery on the third floor. Mrs Price's room was empty but the adjoining door to the old nursery was wide open, and there she was, the Missus, hanging from the gas mantle, a stool knocked over and her feet swinging back and fore like a pendulum.

Nelly felt faint then sick. She was rooted to the spot, hardly able to utter a sound. A breathless Mr Cornelius arrived and let out a piercing scream, 'Aggie. No, my Aggie.' Rushing over he hoisted the limp body up in his arms and, stretching, unhooked the rope

KENSHŌ   House of Secrets

from her neck collapsing with her on the floor. There was nothing to be done. They were too late. By now Mrs Price had made her way up to the top floor. It was she who carefully pulled the engraved solid silver rattle from Agatha's clenched hand.

…at this point Mika could read no more. It was heart breaking. She thought of her own reaction to the silver rattle and wished she'd not thrown it away so casually. It was dawn already. She knew she must sleep but it was hard to rest. All she could think of was that poor woman desperate for children and so unhappy with her life she'd ended it. As Mika buried her head in the pillow the house seemed to groan as if it was opposed to giving up any further secrets. Yet Mika knew there was more to come.

CHAPTER 22
Julian and Rhianna

Julian had almost given up trying to contact Rhianna. A month had gone by. Despite continually trying her mobile he'd now been informed the number was out of service. He'd contacted her flatmates, but all they said was that she'd packed up and gone with no explanation or notice. There was her home, of course, but Julian was wary of getting her parents involved. Desperate as he was, he knew he must find out what was happening. Maybe someone more official like the Bursar could make enquiries.

However, an over exercised Bursar was not in a cooperative mood, saying curtly, 'Professor Blenkinsop, you know quite well students come and go particularly in their first year. But, as you are so worried, I'll make time this week to contact Rhianna or her parents. Will that satisfy you?'

Julian was well aware that Rhianna was an only one, the product of mature and extraordinarily rich and influential parents, and probably the apple of their eye. They would create the most enormous furore if they had the slightest inkling their daughter had been having an affair with her Professor. It would be the end of his career and the comfortable life he'd built up.

The Bursar didn't rush to get back to him. Julian began to slowly go to pieces, bungling his lectures and losing track of his tutorial students' work. He was not sleeping and every day came into work hollow eyed and exhausted. Finally, at the end of the week the Bursar stood in the doorway of his office and said laconically, 'Morning Professor. I did manage to find some information about Rhianna Fortescue-West. However, it was second-hand through her families' housekeeper.' She paused as if for effect.

Julian practically passed out and stammered, 'What did she say?'

KENSHŌ House of Secrets

'Just that Rhianna and her parents had gone to New York Christmas shopping. There was nothing else. I suppose we can just chalk it up to the many reasons students drop out,' she added sardonically.

'What reasons?' Julian asked nervously, blotting his sweating hands under the desk with his handkerchief.

The Bursar, ever the consummate professional, enumerated them with her fingers. 'Well let's see. Number one: homesickness, particularly first years who miss home comforts and their mothers. Number two: illness either mental or physical. Number three: change of course or university or both. Number four: family reasons. Number five: university is not what they imagined. Number six: financial reasons, Number seven: they fail their first year exams if they've got that far and finally the usual doozy.'

Julian looked up enquiringly.

'Well, the Biggy – getting pregnant by a fellow student or,' she chortled mockingly, 'by one's Professor or Tutor.' Adding hastily, 'Though of course not in your case, Prof. No disrespect meant.'

She whizzed off, eager to put some distance between them before she put her foot in her mouth any further. Come to think of it, the poor man had been more than shocked by that last remark and turned very pale. As far as she knew he was definitely not one of the latter types of Professor. There was no doubt he had an eye for a pretty face and probably favoured the attractive students to some extent but she was confident he never went beyond that. It was probably just undue concern for his student. He was known to have a good record of first year passes. That's what was probably making him twitchy. Dismissing any slight misgivings, she rushed on to her next meeting.

After she'd gone, Julian put his head on his desk and let out a groan. Janice called from the outer office, 'Everything alright in

KENSHŌ   House of Secrets

there, Prof? Anything I can do? Perhaps a chocolate biscuit and a cuppa would help.'

Julian let out a squeaky, 'No thanks Janice, I'm fine.' He needed to think. What was going on with Rhianna? Had she lied to him? Was she trying to scare him and make him leave Phoebe? He had no way of finding out. Perhaps a carefully phrased letter on official paper about her sudden departure might be effective. Calling Janice in, he dictated a suitable letter enquiring as to whether Rhianna was likely to return or had left for good. 'What do you think Janice?' he asked.

Never having been asked to voice her opinion before, Janice mused what's up with the Prof? He's losing it, perhaps this girl was one liaison too far, but she piped up brightly, 'What about a brief handwritten message of concern at the bottom, after all you are her personal tutor?' attempting to control a snicker as she said it.

'What sort of message?' a dejected Julian asked.

'Well, maybe something like, '*Do hope things are alright. Give me a ring when you can. I'd be happy to discuss future options with you,*' and then sign it 'Julian Blenkinsop' so it's not too informal.

'Good idea,' a relieved Julian said. 'Carry on, Janice. Let's see if that elicits any results.' By the end of the day Julian was glad to be going home to good old dependable Phoebe although at the moment she was not as dependable as she used to be. It was as if she was going through some sort of mid-life crisis although surely she was too young for that. He didn't know where he was with her anymore. What had happened to those bad old days when he could have his little adventures, and then return to his submissive adoring wife?

CHAPTER 23
The submissive wife

At that very moment, back at Kenshō House, Phoebe was relishing her metamorphosis. Perhaps thirty was the new twenty after all and she'd at last come into her own and blossomed into womanhood. Her twenties had passed her by, taken up with childbearing and parenting. Why shouldn't she enjoy her thirties? Lunch with Geoffrey had been followed up by several more dinners and trips to the theatre. Bypassing Daisy, Phoebe got into the habit of bathing and putting the children to bed early, leaving Daisy to prepare Julian's dinner instead. Initially Daisy was hurt at not having her usual contact with the kids, but she soon began to see the advantage of having Julian to herself.

Julian was far too wretched these days to notice things had changed. However, he did wake up enough to comment to Phoebe, 'You've become such a gadabout. I can't keep up with you and your new clothes. Do you realise you didn't come in till past eleven thirty last night? What will people think? Where were you?' It was typical Phoebe thought for Julian to be more concerned about other people's opinions than asking her where she'd been. So much for his priorities. He hadn't changed. Evasively she replied, 'The theatre and dinner with friends.'

'What friends? Anyone I know?'

'No, Julian, friends from the University Archaeology Society. They're a lively bunch and like to eat out and socialise.'

'How peculiar,' he grumbled, 'for people who mainly grub in the earth. I can't imagine archaeologists are a stimulating bunch. It's hardly 'Raiders of the Lost Ark' in Oxford, more like digging up bones in old burial mounds.'

Phoebe laughed merrily, 'You'd be surprised. There is the odd ageing Harrison Ford amongst them.'

KENSHŌ House of Secrets

Looking her up and down, Julian was suddenly aware of what a striking young woman Phoebe had turned into. Maybe it was stupid of him to keep on with these extramarital liaisons. What was that quote of Paul Newman's, 'Why go out for hamburgers when you can have steak at home?' Seizing his opportunity, he said, 'We should go out for dinner sometime like we used to.'

Phoebe's face lit up, 'That would be nice, Julian. Yes, why don't we? Daisy will always stay and babysit.'

'It's a date then,' Julian laughed hollowly. It would be a change to have a date night with his actual wife.

Phoebe was thrilled. As much as it was wonderful to be wined and dined by the charming Geoffrey, a part of her was still in love with her errant husband. If only it was like the old days before they were married when they went on secret dates away from the campus. Julian had been so romantic and thoughtful then, always buying her gifts of flowers and chocolates. What had happened to their marriage? Since the children they seemed to have drifted further and further apart. Surely the children should have brought them closer together.

There was also the ever present problem of Geoffrey, who was becoming more and more amorous. Phoebe wondered how she could hold him off much longer. There wasn't a week that went by when he didn't drop heavy hints about having a trip away. He'd informed her only last week that he had a conference in London coming up. 'Phoebe darling, this would be an ideal chance for us to get away. It's all expenses paid,' he chuckled, ' so we could really go for it and stay at the Savoy or the Ritz.'

Phoebe had prevaricated, 'Geoffrey, I can't go off for a whole weekend like that. What about the children and what would I say to Julian?' The dilemma was she was still attracted to Geoffrey. When they were together and he was not too ardent in his feelings, it felt like the easy relationship they'd had when they

KENSHŌ   House of Secrets

were students. Not wanting to discourage him altogether, Phoebe added, 'Let me think about it, Geoffrey.'

Looking crestfallen he said, 'Phoebe darling, you do still like me don't you? I'm beginning to wonder. You often seem distant, yet at times it's like we'd never been parted. I've never stopped loving you. I just wish I'd made more effort to keep you out of Julian's clutches when we were students. I knew you were in awe of him but never realised you'd allow yourself to be seduced by such an arrogant smarmy old git like that. Goodness he was more than twenty years older than you, what were you thinking?'

Phoebe could feel her hackles rise, 'Please don't talk about Julian like that. You and I were just friends. Julian made me feel like a grown up, someone who valued my opinion and treated me with respect.'

'I think we were more than 'just friends', Phoebe. We spent several nights together if my memory is correct. You told me I was your first. Really you betrayed me with him.'

'I did no such thing,' Phoebe protested indignantly. 'You were only too clear, telling me ours was a casual arrangement and nothing more. When you accepted the Harvard scholarship at the end of our first year, you certainly didn't consult me but vanished without a word. All I heard from you was a one line postcard saying, *Sorry, had this chance and couldn't turn it down, Love Geoffrey.* That was the last I heard from you in ten years.'

Geoffrey had the grace to look sheepish, 'You're right. I did abandon you. I was a selfish young man in those days. But it was a long time ago. I want to make up it up to you.'

'Don't you think it's a bit late?' Phoebe said angrily. 'You really had no idea what I went through. Julian was always there for me.' In fact, we got married shortly after you shot off to the States. I was at a low ebb and needed someone I could rely on. As you

KENSHŌ House of Secrets

know, I was an orphan and had no family of my own. There was no one else to turn to.'

Momentarily Geoffrey looked shocked, 'I hadn't realised...' he mumbled. 'What a heel I was. I'm sorry, Phoebe. I can't apologise enough. You must tell me everything you went through.'

Phoebe shrugged, 'It's not worth talking about now. I just want you to realise how much Julian has done for me. He and I were so happy at the beginning, then the children came along one after the other. It was difficult with three children under five. I don't think Julian signed up for that much family life.'

Concerned Geoffrey asked, 'Are things that difficult in your marriage? Surely you don't have to stay with Julian if you're not happy.'

'I didn't say that exactly,' Phoebe was riled. 'It's just we lead separate lives. Julian finds fatherhood a problem, probably because his own father, the Colonel, was such a distant parent. Julian was packed off to boarding school at a young age. These days he spends most of his time at college and we hardly see him, however, he is the father of my children. I do have feelings for him. I'm not sure about the 'love' thing anymore. Let's just say I'm used to him. I was so young and naïve when we started out, I really don't know any different.'

'That's hardly a reason to stay.'

'But the children are. Family is everything to me. The last few years I've been very negligent with the children, leaving them to Daisy, whilst I studied with the O.U. I think I regretted dropping out of my degree and was trying to make up for it. But I've turned over a new leaf lately, realising I must take responsibility for my children before they grow up and resent me.'

KENSHŌ   House of Secrets

Geoffrey said quickly, 'I'd like to meet them. I must admit I've had little or nothing to do with children but I'm sure yours would be a delight.'

'I don't know about that,' Phoebe smiled ruefully. 'Ptolemy is nine going on ninety. A real character with a mind of his own. Sadilla is seven, cute as a button, dark and a looker like her father whilst Kepha the baby is just four and a real sweetie. Though am sure I'm prejudiced.'

'Unusual names,' Geoffrey commented. 'I guess all to do with your Middle Eastern studies I suppose. Anyway, they sound charming. Why don't I arrange a day out for the kids? Maybe the ice rink or perhaps a walk and a winter picnic?'

Phoebe was taken aback, 'Sorry Geoffrey I've been talking too much. I've let my mouth run away with me. I'm not at all sure it would be a good idea for you to meet the children. Anyway, who could I say you were?'

'Why, an old friend, of course. Someone from your student days. Kids rarely ask questions, I find, if you present them with the facts.'

Phoebe winced, 'Not Tolly, I'm afraid. He's an astute little boy, only too eager to know everything. He fancies himself a detective so wouldn't make life easy for us. Let me think about it. I'll let you know.'

Keen not to push Phoebe any further, Geoffrey backed off. There was no doubt in his mind he wanted Phoebe in his life again. Perhaps one of the ways of seducing her was to win over her children, although whether he was prepared to take on a readymade family was debatable. For now, slowly, slowly, was the way to go. Reassuring Phoebe he said, 'I'll abide by your wishes, darling Phoebe, but let's arrange this trip to London. Can you make some excuse to get away? Maybe a trip to a museum

KENSHŌ   House of Secrets

for an exhibition or a visit to an old girlfriend? Please try. I can assure you we'll have separate rooms if that's what's worrying you. I just want to show you a good time.'

Phoebe could feel herself weakening. Perhaps a weekend away with Geoffrey would help resolve her conflicted feelings one way or the other. Then she could happily settle down again with Julian and the children or consider the other option. Having no family or close friends to talk to was hard. Most women would be thrilled to have two men to choose from but Phoebe, never a flirt, found all this upsetting and unsettling. She certainly didn't want to revert to the old Phoebe, subjecting herself passively to Julian's every need. But did she actually want to break free and tie herself to another man, and one she barely knew? And what about the children? Could she overturn the only world they knew?

Returning home, the first person a chastened Phoebe bumped into was Tolly. Running up to her he threw his arms round her, 'Mum. Mum, where you been? We missed you today. Come and have tea with Mika and I. Daisy's bathing the little ones.' He dragged Phoebe by the hand to the kitchen where Mika was brewing the ritual tea, 'See Mika, Mum's going to join us today. Tell her about the tea ceremony.'

Mika beamed at Phoebe, 'This what we do most afternoons. Tolly he Japanese expert tea maker.' She bowed and indicated for Phoebe to sit on the cushions they'd borrowed from the dining room.

Phoebe looked fondly at Tolly as he busied himself with the preparations, his blonde curls vibrant with delight. For a fleeting moment there was a distinct likeness… Could it be? There was certainly something. What was she to do? She needed to think.

KENSHŌ   House of Secrets

CHAPTER 24
Daisy comes into her own

These days Daisy was enjoying herself. There were so many evenings when Phoebe was out and she was left to make dinner for Julian. At first she would deliver his meal to the dining room and eat her own in the kitchen, but one evening she ventured to say, 'You must be lonely eating on your own in here. Would you like me to stay and eat with you?' To her astonishment he nodded, 'Good idea, let's do that when Phoebe's on one of her inveterate evenings with the Archaeological Society crowd.'

Julian was reasonably docile these days, in fact extremely subdued. There seemed to be something perpetually on his mind. Daisy wondered if it was something to do with Phoebe. She was certainly gallivanting about dressed to the nines. Daisy suspected another man but wouldn't dare say anything to Julian. Anyway, why should she when she could have him all to herself? As the evenings drew in Daisy took to warming his slippers by the fire and having an aperitif waiting for him in his study. In the dining room she would draw the curtains, place a few discreet lamps and light candles in the silver candelabra she'd rescued from a cupboard and polished. The best china was brought out. A white brocade tablecloth covered up the ink stains and scratches on the once beautifully veneered oak dining table. A little Mozart would be playing in the background whilst she served up Julian's favourite steak au poivre.

Julian made no comment about the arrangements, appearing to bask in the attention as if it were his due. He and Daisy began to have more intimate conversations than they'd ever had. One night he asked her about her family. Daisy wasn't at all keen to talk about her wretched home life. What could she say about an alcohol fuelled, violent father and a wilted, useless mother? On the spur of the moment she decided to invent a life for herself. Fiction was always more interesting than fact.

KENSHŌ   House of Secrets

'Father was in the Foreign Service. He and my mother were posted to Suriname just after I was born and left me with an elderly aunt. As I got older she became ill, and I ended up in an orphanage.'

Julian looked appalled, 'My goodness that sounds a lot like Phoebe's early life. She was orphaned at an early age too. But what about your parents? Why didn't they come back for you?'

Disconcerted, Daisy thought for a minute, then getting more and more carried away, said, 'Some years before they'd been taken hostage by guerrillas. The British government refused to pay the ransom, so they disappeared into the jungle and were never heard of again.' Daisy wondered if she'd gone too far, but apparently for an intelligent man Julian was more gullible than she thought.

He nodded sagely and said compassionately, 'You poor girl, what about schooling?'

Airily, Daisy said, 'I didn't have much and left school when I was sixteen to start cleaning in some of the big houses in Oxford. That was until I came here to look after the children. I'm pretty ignorant but would have loved to have gone to college or university. 'Spect it's too late now.'

'It's never too late,' Julian assured her. 'I'll help you. I'll see what I can find in the way of books. What subjects are you interested in?'

Daisy, never having given education a second's thought, said, 'I'd like to know more about your subject, Japan and Japanese history. It would be useful with Mika.'

A delighted Julian beamed from ear to ear, 'That would be marvellous. I've plenty of books to lend you. We'll be able to have some interesting discussions afterwards. Perhaps some basic Japanese phrase books would help as well. It will be wonderful to share my interest with someone in the house. Phoebe is only concerned with old ruins.'

Inwardly, Daisy pulled a face at what she'd let herself in for. However, any sacrifice was worth it to spend evenings with this handsome, charismatic man. She just hoped he wouldn't expect too much of her. Never one to have applied herself to study or reading, it would be a chore to sit and study Julian's books. She'd been the class clown at school, always told off for lateness or talking too much. An interested teacher had once gone to the trouble of having her assessed and Daisy had been made aware that she had ADHD. However, suffering from a short attention span would hardly capture Julian's interest. One thing she did have in abundance though was underlying cunning and common sense. Hopefully, those and her cookery skills would stand her in good stead.

Determined to make the most of their time together, Daisy tenaciously ploughed through several books on Japanese history. Reading was not her strong point, and it took all her willpower to read page after page. Finding it excruciatingly dull and boring, she decided it might be less painful to seduce Julian through his stomach instead. Each night she would produce a different cordon bleu dish. The courses were accompanied by the correct wines with brandies to follow. A replete Julian started to look forward to the evening's repast, to help him blot out his worries about Rhianna. Daisy would note down Julian's favourites and occasionally tempt him with aphrodisiacs like truffles, oysters or caviar. Of course, Julian had no idea he was the one actually paying for all these luxuries, as Daisy regularly raided the housekeeping allowance Phoebe had left with her.

Julian would say, 'You've surpassed yourself tonight, Daisy. I can't remember having such a feast even in Hall.' Quaffing yet another glass of brandy, he asked, 'Tell me how you're getting on with the books. What I need now is a stimulating discussion to round off a perfect evening.'

KENSHŌ House of Secrets

Under pressure, Daisy racked her brains, wondering how to keep this handsome man entertained. Prevaricating, she said, 'Why not relax instead and tell me something about your first wife. I hear she was a beauty.'

Julian, only too eager to oblige, began a long exposition about Lucy, his dead wife. Only half listening, Daisy became absorbed in her own thoughts. According to the information she'd gleaned from Phoebe, Lucy was not only a beauty with brains but a well-heeled lady to boot. Apparently, Julian had worshipped her and wouldn't allow Phoebe to change anything in the house when they married. Perhaps Lucy was the key to seducing Julian. Daisy knew she'd never compete on the brains front but she flattered herself she was a hit in the looks and sensuality department. She must make it her business to find out more about Lucy and what hold she'd had over Julian.

A week later when everyone had left the house for the day, Daisy crept back into Julian's study. Lucy's photo was still in the wooden box at the back of the drawer. Squinting at it in the sunlight, Daisy couldn't see what the fuss was about. She was a blonde pretty young woman but nothing to write home about – just like any other young woman of that age. However, a much younger and even more gorgeous Julian was gazing down at his wife lovingly as if he'd discovered the Holy Grail. Daisy ground her teeth. Maybe there were more clues in the box.

Leafing through the dusty papers, she found a copy of Lucy's death certificate. It was shocking to think Lucy was only twenty six when she'd died of a heart attack after being diagnosed with breast cancer. How could she have died so young? Shuffling through the rest of the papers, there was little else. As Daisy locked the box and proceeded to put it back, she noticed a crumpled paper. Smoothing it out, she saw it was a letter from the university asking for Lucy's final doctoral thesis, reminding her it was overdue. The date was two days before Lucy's death. Julian had probably sent the thesis in, but had he and why wouldn't he?

KENSHŌ   House of Secrets

Perhaps Lucy had been too ill to finish it, but then why keep this letter? Why not reply and throw it away?

Her nerves jangling, it was as if her gut was trying to tell her something. Daisy sensed a mystery. Perhaps her beloved Prof wasn't as squeaky clean as she supposed. Taking possession of the letter, Daisy replaced the box and returned to the kitchen. Staring at it she resolved to find out about it. Maybe it was nothing. On the other hand, any ammunition might help. She could draft Mika in as an accomplice to do some research for her at the college and the Bodleian, though the less she told Mika the better.

KENSHŌ   House of Secrets

CHAPTER 25
Mika is in demand

Mika had little time for anyone these days. The goings on in the nursery had ceased since Mika had read Agatha's story. It was as if the yūrei were appeased for the moment. However, Mika was still nervous about the nursery and kept mainly to her bedroom. Not wanting to find out more of the house's horrors, she hid the manuscript under her mattress away from prying young eyes. Now the Christmas holidays had started, Tolly and the younger children were all over the house, racing everywhere with Dot and Dash in hot pursuit.

There was still, of course, the Colonel's diary. Glancing though it Mika attempted to decipher the tiny script. It was barely legible. It appeared to be a record of the Colonel's time as a Japanese prisoner of war. The odd underlined word in block letters, 'BETRAYAL' and 'GUILT', stood out. Three quarters of the way through the diary the writing dwindled away, as if the writer had lost interest. There were a lot of blank pages but on the final page was the poignant sentence, 'I will never forget or forgive myself'. It was the cry of a wounded soul and Mika shuddered. She felt she'd trespassed into someone's personal world of pain. Somewhere she shouldn't be. Mika was of two minds. Should she destroy the diary as no one knew it still existed, or return it to the Colonel? The Colonel was a private man and wouldn't want anyone else to have his diary, but after the incident with the sword Mika was aware the Colonel's health was precarious. What if the diary, and particularly the last page, prompted a heart attack or stroke? The best course of action was to give it to Sanshō and let him decide.

Approaching the gargoyled door again on the second floor, Mika felt the same apprehension as previously but knocked lightly. The door opened and the imposing figure of Sanshō was revealed again. He bowed and waited.

KENSHŌ   House of Secrets

Mika swallowed nervously, 'Plees when in attic I find,' she produced the ancient blue leather book. 'I think Colonel san's diary from war.' Before she had a chance to explain further, Sanshō snatched the book from her hand and growled, 'I hope, Miss, you've not had the temerity to read anything so personal.'

Shuffling, Mika lied, 'No, no, writing small. Accidental saw last page. So velly, velly, solly.'

Sanshō flicked to the last page. His usual yellowish complexion turned a greyish green, 'Yes, see what you mean. I'll pass it on to the Colonel. Thank you, Miss.' He went to shut the door, but Mika stood her ground.

'I have history of house too. Colonel san, want me to report.'

'Leave it for now, Miss. The Colonel isn't well. Best not to get him too excited. I'll tell him. Wait for a better day.' This time he shut the door forcefully, making Mika jump back out of the way.

Mika returned to her floor. There was so much work to do before the Christmas vacation. Would she ever be ready? Neither Jack nor her grandfather seemed to understand how difficult the course was for her. These days, Takeshi wrote every week urging her to do well and make him proud, whilst Jack continually complained, 'Honestly Mika, I never see you these days except at lectures or in the library. Please, please, take an afternoon off and come for a ride with me in the countryside. At this rate you'll see nothing of England before you go back.'

But Mika was inflexible, 'I study, Jack. It my duty and owe grandfather. Will stop at Christmas.'

'And what will you do for the vac?' Jack asked grumpily. 'I suppose you'll have to spend it with that strange Blenkinsop family. Much fun you'll have with them. What about me?'

KENSHŌ   House of Secrets

'You fly home Boston see father. He glad to see you.'

'Spend Christmas with the old man, I don't think so. He's like you, working all the time and locked in his study. Mom left me a bit of money so perhaps I'll take off for Europe. Why don't you come with me?'

'No Jack. I stay here, work. Perhaps find out about Kenshō House.'

'I don't know, you seem to be fonder of that old house than me. I thought you and I had an understanding? There's so much I want to tell you about what I'm doing these days if you'd only listen.'

'Solly Jack, no time. Finish essay. We talk later, yes?' She patted his arm reassuringly.

'I suppose so,' Jack said frostily. 'It would serve you right if I found another girl.'

Mika sighed heavily. Relationships were far more complex and demanding than she'd realised, 'Up to you, Jack. I not your property. Do what wish.'

Hesitantly, she walked off, half hoping he'd stop her. Why had she said that? Jack meant everything to her. Yet she was wary of involvement. What was wrong with her? One minute she was longing for him to kiss her and show his feelings, the next she was brushing him off. She was confused.

No one was happy with her these days. Even Tolly was scowling when he saw her. Due to her workload, she'd had to abandon their afternoon tea making.

'You're no fun, Mika. I think you're not my friend anymore,' he said vehemently.

KENSHŌ House of Secrets

'So solly, much work, Tolly. Still friend. I make time tomorrow. We take tea?'

'If you want, I don't care,' Tolly said sullenly, kicking viciously at the door as he left.

The next day Mika found she had a late tutorial and had to apologise to Tolly yet again. He shrugged as he ran off, but she saw his lower lip quiver and an unwilling tear escape down his grimy little face. Mika felt ashamed. She was letting everyone down. At this rate she wouldn't have any friends left.

Next it was Daisy lying in wait for her one late afternoon, 'Mika, I must talk to you. Please, I need a favour.'

Mika, weighed down by all these demands on her time, fled upstairs to her sanctuary. Even the yūrei were preferable to these needy people. To think how lonely she'd felt when she'd first arrived, now there were people and relationships everywhere. It was sad to say, but all those years living with her grandfather in solitary isolation had not equipped her for such relentless attention.

KENSHŌ House of Secrets

CHAPTER 26
Sanshō's dilemma

The day Mika handed Sanshō the Colonel's diary was not an auspicious one for Sanshō. The Colonel had not been well the previous day and Sanshō had been reluctant to leave him at night. Trying to make himself comfortable in an armchair in the Colonel's bedroom, he attempted to doze off as the Colonel tossed and moaned in his sleep. There was a great deal of shouting and at one time a terrible scream that pierced Sanshō to the quick. He tried rousing the sleeping Colonel, but the old man was too far gone. Eventually the old man grunted and turned over, falling into a deeper and calmer sleep. Sanshō was exhausted, feeling his age and wondering how much longer he would be able to carry on. He desperately needed help, begging Julian to bring in a night nurse, but Julian, always thinking about money and his inheritance, quibbled, 'Goodness Sanshō, you've managed so far. I don't suppose my father will last much longer. Then you'll be free.'

It was shameful that Julian and his family lived in the house for free yet were unwilling to lift a finger for the old man. Julian was just waiting to cash in, then, Sanshō thought gloomily, then no doubt he'll sell the old house and buy something modern in the city centre. I'll lose my home and my income. Julian was not a man to care about old Sanshō, probably expecting him to decamp to an old peoples' home or the like.

As the Colonel grew restless again, Sanshō made up a mixture of herbs and with a shot of brandy persuaded the Colonel to drink a little. It was a long time till daybreak. Eventually both slept. Later that morning the two old men, shrouded in blankets, sat either side of a tiny electric fire. Finally, the Colonel roused himself, 'I'm sorry, Sanshō old friend. I know this is hardly what you signed up for.'

KENSHŌ   House of Secrets

It was a rarity, Sanshō thought, for the Colonel to apologise for anything. He must be feeling bad. 'Don't worry Colonel. It's just one of those things. You'll be back to yourself in no time. I'll make up another of my concoctions for you.'

The Colonel shuddered, 'If you must, but I feel better already. What about our meditation practice? Do you think that would help?'

'Leave it today, Colonel. I don't think sitting in that uncomfortable position would help. Let me run you a warm bath. I'll give your old legs a massage, then you can take a nap.'

'Honestly, Sanshō, you treat me like a baby. Forget that. Just leave me awhile. Go back to the coach house with Bakti and roll into bed and catch up on your sleep. I'm warm now and will sit here and think, then perhaps get back to work.' He looked longingly at his manuscripts.

Sanshō followed orders and returned home, with Bakti dragging behind him, stopping to investigate every new smell en route. 'I don't know, Bakti,' Sanshō said. 'What shall I do about that diary the girl gave me? I don't think the old man is up to seeing it at the moment. Of course, I don't know what's in it. What do you think?' Bakti sat up on his hind legs as if he were listening intently and then thrust his head into his master's hand. 'Perhaps you're right,' Sanshō agreed. 'I better read it first. It might be the last nail in the old man's coffin, who knows? I wouldn't want that.' He looked enquiringly again at the dog but Bakti had lost interest and was bounding towards the house thinking about food. 'Good thinking, my friend,' Sanshō laughed. 'Let's put it to one side for now. You and I will consider it later.'

Heading for the bedroom he carefully bent his aching knees and lay down beside a well fed Bakti, who'd already made himself a cosy nest in the middle of their pallet. 'Move over, old friend, make room for me.' The dog snorted and quivered in his sleep.

KENSHŌ   House of Secrets

Sanshō exhaled with relief as he stretched out his aching body. The sitar music ebbed and flowed through the room as the pair slept, curled around one another. Much later in the day, Sanshō and Bakti returned to the house and quietly crept into the study. The Colonel had taken Mika's Muramasa sword out of its case and laid it across his lap. Appearing to be in a daze, he slowly stroked the curved blade as if it were a pet. Soundless tears poured down his face as he stared into the far distance, reliving another life, another time, another place.

Sanshō quietly retired to the kitchenette and, finding a bone for Bakti, proceeded to make the Colonel's favourite Oolong tea. Whatever was going on with the old man? Perhaps it was to do with the Japanese camp. Sanshō had wondered over the years but been too wary to ask. It was if something terrible had happened when he'd been laid up with dysentery. The men had shunned the Colonel ever after. The Colonel, a broken man, spent most of his time head in hands, ragged and malnourished, refusing food. Sanshō never found out what had happened. The men had kept their silence. The diary might provide an insight. Sanshō was hesitant about reading a private journal, but it might enable him to help the Colonel.

Tiptoeing into the study, Sanshō laid the tea tray on the desk gently removing the katana from the Colonel's grasp. He took his time replacing it in the display cabinet, giving the old man a chance to compose himself. Bakti, always sensitive to an atmosphere, sidled in, wrapped himself round the Colonel's feet and reached up to shyly nuzzle the Colonel's hand.

The Colonel smiled and stroked the dog's ears, 'Teatime already Sanshō. I don't know where the day's gone. Sit and talk to me, old friend.' Sanshō breathed a sigh of relief. Everything was back to normal for now at least, but, whether he liked it or not, he would have to read that diary.

KENSHŌ   House of Secrets

CHAPTER 27
Julian hears from Rhianna

Julian hadn't had any response to the letter he'd sent Rhianna and was still in the dark as to what she planned. He wished he'd never got involved with a first year and particularly this first year. She was highly strung and neurotic. Who knows what she'd do next? Why hadn't he had more sense and nipped it in the bud before it all went too far?

Her reply came the week before Christmas. Marked 'Personal', it was brief and to the point,
'*Dear Julian,*

Thank you for your concern but have decided to complete my degree elsewhere. Please send my transcripts to whoever requests them. Our little problem is still with me and I haven't decided what to do about 'it', but you will know my decision when it is made. I want nothing from you. Please do not contact me again. My parents have been incredibly supportive. I will be staying with them indefinitely.

Enjoy your Christmas, as I shall,

Rhianna

Julian was beside himself. In some ways his difficulties were over but reading between the lines was illuminating. Obviously, Rhianna had confided in her parents about the 'b...'. God, he couldn't bring himself to say it out loud. Worst of all, she hinted she still had 'their little problem' and hadn't decided what to do about it. Surely it was much too late now to do anything. Did that mean…argh…he couldn't bear to contemplate it. Imagine if Phoebe found out. That would be the end of their marriage. But more dire than that was if her parents complained to the Dean. Julian could see his Oxford career in shreds. No other university would employ him after that. What could he do? If only he'd handled the situation better that afternoon in his office when he'd offered to pay for the abortion. Rhianna had become hysterical, calling him a 'Baby Killer'. He should have been reassuring and helped her but this type of thing had never happened to him

KENSHŌ   House of Secrets

before. All his other conquests had been more worldly wise and vanished when he'd ended the affairs.

There'd been sweet little first year Phoebe of course and, when she'd got pregnant, he'd married her. She'd been such a contrast to his dear Lucy, but in some ways it had been easier. Lucy, though he adored her, had been far superior to him intellectually. Her beauty attracted men to her like bees to a honeypot. Competing to win Lucy had made him feel inadequate. After they were married he never felt he could live up to her or satisfy her. On the other hand, his and Phoebe's marriage was like a pair of well-worn slippers, comfortable without demands. Regrettably, once the children came along, the marriage had started to falter. By then, of course, his attentions had already strayed.

It had always been difficult to ignore all those gorgeous young girls queuing up and desperate for his favours. This time maybe he'd come to the end of the road and should look homewards for his treats. Certainly, Phoebe now looked the part of an aspiring academic's wife and Daisy, well Daisy, with her cooking and sensuality seemed to be offering a whole lot more though of course he might be mistaken. After all he'd slipped up with Rhianna and couldn't afford further lapses in judgement. However, before he considered any entertainment on the home front, he must resolve the Rhianna situation.

Janice might be the person to turn to. She was a level-headed, objective woman who'd been with him years and probably knew more about his life and what was going on in the college than he did. Two heads would certainly be better than one.

After reading the letter, Janice sat back in her chair and said thoughtfully, 'This needs further investigation, Prof. I tell you what, I know a girl in Rhianna's year who was her best friend. I'll talk to her and let you know what I find out.'

KENSHŌ   House of Secrets

A grateful Julian said, 'That would be wonderful, Janice. I owe you one.'

Savouring his discomfort, an amused Janice told herself inwardly you certainly do, Prof. and you'll find yourself paying for it when staff reviews comes round.

Following Janice's enquiries, it turned out Rhianna's friend had lost touch with her. All she'd heard on the college grapevine that Rhianna was applying to other universities the following September and taking a year out. Janice passed the news on to the Prof. He didn't take it well, sitting with a furrowed brow, and moaning to himself.

Janice, never one to mince words, commented, 'I thought you'd be relieved, Prof. She'll be out of your hair for good. No more bouts of hysteria. She'll be someone else's problem now.'

Julian continued to languish at his desk in a state of dejection, 'There's a bit more to it, Janice, than that. It's personal. I'm sorry I can't share it with you. In fact it's not my place to say anything.'

A riveted Janice went back to her desk. So what was it the Prof was so worried about? Could it be the unthinkable…a baby? Surely not. You'd think he'd have more sense considering the number of liaisons he'd conducted since she'd been there. This could be the end of his career if the Dean and Senior Fellows found out. She must keep her mouth shut though. This job was a bit of a doddle, and she needed to keep on good terms with the Prof.

Next door Julian sat and considered his life. It was imperative to get his marriage back on a better footing. Perhaps he should begin by taking Phoebe flowers. Women were always seduced by a few roses, then maybe dinner at her favourite restaurant. The children, of course, were the key. They were Phoebe's be all and end all. He should find out what they wanted for Christmas. perhaps put

KENSHŌ House of Secrets

himself out personally to buy their presents rather than leave it to Phoebe. That would go down well.

There was however still the matter of Daisy. Over the last weeks she'd managed to insinuate herself into his evenings with her mouth-watering meals and home comforts. It would be hard to give all that up. Strange but in the past he'd barely noticed Daisy, yet lately it was if she were always at hand looking fresh, young, sexy and very trendy. There was a certain voluptuousness about her that was hard to miss, particularly when she flaunted it in his direction. An affair at home was definitely not be a good idea now particularly as he needed to ingratiate himself with Phoebe. Daisy would keep. Perhaps he would have a rethink about her after Christmas when things with Rhianna were settled.

Having clarified his thoughts, Julian called through to Janice, 'Make sure my Christmas is clear of appointments, there's a good girl, I want to spend more time with the family this year.'

I bet he does, Janice smirked, as she pencilled out the holiday in his diary.

CHAPTER 28
Planning Christmas

'I think we should have a good old traditional English Christmas this year,' Phoebe declared. 'I don't know what Mika and her grandfather do, but we owe it to her to really push the boat out as it's her one and only Christmas here. What do you think Julian?'

In one of his absentminded moods, Julian said, 'Why not? The children will be delighted. Perhaps we should ask my father and Sanshō down for a change. They usually make an appearance for Christmas dinner. Perhaps we can persuade them to stay all day. I know they like to hide away through the holiday season but this might be the old man's last, you never know. I'll try to get him to fork out for more appropriate presents for the children this time. Buddhas and shells are hardly suitable.'

Phoebe, full of enthusiasm, was only too eager to agree, 'I'll get Daisy to organise the food, she's better than I am. The children and I can take on decorating the house. Julian, can you get us a tree and the largest turkey you can find. At the very least there'll be eight of us to feed, maybe nine with Daisy. I think we should include Daisy, don't you? Particularly with her home life or lack of it. I'm sure her mother won't mind. Anyway she's practically one of the family.'

In a begrudging manner, Julian said, 'I suppose so.' Then somewhat puzzled, he asked, 'What do you mean about Daisy's 'mother'? I thought she was an orphan with no relatives.'

'You must be confused, dear. She lives on the other side of town on the Blackbird Leys estate. I believe her mother has health problems, though I'm sure she won't begrudge Daisy coming over here on Christmas Day to help out and have lunch with us. The girl has so little fun.'

KENSHŌ House of Secrets

Julian was flabbergasted. What about that story Daisy had told him about her parents being in the Foreign Service and being sent to Suriname? Had she made that up on the spot? She must think him naive, though he admired her bravado. It was the sort of thing he'd do if he found himself in a tight corner. However, the less Phoebe knew about his and Daisy's evenings together the better. Giving Phoebe his full attention, he said, 'I hope you're not planning on going overboard with the spending, darling. We still have to live in the New Year.'

Phoebe wanted to blot out the New Year. So far she'd managed to evade Geoffrey's conference in London, but she was only too aware there were decisions to be made in that direction. Geoffrey was indefatigable in his pursuit of her. He'd conceded over the London trip, but she couldn't avoid him for ever. At least over Christmas she'd have some respite, as he was flying back to the States to sort out business. For now she was just going to concentrate on generating Christmas cheer. Recruiting Daisy and Mika to plan menus and food, Phoebe dug out the old ornaments and decorations. They'd certainly seen better days. Many of them dated back to Lucy's time and Phoebe wanted no reminders of Julian's first wife. This year she was going to do things her way whatever Julian said. Everything must be pristine and new.

Surprisingly that evening, Julian came home early and presented Phoebe with an enormous bouquet of early Christmas roses, saying, 'Leave Daisy to see to the children and the dogs. I've made a reservation for us at Chez Michel's. You always liked it there. I thought we'd discuss our plans for Christmas. Please tell me there's no jollies with the Archaeological Society tonight.'

An astounded Phoebe was thrilled, 'These are wonderful.' She was almost tearful as she clutched the white roses to her chest. Whatever had come over Julian? 'I'll get Daisy to put them in water before she sees to the children. Chez Michel sounds marvellous. I've nothing organised for tonight. Just let me change. This is such a surprise, so unexpected.'

KENSHŌ   House of Secrets

A sheepish Julian said, 'Sorry, my dear, I know it's been a long time,' and stuttered, 'work you know, pressure of work particularly with the Christmas vac on the horizon.'

Daisy emerged from the kitchen as Julian pushed past her, ignoring her as if she was part of the furniture. Daisy was dumbfounded but didn't have a chance to catch her breath before Phoebe thrust a bunch of roses at her, saying, 'Be an angel, Daisy. Put these in the Chinese vase for me. It will set them off beautifully. I've got to change. I'll leave the children to you tonight. Julian's taking me out to a fancy French restaurant we both like, can you imagine?' Daisy literally seethed. Steam practically burst from her ears. What was this about? Wasn't she the one who'd cooked for Julian for the last month and catered to his every need? How dare he snub her and start courting his wife again. This wouldn't do, wouldn't do at all. Something drastic was required.

Julian hummed to himself as they drove into Oxford. 'You seem relaxed tonight, darling,' Phoebe said, 'it must be the thought of Christmas.'

'Absolutely,' Julian said. 'You must tell me your plans and how I can help. I thought I might take on the Christmas shopping for the children's presents myself this year, being as you want such an elaborate festival.' Phoebe hadn't the heart to tell him she'd already bought the majority of the children's presents.

 As they sat sipping Prosecco, she said, 'You could buy some surprises for the children. They'd love it if they came from you. You know how much in awe they are of you.'

Julian frowned, 'I wouldn't like to think my children were frightened of me.'

Hurriedly, Phoebe continued, 'No, that's not what I mean. They look up to you is all.'

KENSHŌ   House of Secrets

'That's a funny turn of phrase, Phoebe - not even grammatically correct. Sounds like the Southern States of America. Where did you pick that up?'

Flustered, Phoebe suddenly thought of Geoffrey. Had she absorbed some of his speech patterns, yet as far as she knew he'd never lived anywhere other than California. Quickly she said, 'Oh it's off the TV I expect. All those American cartoons I watch with the kids.'

'Good to know,' Julian said drily, 'I wouldn't like to think you're chumming up with some American at the Archaeological Society behind my back. You know what I think of our American compatriots.'

'Certainly not,' Phoebe said, trying to muster some righteous indignation. 'They're all true blue British archaeologists and academics.' Hastily changing the subject she added, 'I thought you wanted to discuss Christmas and the children.'

'Let's,' Julian said in a sullen tone as he poked at his steak tartare in dissatisfaction. 'I'd quite forgotten what this was. My schoolboy French was never up to Michel's menu.'

'Shall I order you something else?' Phoebe offered in an appeasing manner.

'No,' Julian said forcefully, not keen to be shown up in front of Michel. 'I'll wait for the main course. At least I know what to expect with coq au vin. Anyway, back to presents. What can I buy the children this year? Don't make them anything too obscure or so popular that I can't get it locally. I haven't the time or the inclination to trek up to Hamleys.' Honestly, Phoebe thought resentfully, he makes it sound as if he buys the presents every year. There's never been a single Christmas or birthday when he's shown an iota of interest in gift giving. Determined to keep the peace, she patted Julian's hand and said, 'A doll for Sadilla, maybe

KENSHŌ House of Secrets

a Japanese one in a kimono, as she's so taken with Mika. Kepha is easy enough to please. Anything he can wheel along or float in the bath will suit him. Tolly is the problem one. He's such an intelligent boy, curious about everything. He'd probably love a detective set, one where you take fingerprints or look for clues. If that's too difficult, then a couple of Sherlock Holmes books will keep him happy. I'll leave it to you. You can enjoy choosing.' Julian was not too sure about the 'enjoy' bit, never having been keen on shopping. His ace in the hole was Janice. He could bribe her with an afternoon off and she could do all the trudging about. But he'd keep that to himself. It would never do for Phoebe to find out her beloved children's Christmas shopping had been delegated to a mere secretary. By the end of the meal the pair of them had come to a reasonable accommodation, even if only in their own minds. Phoebe felt happier they were making efforts with their marriage and Julian was relieved he had Phoebe back on side. Whatever furore Rhianna caused now, he was convinced Phoebe would stick with him. He might need her support and understanding in the future.

When they finally got home, a sullen Daisy was already putting on her coat, 'You're late,' she grumbled. 'It's been a long day.'

'I'm sorry. Come in later tomorrow,' Phoebe said affably. 'Do you want Julian to see you home?'

'No thanks, I'll find my own way.' Behind Phoebe's back, Daisy tightened her lips and narrowed her eyes at Julian as he again avoided looking at her. Making for the kitchen, he whistled quietly under his breath. Daisy was incandescent with rage. No man was going to treat her like this, especially one she'd spent weeks pandering to. She'd invested too much time and effort to be abused and overlooked in this way Practically foaming at the mouth she mouthed to herself, you just wait Professor and see what I find out about your past. There's bound to be a few skeletons in your closet. You might have second thoughts then. I'll make you pay one way or another.

KENSHŌ House of Secrets

CHAPTER 29
Jack flies home to Boston

It was a week before Christmas. Mika and Jack had not spoken since Mika had walked away. The night of their tutor's Christmas cocktail party they managed to stand on different sides of the room, clutching glasses of punch as if their lives depended on them, and, looking at everyone except each other.

Dr Margaret, a cheerful, extrovert character, spotted the lurking Mika and advanced, 'Come on, Mika. You can relax now. No more work till next term. Enjoy some Christmas cheer. Now who do you know? Look, there's Jack hiding in a corner. Come on, Jack. Keep Mika company. I don't want my two brightest students becoming party poopers.' Practically forcing them together, Dr Margaret excused herself with an amused glint in her eye, 'Sorry, my dears. I see the Dean beckoning.'

Mika looked at Jack. He stared down at his glass stonily. Finally she summoned up the courage to say, 'Solly, Jack. I velly stupid and rude last time. I no want you to find other girl…' her sentence petered away as she bowed her head in shame.

Jack's face visibly brightened, 'I don't want another girl, Mika. We're friends and I hope much more. Let's bury the hatchet, shall we?'

Mika looked bewildered, 'Hatchet'! Sound dangerous. Is like sword? And where to bury? In my head?'

Jack doubled over laughing, 'Just a turn of phrase. It means let's forget the past and be friends again.'

'I like that, Jack. Please forgive. We start again. What you do for Christmas? Still go to Europe?'

KENSHŌ House of Secrets

Pursing his lips, Jack said, 'No, unfortunately, the old man seems to want me home. I'm flying to Boston tomorrow. He says there's something he wants to talk to me about.'

Mika looked alarmed, 'He want you leave Oxford?'

'I don't think so - well not till I get my degree. No doubt he has plans for me. As this is my last night before the holiday, let's get out of here and go for a meal.'

'Not good manners, Jack. Look bad.'

Dr Margaret won't mind. She's an understanding soul. I'll go and make our apologies. Wait for me outside.'

They departed for their usual Italian bistro. As they sat in one of the booths, Jack said, 'As I won't see you on Christmas Day, I've brought your present with me. I was hoping you'd be at Dr Margaret's party.'

A shamefaced Mika said, 'Didn't buy you present, Jack. We not speaking. I not know what to do. Why you buy me present when I so bad to you?'

'Don't be silly, Mika. It was just a spat. I never stopped liking you.' (He swallowed hard to stop himself saying 'loving you' in case he frightened her away again). 'It doesn't matter about all that now. Please open it.'

Mika carefully unwrapped the black velvet box. A pair of jade drop earrings sparkled up at her. She gasped.

Jack continued, 'Remember when you wore that beautiful cheongsam dress with the green dragons. I thought these would look good with the dress if you wore it over Christmas.'

'But Jack, this too much. How you afford?'

KENSHŌ   House of Secrets

Jack smiled, 'I saved some of the money I was going to spend in Europe and spent it on you. This is why I'm going home for Christmas, and to see my father of course. You're worth it. There was a special reason I chose jade; do you know why?'

'No,' Mika said, completely overawed by the gift.

'It's supposed to bring the wearer luck, happiness, harmony and encourage the dreams of the heart.' Jack blushed bright red with embarrassment as he said it.

Instinctively, Mika leaned across the table. Taking Jack's hand she drew him towards her and kissed him full on the lips. Astounded at her own audacity, she attempted to pull away but he moved in closer and breathed into her neck, 'I've been waiting for that. Does this mean what I think it means?'

Mika struggled from his embrace, lowering her head, 'Plees to forgive. Not know what thinking?'

But Jack knew, 'You really do like me then?' he persevered.

'Of course,' was the only answer he got.

'That's all I need to hear,' he said, sitting back in his chair and beaming from ear to ear.

'Plees to change subject,' a flustered Mika said.

Later that evening when they reached the end of the drive leading to Kenshō House, Mika allowed Jack to kiss her thoroughly. She was dizzy with excitement. What had happened to her? Where were all those years of control and restraint now? What would her grandfather think?

Promising to write and phone, Jack returned to his lodgings to pack ready to fly to Boston the following day.

KENSHŌ   House of Secrets

CHAPTER 30
Jack confronts his father

Arriving back at the gloomy old house in the Boston suburbs, Jack wondered why he'd bothered. There wasn't a single sign of Christmas or any other form of welcome. A strange maid opened the door and he had to explain who he was. She scuttled back to her warm kitchen whilst he dumped his rucksack in the hall and made for his father's study. Slivers of light filtered through the edges of the door but the door was firmly closed. Jack knocked and received a 'Come'. As ever, his father had his head down studying piles of documents. 'Just put the tray down over there, Millie,' he said peremptorily without raising his head.

'It's me, father. Jack. I'm home for the holidays.'

A surprised Mr Sylvester looked up with a start. He was a tall lean grey haired man of indeterminate years always clad in a Brooks Brothers dark suit, shirt and tie, even when working at home. Standing to his full height, he strode round the desk to shake hands with his son. 'Welcome home, my boy. I was expecting you tomorrow, the twentieth.'

'Today's the twentieth,' Jack said wryly. 'I expect you lost track with your work and the time difference of course.'

'That must be it,' the older man said wearily. 'I just hope, Jack, when you join the firm you'll be able to take some of the burden of all this paperwork off my shoulders.'

Jack winced. It had started already. Nevertheless, now was not the moment to have a row, not when he'd just arrived. They had to survive Christmas yet. He adroitly changed the subject, 'I see we've got a new maid. What happened to Suzie?'

'She wasn't suitable. Far too informal in her manners. You'll notice a few other changes round here too. Buddy, the old

KENSHŌ   House of Secrets

gardener, has retired and so has Lou, our housekeeper. Both pensioned off. There's a very efficient lady called Effie who's come in to run the household. Ask her if you want anything.'

'What about Christmas? Anything special happening?'

'No, the usual firm's party at the Four Seasons on Christmas Eve, to which of course you're invited. But I'm afraid it's just you and I on Christmas Day. Effie's coming in early to prepare lunch at one. Then we'll be left to our own devices. Perhaps church in the morning if you're so inclined, a walk in the afternoon. I've a few things to discuss with you. But settle in. I'll see you for dinner at seven.'

Realising he was dismissed, Jack headed for his rooms at the top of the house. It was going to be as grim a holiday as ever, especially with that talk on Christmas afternoon to look forward to. Having nothing to do, Jack visited his mother's old bedroom. His father had kept it exactly as it was and moved into another room. Delicately, he touched the ornaments and sniffed the evaporated perfume bottles. Though his mother's fragrance was familiar and evocative, there'd been little affection between them. His parents were like cardboard cut-outs, having little or no depth. Their friends and hangers-on were mere acquaintances and superficial ones at that and had all fallen away since his mother's death, once the parties and social life stopped. No relatives or past memories of his or his parents' childhoods were ever mentioned. It was as if his parents had come from nowhere.

Christmas Day arrived. Jack and his father sat down to their heated up turkey lunch, making an effort at strained small talk and a pretend jollity as they pulled gold embossed crackers. After lunch Jack volunteered to clean up and load the dishwasher, whilst his relieved father vanished back into his study. Keeping himself going by humming Christmas Carols, Jack sorted out the kitchen and then sat down at the table to quaff the rest of a rather good brandy that had not been on offer.

KENSHŌ House of Secrets

At three o'clock on the dot, just as Jack was getting pleasantly squiffy, Mr Sylvester made an appearance, 'Shall we take that constitutional now, Jack. Grab that old fur parka of mine and a scarf. It's freezing out there.'

The conversation started amiably enough. Mr Sylvester Senior asked about Jack's life at Oxford. Without thinking and being more than a little tipsy, Jack said, 'I've met a girl. I think it might be serious.'

His father nodded sagely but said, 'It probably won't last, Jack. These college romances rarely do. Just enjoy it while you can. There'll be other girls. Once you qualify as a lawyer and join the firm, you'll meet the right class of wife to help you socially with your career.'

'No, this is the right girl for me,' Jack was adamant. 'I'm sure of it. I've never felt like this before. I adore her though I'm not certain how she feels about me.'

Mr Sylvester sighed, 'It'll pass. Where does she come from? Who are her family?'

'Her name's Mika. She's from Japan, a place called Wajima on the Noto Peninsula, and lives with an ageing grandfather.'

There was an over-long silence. A shocked Mr Sylvester, suddenly looking older, quite out of character, shouted, 'It won't do. It won't do at all. What were you be thinking of? You must finish it as soon as you return. Promise me.'

'I'll do nothing of the sort,' Jack said with controlled vehemence. 'Why should I?'

'There are things you don't know,' Mr Sylvester hissed angrily. 'This can't happen, you hear. I won't have it. A Jap of all people.

KENSHŌ House of Secrets

If your poor mother were alive…or your grandfather for that matter…he'd turn in his grave.'

'What is this about? What about mother? Do you hate the Japanese or something? You weren't even old enough to be in the last war. I can't believe a man of your standing and education would have such prejudice. For goodness sake, the war's long over. Who cares about it now?'

'Some of us still care,' his father said bitterly, 'particularly the ones who survived Pearl Harbour. This romance cannot happen. I forbid it. I think you should give up Oxford and transfer to a law degree here in Boston.'

'I certainly won't,' Jack was furious. 'I got a scholarship to Oxford. I intend seeing it through to my degree and being with Mika. As for law, I never wanted to be a lawyer or join your firm. That's all your idea. I've absolutely no interest in the law, and plan to be a writer.' Stalking off, he left his father aghast and open mouthed.

Returning to the house there was nothing for it but to pack and return to Oxford earlier than he'd envisaged. He needed to put distance between himself and that cold depressing sepulchre of a house, and his emotionless automaton of a father. Some Christmas this had been.

KENSHŌ   House of Secrets

CHAPTER 31
Christmas Day at Kenshō House

Events at Kenshō House proved to be more joyful on Christmas Day than in Boston. Phoebe, besieged by small children fighting hordes of wrapping paper and an ecstatic Dot and Dash racing up and down, wondered how she would ever get the Christmas dinner on the table.

Since early morning, the Colonel, Sanshō and Bakti had taken up residence in the dining room, patiently awaiting their call to lunch. Sipping sherries and munching cheese and olives on sticks, they resolutely avoided the screaming children and panting dogs. For once the Colonel had outdone himself by buying the children the right sort of presents, although the drum for Kepha was proving a nightmare with the banging. However, the rag doll for Sadilla and the magic set for Tolly were well received. Even Julian had found suitable presents for the children plus a beautiful emerald silk scarf for Phoebe, an antique Japanese lantern for Mika and perfume for Daisy. Janice had come up trumps as usual and been duly rewarded with an extended holiday, a bonus and a second-hand fruit basket Julian had received from Nissan.

Shattered by all his efforts at showing paternal interest in his children, Julian felt he'd done enough and retired from the fray, shutting the sitting room door firmly behind him. As it was the season of goodwill, the next port of call was his father and Sanshō. Never sure of what reception to expect from the old man, Julian enquired solicitously, 'How is the arthritis these days, father? Are you managing much research?'

Brusquely, the old man said, 'Sanshō looks after me well enough and keeps me mobile. As for the research, it's progressing.' Striving for a pleasanter tone, the Colonel attempted to return the compliment asking, 'How about yourself? Published any papers lately?'

KENSHŌ House of Secrets

'No, I've no chance,' Julian puffed himself up with pride. 'It's a lot of work being head of the Institute. So many calls on my time.'

'I suppose so,' the Colonel said with a leer, only too aware of his son's predilections. 'Let's hope they're not all feminine ones.'

Julian scowled. He was no match for his father when the Colonel was on form. Apparently the sherry was doing its work. Knowing he was bested Julian retired to the kitchen, which was a sweltering hive of activity. Phoebe was basting a gargantuan turkey that barely fitted in the Aga, as Mika and Daisy peeled mountains of potatoes and vegetables. All three, continuously mopping their brows in the steaming kitchen, had rolled up their sleeves to cope with the heat.

Making an effort at fake geniality, Julian asked, 'Would any of you hard working ladies like a drink?'

The only one to pipe up was Daisy. Staring at him seductively from under her dark, heavily mascared false eyelashes she quipped, 'We certainly would, wouldn't we ladies? (emphasising the word 'ladies' in an imitation of Julian's posh upper class accent).

Ignoring the mockery, Julian continued, 'What would you like?'

'Surprise us,' Daisy said, licking her lips lasciviously at him from behind Phoebe's aproned back.

Julian, made a speedy exit, returning post haste with brimming cocktails. Dumping the drinks on the only uncluttered surface, he mumbled 'must get back to the kids' and beat a rapid retreat. That Daisy had some gall flirting with him. What if Phoebe'd noticed? It wouldn't do. He'd have to nip it in the bud. There was no getting away from the fact though she was a very sexy young thing, becoming more alluring by the day, even if she was from the wrong side of the tracks.

KENSHŌ   House of Secrets

Mika, looking up fleetingly from the job in hand, realised she'd had little chance today to talk to the Colonel let alone the children. She, Phoebe and Daisy had been up since the crack of dawn struggling with the preparations. At last when everything was cooking, Phoebe said, 'Mika, thanks so much for all your hard work. I think everything's under control now. Why don't you go and sit with the Colonel and Sanshō in the dining room? It'll be cooler and quieter in there. Help yourself to their sherry before they drink it all, or there's sake in the fridge for you if you prefer. Daisy and I will sort out the children and tidy up their mess.'

Glad to take a breather, Mika was relieved to sit with the two old men. It was like being at home with her grandfather. All the hullabaloo with the children and Dot and Dash in the sitting room was too intense and not what she was used to. Bakti came up and put his head on her hand, and Mika gave him a tentative pat before he resumed his place sitting across the Colonel's feet. The Colonel, afloat with sherry, said kindly, 'It seems a while since our last meeting. I'm still in awe of that magnificent sword. Sit next to me and tell me what you and your grandfather would do on Christmas Day.'

Mika thought for a moment, 'Not like England. Grandfather treat as usual day with Samurai practice. We celebrate 23 December birthday of Emperor. Is national holiday. Christmas Day ordinary workday. But different in Tokyo have Western decorations, lights and trees now.'

'Do you give gifts?' Sanshō enquired.

'No, only gift on birthday. I make Christmas cake as treat not like yours. Sponge with strawberries and cream.'

The Colonel winced at the bleakness of Mika's life. Even in the prison camps at Christmas they'd fashioned gifts from wood or old socks and dredged up some meat, probably boiled rat, to flavour the rice. Seeing the Colonel's expression, Mika said

KENSHŌ House of Secrets

hastily, 'New Year important for us. After 'Ōsōji/big cleaning' of house, families together, eat traditional food, light lanterns, visit shrines and temples.'

By now Sanshō was lightly snoring as he nodded off in one of the large armchairs The Colonel, enlivened by the sherry, said, 'You never did come and tell me what you found in the attic about my ancestors. Are the yūrei still around?'

Mika dropped her head in penitence, 'So solly, heard you not well. Not want to trouble. Yūrei quiet now.' She was hesitant to mention the account she'd read of Agatha's suicide. Some things were best kept to oneself.

'So what did you find?' The Colonel was nothing but insistent, now his interest was piqued.

'Old folders, bills to do with house. Not important.' Mika was not sure whether to mention the Colonel's old diary. She looked across at Sanshō who was fast asleep. Obviously, he'd never given it to the Colonel. What should she do or say about it? Perhaps silence was the best policy.

The Colonel seemed satisfied and shook his head, 'It was just a thought. I was hoping you might uncover something that would give us some clues to the history of the house.' He started to ramble on reliving the past. Mika smiled and nodded encouragement though she could barely follow...'My Aunt Violet lived in this house all her life. I believe she moved in as a child with her family in 1901. I never met her. I suppose it was because Mother, the youngest in the family, the baby, eloped at fifteen and was disowned by them all. Mother, poor soul was never given a name but known as Baby all her short life, which can't have been much fun. I was eighteen when I joined the army and Mother died just after, so I had no chance to find out about her family. Then it was war...(he gulped, omitting his time as a prisoner of war). By the time I left hospital in 1946, Aunt Violet had died and left me

KENSHŌ House of Secrets

the house. Apparently I was her sole heir. I must say I was glad of it. Things were not easy for me. My wife had died in the London bombing, and Julian was just a baby living with my in-laws. I secreted myself away here like a hermit with my books. Sanshō joined me later. This house has been our life and my deliverance.'

Just then Sanshō began to stir and the Colonel tapped his nose, 'That's all between you and me, Mika. I feel I can trust you.'

Mika wondered why, when he hardly knew her, and why did people feel they must keep secrets from one another? Perhaps it was as well she'd not told the Colonel about finding the diary. His past might be too painful to reread and she wouldn't like to be responsible for his collapse. It was confusing. She wished she understood the spoken language better, as there appeared to be so much more going on beneath the surface.

Tolly came scrambling into the room, breaking into the quiet to announce in an ear-splitting roar, 'Lady and gentlemen. Mum says dinner's served. Please takes your places.'

Sanshō gallantly pulled out a chair for Mika and heaved the Colonel into a seat beside her. The table had been laid earlier by Daisy and Mika who'd designed the table decorations and added crackers. Marshalling the two younger children, Daisy provided them with bibs and cautioned them to sit still. Tolly was already pulling and shaking crackers with his father as his mother brought in the food. Once the turkey arrived, Julian, full of self-importance, set to work making a great show of sharpening knives and carving.

Trying to divest herself of her apron, a flustered Phoebe apologised about the lack of starters, 'The girls and I have had too much to do. We thought Christmas dinner and plum pudding to follow would be enough.'

KENSHŌ   House of Secrets

The Colonel raised his wine glass, 'Relax Phoebe, my dear, everything looks magnificent. Here's to you and your helpers.' (acknowledging Daisy and Mika). 'I congratulate the three of you. Happy Christmas, my dear, to my family and our guests.'

Phoebe blushed and stammered, 'Thank you Colonel, and for the lovely gifts. I'm sure the children are delighted, aren't you children?' No one was listening as they tucked into enormous plates of turkey with all the trimmings.

An irrepressible Tolly piped up saying, 'I loved my magic set, Gramps, and my private eye kit, Dad. As a reward I'm gonna fingerprint everyone after lunch.' The Colonel grimaced. Sanshō flinched. Any mention of fingerprints always made him think back to his time in that Indian jail.

Phoebe, noticing the two old men's reaction, said sharply, 'Get on with your meal, Tolly. Don't call your grandfather 'Gramps'.' Tapping his hand, she added, 'Not another word.' Attempting to distract the table, she said brightly to Mika, 'Have you had a chance to phone your grandfather today? You know we're happy for you to use the telephone whenever you like.' This time it was Julian who recoiled calculating the cost of calls to Japan.

Doing her best to hide her Brussel sprouts under a mound of roast potatoes, Mika replied, 'Arigatō Phoebe. Grandfather wrote last week. He away in New Year. I think he visit Nagasaki. He not say why. Secretive man.'

A deathly silence descended on the table as each of the adults absorbed what she'd said. Even after fifty five years the name 'Nagasaki' resonated. They all studiously avoided Mika's eyes, concentrating on their plates. Only the low murmur of the two younger children's voices could be heard as they innocently prattled between themselves.

KENSHŌ House of Secrets

CHAPTER 32
Kurisamu - Takeshi visits the past

Takeshi had never realised quite how much he needed Mika until Christmas and the New Year. It was if a part of him was missing. Was it the sound of her sweet voice trilling the latest pop song as she made tempura batter, or the click clack of her geta sandals on the path or just her unassuming quiet presence? Somehow through the years she'd provided the lightness in his life. Over the last months despite the discipline of his Samurai rituals, there'd been something lacking. Of course, they talked occasionally on the telephone and wrote letters but his heart ached. He knew he'd been too distant, showing Mika only order and self-control. Why hadn't he been able to show her love or affection? It was as if he were too frightened to reveal that side of himself in case he lost her, as he'd lost his beloved wife and then his son. Had he left it too late to change? He must consult the ancestors for guidance. Perhaps it was time to return to the past and revisit Nagasaki. Then maybe his wounds would heal.

Ignoring Christmas Day, Takeshi carried on with his rituals as normal, wondering how Mika was enjoying an English Christmas. The West made so much fuss over the Christian festival that now even Japanese cities were adopting its traditions with trees, lights and presents. Preparing for the New Year, Takeshi carried out the customary 'Ōsōji/ big cleaning' of his and Mika's katei. It was a chance to clear his mind before he embarked on the long journey to Nagasaki.

On the day of his departure he reflected on how strange it was to be travelling by train. All those years ago he'd walked or limped most of the way to Sakura's home. After the two atomic bombs and the surrender in August 1945, Japan was in chaos. Avoiding the American troops, Takeshi had surreptitiously changed out of his Imperial uniform, dressing himself in tattered peasant clothes. He knew if he were caught out of uniform it would mean a dishonourable death. But all he wanted was to find his beloved

KENSHŌ House of Secrets

Sakura and his twelve month old son. His feet, unaccustomed to the geta, were blistered and bleeding by the time he reached Nagasaki.

Why oh why had he sent them to her parents in Nagasaki? It seemed for the best because of the Tokyo firebombing, but had his family survived? What would he find when he reached Sakura's home? At the time, when he'd reached the city, he'd been unaware the bomb had been dropped on the north of the city in Urakami, where Sakura's family lived. The Nagasaki bomb, more powerful than the Hiroshima bomb, had unleashed twenty one tons of plutonium fifty three seconds after its release. Its fireball, half as hot as the surface of the sun, had incinerated seventy thousand people.

It was no use dwelling on past memories, Takeshi had to start his journey. Packing his few possessions in an antiquated leather satchel, grabbing his hantan jacket and sushi for the journey, Takeshi set off for the train. It had been fifty six years since that last trek to Nagasaki in 1945. In latter years he'd never travelled further than Tokyo. Now he was to embark on this eleven hour train journey into his former life. Though a man of iron control, Takeshi felt the first stirrings of fear. What if this was a mistake and there was only pain at the end of it? Yet it had to be done. He owed it to Mika. All through her childhood and growing up years, he'd deprived her of any photos or anecdotes about her parents or grandparents. It had been an austere life for a child. He could see that now. Mika had paid the price for his anguish, his guilt, and his grief. How would this affect her in the future? He decided everything would be different when she returned from Oxford. Once he'd relived the past on this pilgrimage, he'd share everything with her. Perhaps she would eventually forgive him.

Sitting opposite him on the train was a dapper business suited little man who jumped to his feet at the beginning of their journey and, bowing deeply, said, 'Ohayou gozaimasu sama', and offered help with Takeshi's bag. Takeshi was incensed. Why did this man

KENSHŌ House of Secrets

think he needed help? Surely he didn't look that old and frail. With his daily practice he was probably far fitter than this man with his middle-aged paunch and sallow complexion. Shaking his head he shrugged off the man's attempts to make conversation, eager to return to the past.

The eleven hours sped by despite all the changes of trains. Eventually, Takeshi disembarked at Urakami Station. He was shocked. The area was so built up he recognised nothing. Hordes of his countrymen and gaikokujin rushed past him intent on sightseeing. Everywhere there were signs to memorials of the bomb, the rebuilt Urakami Cathedral, the Peace Park and the Hypocentre Park, the epicentre of the bomb.

It was late to find a ryokan but eventually Takeshi found a small family inn down a backstreet. Exhausted and declining food, he lay down on a mattress on the tatami mat, pulling the duvet over him. His bones ached. He felt his age. The journey had been long, but it was the people that had drained him. His solitary life had not equipped him for the throngs, the noise, the smells and sights of a city. He longed for the peace and tranquillity of his dōjō, the sweet smell of jasmine in the garden, the fading echoes of the singing bowls, the tinkling of cups as Mika prepared afternoon tea and above all sound sleep. There was a lot to do in the next days. But all night long he was plagued by the ancestors. His great grandfather, one of the last Samurai warriors before the Meiji revolution to carry a sword and wear a topknot, brandished his fist at Takeshi as if to warn him. Could this have anything to do with Mika?

Next morning Takeshi woke weary from dreaming but allowed himself to be refreshed by a hearty breakfast. The meal of steaming rice, miso soup, grilled fish, eggs and hot tea invigorated him enough to set out for the Urakami Cathedral. His wife and her family had been practising Catholics, and he wanted to begin his pilgrimage by honouring their religion and their spirits. One of the priests came forward and bowed, asking, 'Ikaga

KENSHŌ   House of Secrets

nasaimasuka okyaku- sama?' ('Can I help you, sir?'). Takeshi, deep in thought, didn't hear him and moved to the altar to light a candle for his beloved Sakura. Later, wandering round the streets of Urakami, Takeshi wondered if he would ever be able to find the location of Sakura's home. She'd been so fresh, young and delicate like cherry blossom when he'd met her. If only he could talk to her now or see her once more.

The visceral pain of loss flooded back to that day in 1945 when he'd reached the city. Of course, there was no city then just a wasteland of devastation. Thick black smoke hung like a curtain in the atmosphere. Desperate and fraught with grief, Takeshi had finally found the remains of Sakura's home. Dropping to his knees, he'd started digging in the ruins with his bare hands but there was nothing. It was futile. Later he'd been told that anything or anyone within half a mile of the explosion had been vapourised. But that day Takeshi wouldn't stop digging. As night fell and about to give up, his nails clinked on something hard. Piece by piece he unearthed what was to be the kintsugi bowl. It had been an anniversary present to his wife. An azure blue bowl adorned with a graceful hand painted sprig of cherry blossom. All that was left now were shards. He clasped the fragments to his chest, utterly tormented, shedding burning tears for his lost love. What about his son? A twelve month old baby could never have survived this, surely.

Later that day, wandering aimlessly round the bonfires where relatives were burning their dead, he began to hear miraculous stories about babies that had survived. One tale was about 'a baby that had crawled out from between Assistant Police Inspector Yamasaki's feet covered in dust'. Influenced by the stories and convinced his son Riki was still alive, Takeshi frantically tracked down all the orphaned babies to City Hall and then to Togiya Elementary School. This was where he found his son. He recognised him immediately. The nursery schoolteacher said it wasn't possible, but Takeshi knew. It was an instinctual ache in his guts – something primeval. As there was no one to claim these

KENSHŌ   House of Secrets

orphans, and despite the teacher's protests, Takeshi spirited Riki away to an isolated minka he'd bought outside Wajima and away from all the madness and desolation. Japan was now under the control of the Americans and rebuilding had begun but Takeshi cared little about that – his focus was his son.

For months the baby flourished, then his belly began to swell with the effects of the radiation, but Takeshi never gave up. Over the years he nursed his sick son through every illness with countless visits to Kanazawa hospital. Eventually, against Takeshi's wishes Riki met and married Mariko, another 'hibakusha' (survivor of the atomic bomb). Despite his reservations, Takeshi's heart was full when they announced they were having a baby. What a miracle. Something pure was going to come from all the destruction. But it was not to be. Riki never lived to see his baby born, and Mariko was too weak to survive the birth. But Mika was a healthy bouncing baby from the start and Takeshi found himself with a new reason for living.

The last place to visit on Takeshi's pilgrimage was the Akgi cemetery. It was there on that fateful day in 1945 that he'd placed the stones and crosses for Sakura and her parents. At the time he'd been so drained with emotion, only sustained by the guzoni broth one of the priests from the monastery had given him, that he'd barely been able to make it to the cemetery. This time, after searching for hours, he found the simple little crosses and wooden plaques on which he'd inscribed their names. How he wished he could feel their presence. It would have been comforting, but they'd long gone. There was nothing of them, except in his heart. This is what he should have passed on to Mika, allowing her to know and mourn her dead mother and father, her grandmother and great grandparents. What wounds had he inadvertently inflicted upon her? He'd been so wrong and Takeshi knew the ancestors wouldn't rest until he righted the wrong. He must return home and meditate on how to make amends.

KENSHŌ   House of Secrets

CHAPTER 33
New Year and Jack's return

For once the Blenkinsop family, together with Mika and Daisy, celebrated New Year's Day by having breakfast together. Even the children had been allowed into Julian's sanctum sanctorum – the dining room. When the phone rang, Tolly sprang out of his chair and came running back shouting to Mika, 'It's someone called Jack. He wants to talk to you urgently. He's calling from New York.'

A blushing Mika raced to the phone. Jack's voice could barely be heard above the hubbub in the dining room as the children chanted, 'Mika's got a boyfriend. Mika's got a boyfriend.'

Jack said, 'Listen Mika, I'm coming back early. I stopped off in New York to see an old family friend of my mother's. Can you meet me tomorrow in London? I'm stopping there for a few days to do some research. If you get the eleven thirty two, that's the most direct train. I'll meet you at Paddington.'

Mika didn't know what to say, 'But Jack, there is family holiday for week. Will be rude. What to say?'

Impatiently Jack said, 'Sorry Mika, have to go, my money's running out. Am sure you'll think of something.'

A disconcerted Mika returned to the dining room to be greeted by a sea of expectant faces. Reluctant to tell them Jack was her boyfriend, she muttered, 'Solly. Jack, student on course, back from Boston. Want meet in London for research.'

The whole table erupted in laughter. Julian quipped, 'Is that what it's called these days? Research?' and raised his eyebrows.

Phoebe, seeing how embarrassed Mika was, said, 'Take no notice of that lot, Mika. We're glad you have a friend. Please feel free to

KENSHŌ   House of Secrets

go and meet him in London. Let me know which train and I'll run you into Oxford.'

'Much trouble,' Mika mumbled, keen to change the subject. 'Arigatō, Phoebe. He mention eleven thirty two tomorrow. OK?'

Once that was settled Julian turned to the rest of his family, 'So what's it to be, children? How shall we spend the day? Perhaps a visit to one of our historic houses?'

Tolly groaned out loud and rolled his eyes. Picking up on his mood, Sadilla and Kepha began to bang on their plates loudly with their spoons. Phoebe, attempting to soothe the situation, said, 'Look Julian, it's such a lovely day a short walk would be good for us all. Then we can come back, have a cold turkey lunch and enjoy board games.' Julian grunted peevishly. He never felt he received the respect he deserved as head of the family, especially as he'd made so much effort this year. Granted on Christmas Day he'd felt compelled to give way and allow his father the privilege of being head of the household but now those two old codgers were firmly entrenched back on their own floor, he should be the one making decisions not Phoebe.

Recognising his sulky face, Phoebe patted his arm affectionately and said, 'Let's enjoy taking the children out together. Leave Daisy and Mika to sort out the dishes and the kitchen. You can wear that red cashmere scarf I bought you. What about that Cossack hat? I've not seen that this winter and you look so distinguished in it.'

A pacified Julian brightened up, 'Very well, Phoebe my dear. Come on kids. Get your coats and hats. A good long stretch will do wonders after all that food.'

Next day when Mika set off for London, she wondered why Jack had returned so early. Had he and his father fallen out? His father sounded a lot like her grandfather, disciplined, work oriented and

KENSHŌ   House of Secrets

controlling. When she got to Paddington, Jack was standing in the centre of the concourse under the clock. Realising he'd not seen her, Mika studied him from afar. There was no doubt he was good looking with his blonde hair and tall slim build. It was as if she was seeing him for the first time. Her heart leapt, recognising him as the person she loved. At that very moment he turned and saw her, his face full of joy, his smile luminous and came towards her arms outstretched. Without thinking about etiquette or public displays of behaviour, Mika stumbled forwards and fell into his arms. The depth of their kissing shook her. It was as if they were two survivors on a desert island, far from everything and everyone.

'How I've missed you,' Jack breathed into her hair, 'it's been so long.'

Mika laughed, 'One week.'

'We must go somewhere and talk,' Jack said urgently.

'Why what happen with father? Trouble?'

'You could say that.' Jack was curt. Strolling along hand in hand, they found a cosy café down a backstreet that served mugs of hot chocolate. Sitting back they gazed into one another's eyes.

'I had a real row with father on Christmas Day of all days. We were getting on fine. He was asking about my life at Oxford. I told him about you. He was furious.'

'About me?' Mika ventured timidly. 'He no like Japanese. Because of war?'

'I don't know,' Jack said grimly. 'Something to do with my mother and grandfather. That's why I stopped in New York, to see mother's old lawyer. He was tight lipped too. All he would say was my grandfather was an immigrant who came to Britain then

KENSHŌ   House of Secrets

was lent to the US government during the war. He was most emphatic about my forgetting the past and getting on with my own life.'

'But why you stay in London now?'

'I thought I could look through archives and find out what all the mystery is.'

'Do you know grandfather name? Where look?'

'I know an American, who was at school with me, now doing his PhD at UCL. Something about America's involvement in the Second World War. I'm meeting him tomorrow. He might be able to point me in the right direction.'

Mika was distressed. The last thing she wanted to do was cause a rift between Jack and his father. 'Perhaps we stop seeing each other. You and father then together again.'

'Absolutely not,' Jack said categorically. 'Never. Now I've found you I'm not letting you go. Anyway, it's not just about us. He wants me to join his law firm. There's no way I'm doing that.' Afraid his anger might scare Mika, he said gently, 'Tell me about your Christmas. What was it like with the Blenkinsops en famille, and what about your grandfather, have you heard from him?'

'I know you change subject,' Mika said softly, 'but more worried about you and father. Christmas OK but hard work. Much food to prepare not like Japan at Christmas. I receive letter from grandfather. He say he go Nagasaki. I not know why. He say not been since 1945 and bomb. Not understand. He never travel from Wajima. Maybe Tokyo but that all.'

Jack frowned, 'Sounds like some sort of mission. Did he lose family when the bomb fell?'

KENSHŌ   House of Secrets

'He never say. Tell nothing of family or ancestors ever. Know nothing of parents. No good ask either.'

Tightening his lips, Jack said, 'Both our family backgrounds are such mysteries, but I'm determined to find out about mine. Then we'll concentrate on yours.' They fell into silence, holding hands under the table and smiling at one another.

Eventually Jack said, 'I'll be back in Oxford in a few days but let's make the most of today.' Noticing Mika shiver he wrapped her in his padded jacket, 'I know it's cold but it's such a lovely afternoon for January. A good walk round the sights will warm you up. Perhaps we'll stop for a cream tea, it's so English. What do you think?'

Mika giggled, 'Know cream teas,' and told him the story about Daisy coming to collect her from the college when Mika had first arrived, and her use of the phrase, 'stuff ourselves like pigs.' Mika was so confused at the time, she thought it had something to do with eating pork. Laughing their heads off, and arm in arm, they headed for The Mall and Buckingham Palace.

CHAPTER 34
Hilary Term
Daisy reconnoitres

It was well into the New Year before Daisy was able to attract Mika's attention. Mika was elusive these days, disappearing into her room for long periods, with far more important things on her mind than Daisy's obsession with Julian. Mika was continually worried about Jack and what he might find out in London. Had they a future together or was it a pipedream? Nothing could happen between them if Jack's father were so opposed. Also, Mika knew her grandfather would never approve of her relationship with a gaikokujin (a foreigner) either.

Daisy finally tracked Mika down. She was staring into space and daydreaming in her bedroom, an open book of Victorian poetry in front of her. Throwing herself on Mika's bed, a breathless Daisy gasped, 'There you are. At last. I thought you might be out. You're like a ghost these days, Mika. Sometimes you vanish and appear from nowhere.'

Mika glowered at being disturbed and particularly at being compared to a ghost - a sore subject for her at the best of times. She snapped, 'You mistaken, Daisy. I here or downstairs. College not started yet.'

A penitent Daisy mumbled, 'Sorry Mika, didn't mean to upset you. Just wanted a favour when you get back to college.'

'Favour?' Mika asked sharply.

'Well,' Daisy tried to adopt a more conciliating tone, 'I know you work hard but wondered when you were in the library next if you would look up something for me. I'm sure you realise how much I admire the Prof. At one time he mentioned his doctoral thesis to me - the one he wrote at the time of his first wife's death. He and

KENSHŌ House of Secrets

Lucy were students together – so romantic - and were working on the same topic. I'd just like to read his thesis and maybe Lucy's as well. It would be about 1980, I think, maybe a bit before.'

'What is subject?' Mika asked, hesitating about asking why. This was so out of character for Daisy when she only ever read celebrity magazines and had never been known to open let alone read a book? Probably it was some crafty way to engage Julian's attention, as Mika was only too aware of Daisy's infatuation with him.

Daisy was flummoxed and out of her depth at the question. Even her capacity for telling tall tales was strained. 'Maybe some sort of comparison of Japanese and Western culture,' she bluffed.

'Sound more like undergraduate work than doctorate,' Mika mused thoughtfully. 'But interested. Will check microfiche at library.'

Keen to avoid further embarrassing inroads into academia, Daisy squirmed but forced herself to stay and chat about Mika's studies. She felt a surge of excitement. If there was anything shady she was impatient to find out what it was. Maybe Julian (she'd given up calling him Prof now they were on more intimate terms) could be hers after all. If there was a grubby secret she'd unearth it, then they could take care of it together.

It was another three weeks before Mika came back to Daisy. Taking her to one side, Mika said, 'Found Professor Blenkinsop's thesis. Thorough, detailed. English difficult for me. No thesis for Professor wife. Perhaps she die before finishing?'

Daisy was disappointed. This was no good. There was definitely something suspicious here but what? Perhaps she should talk to Phoebe. Absentmindedly thanking Mika, she considered her next move.

KENSHŌ   House of Secrets

Waylaying Phoebe was as difficult as ambushing Mika. Since the Blenkinsops' Christmas get together each family member had retreated back to their own corners. Phoebe, smart and confident these days, dipped in and out. She was either coming from or going to Oxford. If Daisy hadn't known better she might have speculated that Phoebe had a 'fancy man'. Surely not Phoebe with her undying devotion to Julian.

Finally one afternoon, Daisy seized her chance to sit with Phoebe in the kitchen and chat over a cup of tea and a Danish. Casually Daisy opened the conversation, 'The other day I started wondering about the first Mrs Blenkinsop, you know, 'Lucy'.'

'I know 'Lucy' alright. I heard enough about her in the early days of our marriage. Why would you think about her?' Phoebe said crossly, not at all keen to discuss the first Mrs Blenkinsop.

'Oh, I think the Colonel mentioned her on Christmas Day when we were chatting,' Daisy lied blithely.

'What did he say exactly?' Phoebe enquired in a harsh tone. Strangely, she didn't seem to wonder why the old man would talk to Daisy when he barely acknowledged the girl's existence.

'He said something about her having both brains and beauty and that she and Julian had been students together, that they did the same subject for their doctorates after they married. What a partnership it must have been. How sad that Lucy never finished her thesis before she died.'

'That's absolute rubbish. The old man talks a load of rot. He was always in awe of Lucy because she was a lady and came from money,' Phoebe retorted. 'In fact, as regards the thesis, I'm sure I recall Julian saying she was awarded her PhD posthumously.'

'That's good then,' Daisy declared, 'it would have been a shame if all that work went for nothing.'

KENSHŌ   House of Secrets

Without pausing to think, Phoebe moved into a more confiding mood, 'Of course, it was a good ten years before I met Julian,' adding with a hint of cattiness, 'and I think for all his brains he had a hard time completing his own thesis.' Amending her tone, she said more sympathetically, 'Of course he was teaching part time so it must have been a strain. The examining board refused his thesis first time, telling him it wasn't adequate and had to be rewritten. It was just at the time when Lucy's health deteriorated and she died. The poor man must have been at his wit's end.'

I'm sure he was, a gleeful Daisy thought. The pieces were beginning to fall into place. Now all she had to do was to find out whether Lucy submitted her thesis or not.

When the household departed next morning, Daisy slipped back into Julian's study and retrieved the crumpled letter from the drawer. Obviously the person who wrote it would no longer be around but there was a contact telephone number. Putting on her poshest voice, Daisy rang the number pretending to be Julian's secretary. She explained he'd come across the letter in his files and couldn't remember if he'd ever presented his late wife's work. There was a long pause on the phone and the voice said, 'It was 1980, madam. Are you sure you still need to follow this up?' Daisy was resolute, refusing to be put off.

'Very well, madam. We may have that year's records computerised but, if not, it will mean going back through the archives. That would be a lengthy job. I'll have to get back to you.'

During the following weeks Daisy practically lived by the phone, afraid someone else from the household would answer it and wonder what it was all about. She became a nervous wreck, jumping at every ring, terrified to venture far from the house. Over a month went by and there was nothing. Finally, the phone rang and this time it was someone asking for Julian's secretary. Careful to revert to her previous accent, Daisy answered, 'This is she.' An anonymous voice said, 'Regarding your enquiry,

KENSHŌ   House of Secrets

madam, I'm sorry. It doesn't look as if we received any reply to our letter asking for Mrs Lucy Blenkinsop's thesis, so unfortunately I can confirm that Mrs Lucy Blenkinsop didn't get awarded a doctorate by us. Hope that helps.'

It certainly does, Daisy thought, I was right all along. I may never know for sure but it's possible Julian, in his panic, borrowed from his wife's work when he resubmitted his own thesis. Daisy was jubilant. Her perfect man was not so perfect after all. She much preferred him this way. It made him more accessible and less out of her league. He was ripe for the taking now. But a little part of Daisy's mind niggled away at her, wondering if there were other things he was hiding.

KENSHŌ   House of Secrets

CHAPTER 35
Phoebe confronts her feelings

With the turn of the year, Phoebe was forced to make some decisions about Geoffrey. He'd arrived back early from the States and was on the phone to her before she had a chance to think. Full of vim and vigour he said, 'I've missed you, darling Phoebe. When can I see you?'

A harassed Phoebe, trying to dismantle the Christmas tree and pack away the trimmings, said, 'I'm up to my eyes trying to clear up Christmas. I can't get away till next week. There's so much to do.'

Forcefully, Geoffrey said, 'Honestly Phoebe, I must see you. I did what you asked and left you alone over the holidays. I need to know how you feel. Please don't leave me hanging like this.'

Desperate to get him off the main house phone in case anyone in the family came along, Phoebe said, 'Very well. What about lunch tomorrow, but it'll have to be an early one. I need to get the children ready to go back to school.'

Geoffrey sighed deeply, 'I suppose that will have to do. Shall we meet at the usual place at say a quarter to twelve?' Practically slamming the phone down, Phoebe agreed. What was it with men? If you played hard to get they were in hot pursuit and wouldn't leave you alone. If you were available they lost interest. She still didn't know how she felt about Geoffrey. Christmas this year had been like a breath of fresh air with everyone including Julian and the Colonel putting themselves out to be amiable and co-operative. This had only made her appreciate the family more. Did she want to disrupt all that? The impact it would have on everyone's life would be devastating.

At lunch the following day, Geoffrey was more amorous than ever, presenting her with a single red rose. Throughout the meal

KENSHŌ   House of Secrets

he stroked Phoebe's hand, occasionally lifting it to kiss her fingers. Phoebe was hot with embarrassment yet was only too aware no one had ever courted her like this. With Julian it had been a planned seduction, first of all on the couch in his rooms at college, and later at an out of the way hotel where he wouldn't be recognised. Rarely had he bought her flowers, well only from the local garage, and certainly made no effort to kiss her hand or tell how beautiful she was. Had she been missing out?

Geoffrey repeated himself, 'I longed for you so much over Christmas, darling Phoebe. It made me realise what a mistake I made all those years ago. I was a selfish young oaf, loving and then leaving you all for my own ambitions. Can you forgive me? Please let me make it up to you.' From his breast pocket he produced a ring box, 'I wanted to give you this on Christmas Day, but I hope you'll look on it as a New Year's gift now. A promise of a future together.'

Apprehensively, Phoebe opened the box. A sparkling band encrusted with diamonds lay on a satin cushion. Dazed, Phoebe could barely speak but managed, 'Geoffrey, I can't accept this. I'm still well and truly married,' and shut the box forcefully.

'Phoebe darling, I need you to know how serious I am. I'm sorry to have upset you. This was my poor attempt to show you how genuine I am. I thought an eternity ring would show you how much I want us to be together. I know you're married to Julian but I'm sure you feel something for me. Please give us another chance. Keep the ring. Wear it when you've made a decision. In the meantime, I could meet your children. Should I perhaps organise a day out for us all before school starts?'

Phoebe was confused but allowed Geoffrey to close her limp hand round the box. 'I'm not sure Geoffrey, about your meeting the children. How would I explain you?' Inwardly she thought what about Tolly? What right had she to deprive him of a potential father especially as a huge question mark still hung over Tolly's

KENSHŌ   House of Secrets

parentage? Maybe Geoffrey was right about a day out with the children. It might help settle her apprehensions once and for all.

It was easy enough to run the idea past Julian. The Hilary term had barely started but he was already spending more and more time at college. It was as if he'd done his duty by them over Christmas and the New Year and was eager to return to his old routines. Casually, Phoebe said, 'Julian, I thought it would be a good idea if I took the children for a day out. School starts next week and then there'll be no time. I want to make the most of them. What do you think?'

'Please yourself, dear,' Julian said as he checked his Blackberry. 'Good thinking. I've a lot of prep work to do at home before term starts. It would be good to have the children out of the way. Which day were you thinking of?'   Attempting to muster some half-hearted pretence of interest, he asked, 'and where would you go?'

'I thought Wednesday. If we made an early start we could go to Legoland at Windsor. It would be perfect for the children and there's plenty to do for all ages, so we'd be out all day.'

'Wonderful,' Julian was practically ecstatic. 'Wednesday would be ideal. I have a lot of urgent phone calls to make and wouldn't want to be disturbed,' thinking of the Rhianna dilemma. Maybe this would be his chance to meet up with her and check out the lay of the land.

On the Wednesday, Phoebe piled the kids into her ancient station wagon and drove to the rendezvous with Geoffrey at Oxford station. Sadilla and Kepha were wild with excitement but Tolly sat silent and non-speaking. Finally, he cracked, asking in his usual direct manner, 'Why's we going to the station, Mum? Are we's going by train?'

'No,' Phoebe said shortly. This was going to be some outing, if Tolly was in the mood to query everything. 'We're meeting an old

KENSHŌ   House of Secrets

friend of mine from America. He and I were students together, and he's offered to drive us to Windsor.'

Tolly, not one to be diverted easily, was intent on his cross-examination, 'But what man? Has he been to the house? Does Dad knows him?'

'No, no and no,' Phoebe became unnerved and exasperated. 'Look Tolly, just enjoy the day. You can ask Geoffrey, that's my friend's name, all the questions you like when you meet him.' Phoebe ground her teeth. Poor Geoffrey, I've really dropped him in it. How will he cope? A man with no experience of children. Sensing his mother's irritation, Tolly sat back and stared out the window.

On their arrival at the station there was even more for Phoebe to be alarmed about. A nonchalant Geoffrey was leaning on the bonnet of a gleaming white stretch limousine, together with uniformed chauffeur. Before Phoebe could open her mouth to protest, her two youngest had clambered aboard with the help of the chauffeur and started investigating every nook and cranny. Tolly, however, stood well back, disapproval written all over his face, saying loudly, 'Gorblimey, Mum. Who 'xactly is your friend? A film director or summat?' Phoebe flinched visibly, wondering why Tolly talked like a combination of some East End barrow boy and 'Just William'. She and Julian had done their absolute best to knock it out of him but to no avail. Even his private school education barely scratched the surface of his curious linguistics.

Turning her back on her eldest, Phoebe allowed herself to be helped into a seat, followed by a recalcitrant Tolly who stalked in and plonked himself right beside her. Geoffrey grinned and took a seat to the side, 'Well young Tolly, what do you think?'

Tolly said imperiously, 'Don' know. We's not yet been introduced. Who are you's?'

KENSHŌ   House of Secrets

Phoebe said sternly and formidably, 'Kids, this is Uncle Geoffrey. Not a real uncle but Mummy's friend.' Sadilla and Kepha whooped with delight and fell upon the unsuspecting Geoffrey who practically collapsed.

'Sorry Geoffrey,' Phoebe said apologetically. 'My two youngest tend to be overly affectionate and excitable. They'll calm down soon.' Tolly, however, remained unmoved by the razzamatazz, continuing his reticence for the rest of the journey.

Everything went smoothly at the entrance into Legoland. Geoffrey had taken care of all the details and even engaged a helper for the two youngest. They were escorted off to the model village and a boat ride through the fairy tale forest. Geoffrey turned to Tolly and asked, 'What would you like to do? I thought you might like the driving school. The electric cars go round make-believe roads. You can qualify as a driver on the circuit and get a certificate. What do you think?'

Tolly, his nose in the air, said, 'That there's for kids. I think I'll stay with Mum.' Geoffrey sighed, making every effort not to be provoked. Commandeering Phoebe's arm he strolled on, leaving Tolly to drag along in their wake.

Desperate to improve the situation, Phoebe suddenly spotted 'The Scarab Bouncers'. 'Look Tolly, there's a ride that's something to do with Egypt.' Like herself, Tolly always had an interest in the Pharaohs and anything Egyptian. 'We can all do it together,' she announced, trying to sound excited but not at all sure she was keen to be catapulted into the air. But her two men's faces lightened; there was even the slightest trace of enthusiasm in the air. What you have to do for love Phoebe thought, trying to gird her loins for the ride, and murmuring wryly, 'It looks a lot of fun.'

Once they were seated there was a distinct look of anticipation on both Geoffrey and Tolly's faces. Phoebe's heart sank, hoping she wouldn't show herself up by being sick. It was as terrifying as she thought it would be, continuously bouncing up and down, as pictures and sights of Egypt whizzed past - her idea of living hell. But Geoffrey and Tolly were beside themselves laughing and giggling at every bounce. It was disconcerting to see their two heads together. Tolly's blonde curls were so reminiscent of Geoffrey's when he was younger. Even their smiles were similar, the way they both thrust out their chins and showed exactly the same amount of teeth. It was spooky. Perhaps this was the nudge she needed to decide about Geoffrey. Granted Julian had made a monumental effort over Christmas, but he'd soon reverted to his old habits, ignoring her and more importantly the children.

If only she could be sure enough of the dates when her relationship with Geoffrey ended and her affair with Julian began. Why had she let things overlap like that? Of course at the time she'd been devastated by Geoffrey's sudden departure and all but fallen into Julian's waiting arms. There'd been little planning involved.

On the way home in the limo Phoebe started thinking. Geoffrey and Tolly were now chatting away like old friends, discussing Tolly's magic tricks and his detective work with Mika in Kenshō House. It was as if they'd always known one another. Her two youngest were fast asleep. Kepha had found a place to curl up in Geoffrey's lap, and Sadilla appeared to be sleeping, sucking her thumb and clutching Geoffrey's hand. How extraordinary Phoebe thought. It was as if her children had intuitively decided Geoffrey would make a suitable father. At that very instant, Geoffrey looked up and smiled his sweet smile at her, it was then something inside her melted and surrendered. There was such a warm feeling of familiarity and security. Perhaps they had a future together, as a family, after all.

KENSHŌ   House of Secrets

CHAPTER 36
Julian considers his priorities

At the beginning of January, Julian knew he had to turn over a new leaf. It was 2001. He was well into his fifties and couldn't carry on like the Lothario he'd been in the past. It was time to sort things out once and for all with Rhianna. Throughout the holiday he'd become aware of Daisy throwing him knowing glances, as if he and she shared some deep dark secret. But though he was tempted he wasn't at all sure he wanted to go there. It was too dangerous.

On the Wednesday that Phoebe organised the Legoland day out, Julian was sitting in his study wondering what to do about Rhianna. There was a light tap on his door and Daisy appeared with a tray of hot chocolate and left-over mince pies. 'Thought you might be hungry with all that brain work, Prof. Brought you a little snack.'

'How thoughtful, Daisy. That's just what I need, a welcome distraction.'

'You seem preoccupied, Prof. Is the new term worrying you?'

'Not really,' Julian blurted out without thinking, 'it's something personal.'

'Can I help?'

'I don't think so, my dear. It's to do with one of my students. She left rather precipitately halfway through last term and I'm not sure if she's coming back. I don't know what to do about her.'

Daisy's ears pricked up, only too aware of her beloved Julian's reputation. She would bet it was one of his torrid liaisons that had gone horribly wrong. These girl students were no better than they should be, cavorting about in short skirts and low tops, practically offering themselves on a plate to the lecturers. The girl had obviously thrown herself at Julian and what red blooded man could resist a nubile young body. Never mind whatever it was, Julian could depend on his loyal Daisy to step up and sort it out. The poor man must be allowed to get back to his important work.

'Tell me more about her, Prof. I'm a good listener and can tackle most problems.'

'Very well,' Julian said, not overly keen to divulge his role in the sordid affair. 'There's talk round the college that the girl's pregnant. Naturally, I don't want to overstep my position as her tutor but would like to know what her intentions are. For her own good, you understand.'

Daisy nodded wisely. The poor love. He always seemed to get himself entangled with women who were wrong for him. Look at his first wife. Lucy had probably crushed him with her intelligence, beauty and monied background. Phoebe, on the other hand, was a hopeless, disorganised creature, not capable of running anyone's household let alone a prominent academic's. As a consequence yet another of these luscious young students, desperate for approval, had led her darling Julian astray. What Julian needed was a wife like her - young and lusty but with plenty of common sense. Unquestionably she would be good for him, keep him grounded and on a tight rein. He'd be safe with her, in no danger of straying.

'Look Prof,' Daisy said, 'why don't you give me this young student's details. I'll contact her and find out what's going on.'

 A bemused Julian wasn't at all sure he wanted Daisy involved in his private life but he was at his wit's end. At least if he could find out whether Rhianna was really pregnant or not… Surely Daisy would be able to ascertain that at the very least. Nodding hesitantly, he gave Daisy the required information.

KENSHŌ   House of Secrets

'Leave this to me, Prof,' Daisy said confidently. 'I'm ace at sorting out tricky bits of business.'

A few days later, Daisy set off for Rhianna's. She knew Julian would never approve of her visiting Rhianna at home, but this was necessary if she was to frighten the girl off once and for all. It also meant she'd be in possession of yet another of Julian's secrets. Inevitably Julian would be grateful, and Daisy would be only too willing and able to collect on his gratitude. Phoebe was of no account these days as her mind and thoughts seemed to be elsewhere, possibly with a lover.

Rhianna lived in the Gloucestershire countryside, so it took Daisy a while to manoeuvre her Mini up and down the winding lanes of the Cotswolds. Finally there was a sign for 'Blackthorn Farm'. A long driveway delivered her to a formidable looking stone manor rather than an insignificant farmhouse. Tremors of nerves rumbled in Daisy's stomach. For once she felt panic. Could she pull this off? There was lot at stake, so she must. A uniformed maid answered the front door and showed Daisy into an impressive library, saying, 'I'll see if Miss Rhianna's at home.' The whole place was like something out of an historical novel. Daisy quaked in her boots.

A few minutes later a tall fair slim girl came bounding into the room. She certainly didn't look pregnant or as if she'd recently given birth. 'I don't think I know you,' she announced in a superior manner.

'You don't,' Daisy said flatly. 'The Prof sent me.'

For a moment Rhianna looked confused, then blushed to the roots of her hair, 'You don't mean Julian, do you? You're hardly his type. I wouldn't have thought he'd send a lackey,' looking meaningfully at Daisy's short leather skirt, bomber jacket and Doc Marten lace up boots. 'Why didn't he come himself? Shit scared, I imagine, in case I made a scene.'

KENSHŌ   House of Secrets

Unsure of herself and the circumstances, Daisy said tentatively, 'He just wanted to know if you were returning to Oxford this coming term?'

'I bet he does,' Rhianna laughed scornfully. 'I would think he's less bothered about that than whether I was having his baby. He's been fishing for ages by phone and letter but I preferred to keep him on the hook. I do so love these fishing metaphors, don't you? I pick them up from Daddy. He's a great angler, you know.'

Daisy could have strangled her, 'So you're not pregnant then?'

'Am I hell as like? No, of course not. Daddy would have had an apoplectic fit and been up that college in a jiffy. Julian would have been thrown out on his ear. I did have a bit of a scare when my period was late and got in a state. When I told Julian all he could think about was his career. He was icy and caustic denying it could possibly be his, yet he knew full well I was a virgin, when he seduced me on that couch in his study where he's probably made a habit of popping other first years' cherries.'

Momentarily Daisy felt a fleeting pang of sympathy for the girl, but it didn't last. She reminded herself how promiscuous these girls were, leading poor Julian on. 'Oh well,' she said, 'that's that then. What shall I tell him about your returning to Oxford?'

'Bah to that,' Rhianna scoffed. 'I think I'll be better off in one of the redbrick universities. I'm off to Bristol in September. I just want to forget all about that jumped up twit and never see him again as long as I live.' Knitting her brow and frowning she said, 'Why are you doing his dirty work? As far as I remember he has a secretary called Janice whom he used to dump all his 'dirty washing' on. You're certainly not her.'

'No, I'm a close friend of his. In fact, you could say we're more than close. I'm looking out for his best interests.'

KENSHŌ   House of Secrets

'Um,' Rhianna mouthed, 'just be careful with all that 'closeness'. You don't want to be the next one 'up the duff'.'

'I'm sure,' Daisy said tartly, 'that would never happen to me unless I wanted it to.'

'But surely Julian has a wife doesn't he? Where does she fit into your cosy little relationship à deux?' It was becoming obvious to Daisy that Rhianna was determined to extract as much amusement from this situation as she could.

Daisy shrugged with a smug smile, 'Phoebe will soon be history, leaving Julian and I to plan a future together.'

Rhianna doubled over with mirth as she showed Daisy out, 'Good luck with that. Going back to my earlier fishing metaphors, make sure your fish doesn't squirm off the hook. That Julian is a good squirmer.'

An infuriated Daisy strode back to her car. That girl had a cheek talking about Julian like that. He was well rid of her. On the journey back, Daisy's rage subsided as she weighed up the last obstacle in her path. Only Phoebe now, but she was of little consequence. Julian, though he didn't know it yet, was hers for the taking!

KENSHŌ   House of Secrets

CHAPTER 37
Tolly's excitement

Tolly was so excited after his day at Legoland that he raced up the three flights of stairs to the top of the house to tell Mika. She was very brooding these days and not much fun as his friend. Perhaps he could cheer her up. Why she was so gloomy now she had a boyfriend was beyond him. But adults were a mystery and not worth thinking about. Nearing the top of the stairs he started yelling, 'Mika, Mika.'

Mika shot out of her room in alarm.

Tolly continued at the top of his voice, 'Mika, I've summat to tell you.'

'Calm, Tolly, quiet. Not good shrieking. Come, sit, tell me.'

'There's this man Mum knows. From America. I likes him. We spent all day wiv him. Gonna take me riding next week. I's never been on a horse or seen a real cowboy.' Tolly could barely contain himself, 'And there's summat else. I knows another secret.' Pulling his mouth into a jib, he said, 'Dunno whether I'll tell. You and I don't do tea anymore.' Sitting head on hands, arms propped on knees, Tolly deliberated. He stared reproachfully at Mika, 'You got no time for me now you's got a boyfriend. I's your friend first. You dumped me. Everyone leaves me.' However, just as rapidly his dark mood lifted, and Tolly brightened fleetingly and defiantly, 'I's got Uncle Geoffrey. That's what Mum wants us to call him. He's my friend now.'

Mika was only half listening. Her mind was busy thinking about Jack and how he was getting on in London. At last, Tolly's anguished outburst, his hunched shoulders, and downcast glances penetrated and Mika responded. Sitting close to Tolly she put her arm round the boy's scrawny shoulders. It was as if she'd released a dam of emotion. He turned and throwing his arms

KENSHŌ House of Secrets

round her sobbed pitifully, 'Why do no one like me? I got no friends at school. Mum and Dad only talks to me when they tells me off.' Mika was racked with guilt. When she'd first arrived at Kenshō House this little boy had been the only person to hold out the hand of friendship. What had she done but abandon him once she'd settled into college and become friends with Jack? Attempting to make it up to him, Mika said, 'People like you, Tolly. You clever boy, understand many things, maybe too quick for lot people. People little afraid, what you know and see. But I value. Still friend. We start tea ceremony again next week. Dry eyes. Tell me other secret.'

Reassured, Tolly, starting to smile through his tears, was swift to forgive, 'You's think I's clever, Mika? At school they's think am half-wit because way I speaks. But no problem passing exams.'

It was Mika's turn to smile, 'You bright boy. Forget what others say. One day you have important job. Be famous.'

Tolly was overcome, puffing out his chest and beaming from ear to ear. Holding on tightly to Mika's hand, he divulged his other secret, 'It's Sanshō. You know Grandpa's old war diary we's found in the attic. I were looking through my spyhole into their room. Grandpa were fast asleep in his chair, but Sanshō were holding Grandpa's diary and staring at it. Then he puts it his pocket. I members the blue leather cover. Not right. You said we's not to look at other people's stuff.'

Mika was nonplussed. Of course that's what she'd said at the time, although she herself had glanced through it. When she'd given the diary to Sanshō she'd thought he would know best when to pass it on to the Colonel. Perhaps he was being cautious and examining it before giving it to the old man. Thinking this the most suitable explanation, she said, 'Sanshō read first. Too upsetting for Colonel. Colonel old. Bad for health.'

KENSHŌ House of Secrets

'You means might kill him,' Tolly said in a blood curdling tone. 'S'pose so, but he wrote it didn't he – knows what in it.'

'But long time ago, Tolly, in camps,' baulking at adding 'as a prisoner of my people.' How could a boy of Tolly's age understand war, let alone accept what her people had done to someone like his grandfather. The subject was best avoided.

Tolly, not a child to give up easily, protested, 'But Mika, shouldn't you's tell Grandpa?'

'No, leave alone. Adults know best.' Mika felt a hypocrite saying that. Not wanting the boy to fixate on the situation and determined to distract him, Mika said, 'Tell more about Uncle Geoffrey.'

Thrilled to discuss his current favourite person, Tolly gabbled on non-stop about Legoland and the plans he and Uncle Geoffrey would make. Allowing the boy's fervour to sweep over her, Mika picked up on something about 'an American ranch in Texas and lots of horses.' Politely she asked, 'Your uncle own ranch?'

'No,' Tolly said with regret, 'just fusty Professor like Dad, but I is sure he want a ranch. We's can be cowboys together.'

Mika couldn't help herself and laughed out loud. Looking pained, Tolly said, 'I can't see what funny?'

'Nothing, nothing,' Mika said hurriedly, not wanting to upset the boy again. 'Enough talk. Shall we race to kitchen, raid fridge. Christmas cake left.'

With little prompting Tolly was off and running before Mika could finish the sentence. Following along more sedately, Mika wondered what to do about the Colonel's diary. There was also the unfinished manuscript of 'The House'. After the young wife, Agatha's suicide, Mika couldn't bring herself to read anymore

KENSHŌ House of Secrets

and had abandoned the folder. The yūrei had not been in evidence for a while and Mika was not disposed to disturb them. Perhaps they'd disappeared for good. These days she kept away from the old nursery, preferring to work in her bedroom. The old rocking horse, of course, was still in situ. Phoebe had promised on several occasions to have it removed but in her usual haphazard way had probably forgotten all about it. Mika had taken to throwing a blanket over its head, to avoid looking at its one staring eye. But on the odd occasion when she dared visit the room, the blanket would have been removed and lie neatly folded at the horse's base.

Maybe she should steel herself and continue 'The House'. If she could get to the bottom of the mystery perhaps she would not be so scared of that stupid horse; after all it was only a toy. That night Mika got out the folder and took out the yellowing sheaves of paper. Before she started, and feeling braver than usual, she ventured into the nursery. Brandishing the manuscript, she addressed the rocking horse out loud, 'Not afraid. See. Reading next part.' Anyone seeing her would think she was mad talking to an ancient rocking horse. For once she didn't care, but as usual tossed the old blanket angrily over the horse's head. 'Not look at me now,' she warned.

Banging and closing the nursery door securely, Mika scuttled back to her warm bed. Climbing in she wrapped herself in her woollen dressing gown, pulled the duvet up to the tips of her frozen ears, adjusted her furry mittens and began to read…

KENSHŌ   House of Secrets

CHAPTER 38
Part Two: 'The House' resumes its story
'La Grande Maison', 1901

…Mrs Wallander took one look and threw up her hands in horror, 'How could anyone leave a house in this condition? I tell you, Wallander, even though it's in a prestigious part of Oxford I'm not setting foot in this house till we've had the builders in. We're going to need more space too with our lot, maybe an extra wing. Have you seen that old fashioned bathroom with an earth closet of all things, and the kitchen's not fit for pigs. The name's ridiculous. I'm not living in a house called 'Greensleeves' – what a joke. No, I think 'La Grande Maison'. It gives us class, don't you think? A French name shows we're coming up in the world. But I tell you frankly, Wallander, me and the young 'uns will not be moving in until everything's tickety boo. We must have one of those new flushing toilets.'

Mr Wallander winced, 'It's a wonderful house, Eunice, but hardly fancy. A French name in Oxford. What will people think?' not having the heart or guts to tell her 'La Grande Maison' merely meant 'The Big House'. Mrs Wallander, who prided herself on her French, obviously thought it meant 'The Grand House.' It never paid to contradict her. Privately he thought a good solid English name would suit the house best, but once Mrs Wallander had her mind set on something that was that. Conciliatingly he added, 'We've been lucky to get it at such a price, though it's been empty for nigh on ten years. It's a real step up from our villa in Gravesend. But we can't spend too much, Eunice,' adding pleadingly, 'remember the private mortgage I got has to be paid off. As it is, it'll take us years on my salary at the Exchange.'

Ignoring her husband's words, Mrs Wallander continued, 'And why has it been empty so long, I ask you? There must be a catch somewhere.'

KENSHŌ   House of Secrets

Shrinking further into his greatcoat, Mr Wallander, a meek man, attempting to pacify his over-ebullient wife, murmured, 'I believe the last owner's wife died, leaving her grief stricken husband to set sail for India to work on the railways.'

His wife, never satisfied, was determined to get to the bottom of the affair, 'What happened to the wife?'

Drawing on every vestige of courage, Mr Wallander said quietly, 'I believe she killed herself. It was tragic, something to do with being childless, I believe.'

'Killed herself for that.' His wife laughed coarsely, 'Why, we've never had any trouble in that department, have we Wallander? You look dull and lifeless, but you've certainly got what it takes in the bedroom department. Haven't we got ten little darlings to show for it,' she guffawed raucously. 'Anyway, to get back to this death, what were the sordid details?'

Hesitantly Mr Wallander mumbled, 'We best not talk about it. It was a good ten years ago.'

'But I want to know. I'm not sure I'm keen to live in a house where there was a grisly murder.'

'It wasn't murder. The poor lady hanged herself from one of the gas mantles in the nursery on the third floor.'

Mrs Wallander sniffed as if she'd encountered a bad smell. 'There's nothing for it then, we'll put the children up there. If there's ghosts they'll soon see 'em off. In the meantime, husband dearest, get this place habitable, or you'll know all about it.'

The removal to 'La Grande Maison' didn't take place until well into 1901. By then old Queen Victoria was dead and there was a new King on the throne. Mrs Wallander was delighted, 'Thank goodness. Now, Wallander, perhaps we'll be able to get away

KENSHŌ   House of Secrets

from all that mourning old queen in her funereal black veils and enjoy a bit of life. It'll be good riddance to dark furniture and horrible pictures of Scottish Highland cattle and a chance to bring in something lighter, modern and more pleasant to look at.'

On moving day, a vast procession of wagons and horses drew up outside 'La Grande Maison's' front door. A dapper dressed Mr Wallander handed his lady wife out of a rented hackney, followed by their two youngest who were carried out by the coachman. They were immediately handed over to a maid who'd arrived with the other children in a wagonette. All was at a standstill whilst Mrs Wallander walked round inspecting the frontage of the property. Anxious to get things underway, Mr Wallander murmured, 'They've made a good job of that extra wing. Looks like it's always been there don't you think, Eunice?'

His wife snorted, 'Remains to be seen, Wallander. Not at all sure about red brick, makes it stand out too much. Just wait till I've examined the inside, then we'll find out what sort of job those builders have done. It cost enough.'

'But the children, Eunice? You can't keep them penned in that wagonette much longer. It's been a long drive. I'm sure the little ones need to…' his thin voice dwindled away.

'Very well. Let the little darlings loose, Wallander, but keep them outside till I see what's what, d'ya hear? There's an outside lavvy in one of them sheds, take the ones who need it there.'

'Very well, dear,' said the biddable Wallander as he shepherded his progeny towards the outbuildings.

Meantime, Mrs Wallander bustled inside adjusting her skirts as she went, intent on examining the house, room by room. The removers' men swore under their breaths as they tried to settle the wagon horses who were pawing the ground and pulling at their harnesses. It had been made clear to them there was to be no

KENSHŌ House of Secrets

moving of furniture inside, until Mrs Wallander approved the house.

Eager to speed up the process, Mr Wallander left the children to their own devices and raced after his wife. As usual, she was busy shouting a running commentary, 'Look Wallander, this would make a lovely parlour, wonderful for receiving visitors. We can have this as a music room, and of course I shall have to have my salon.'

'Salon!' squeaked a breathless Mr Wallander. 'What's that for?'

'Entertainment, silly,' Mrs Wallander threw out her hands in one of her theatrical gestures. 'Once I become known, we'll be entertaining all the right people from Oxford City. Poets, writers, artists, I don't wonder. It will be a veritable cornucopia of talent and creativity.'

Mr Wallander, still recovering from his exertions, leant against the nearest wall and emitted an enormous sigh. 'But Eunice, I thought you'd put all that idea of entertaining people behind you when you left the music halls.'

'This will be nothing like those coarse ruffians in the stalls catcalling every night. No, Wallander, these will be people of influence and letters. People with reputations, the crème de la crème of society.'

Carried away with her own self-importance, Mrs Wallander proceeded to strut through the house, her billowing skirts swishing along in hot pursuit. She came to a full stop in the hallway where a double staircase led to the first landing. In ecstasy she exclaimed, 'Can't you just see me, Wallander, gliding down these stairs, making an entrance and greeting our guests? Everyone watching me.'

KENSHŌ   House of Secrets

Poor Mr Wallander, by now stupefied with scurrying to keep up with her, could hardly credit what was happening to his wife. This was the woman who'd once been content living in 'Home Sweet Home' villas in Gravesend, producing children every year. Granted she'd shown little interest in the children once they'd arrived - a wetnurse had been employed from the moment they left the womb, and then a nursery nurse. The children were always kept out of sight whilst he and Eunice took tea in the parlour or dined à deux. No wonder they were such a rowdy untamed bunch of hooligans. Not one of them went to school. The two eldest, Violet and Rose, had looked after the rest since the last nursemaid had left under a cloud. To be perfectly honest, Mr Wallander thought, en masse his children frightened him. They were such a mob, and so out of control, that he was glad to escape to his stockbroking job in the City each day.

By now Mrs Wallander had vanished upstairs shouting more instructions down to her distracted husband. Keen to please, Mr Wallander ran up the stairs. Having a wife twenty years his junior should have made him feel younger, instead he felt like an old man. Sometimes he would daydream about sitting by a fireside, lighting one of his many clay pipes, with an accommodating wife warming his slippers and asking about his day. But that was a fantasy. The reality was that Mrs Wallander had reached the top of the house so Mr Wallander followed, wearily ascending the last flight of stairs. 'This will do fine for the children,' Mrs Wallander declared. 'Which room was it where the lady hanged herself, Wallander?'

'I believe it was the nursery,' Mr Wallander said with passive resignation.

'Well, that'll do nicely as a playroom and somewhere for the kiddies to eat. I see some toys packed away in a corner and a rocking horse. There's even a silver rattle, that will do nicely for Baby and save us a quid or two. They can use next door and one or two of the other rooms on this floor for eating and sleeping.

KENSHŌ   House of Secrets

We'll look out for some trestle tables and second-hand truckle beds from the auction rooms. In the meantime they'll have to bunch up on mattresses on the floor.'

'But Eunice,' Mr Wallander protested weakly, 'surely there's plenty of room in the new wing for them to have their own rooms. Now they're older they could eat with us downstairs. I don't like the idea of leaving them up here. These are supposed to be the servants' quarters.'

'Don't worry your head, Wallander. They'll be snug as a rug up here, and they've got the run of the grounds remember.'

'But surely we'll need to get them some sort of nursemaid or governess? We've only got Maisie. She's just a tweeny, much too young to look after the children.'

'Bosh,' Mrs Wallander retorted. 'I agree we'll have to engage another maid. I'll need someone to help me. Then we need a housekeeper and a gardener, maybe a boot boy. But Violet and Rose are quite old enough and capable enough to look after the other children.' Desperate to say more, Mr Wallander thought better of it. The house was his wife's domain, she knew best. By the end of the day, both removers' men and children were allowed inside the house. The men struggled and sweated with Mrs Wallander's explicit instructions, moaning and complaining to one another. The children, let loose at last, were like feral animals, racing through rooms and corridors screaming and shouting with excitement.

Mrs Wallander, finding it all too much, said plaintively, 'Wallander, I think I'll retire to my bedroom now it's all underway. I have the headache. Find Maisie and tell her to bring me some sal volatile and tea and I might manage a little of that fruit cake we brought.' Mr Wallander sighed heavily but did as he was told. That very morning he'd had a foreboding that everything would be left to him to sort out.

KENSHŌ   House of Secrets

CHAPTER 39
The Wallanders (continued)

Tom, the eldest of the Wallander boys, puffed out his chest and in a loud voice yelled, 'Come on you scallywags. Put your backs into it or we'll never get this den built.'

Sulkily, the twins Ruby and Pearl banged about slapping wet leaves over a wonky leaning structure made out of tree branches. Teddy and Horace whimpering about the mud and their wet feet, cried, 'Nough Tom. Can't we go in now? Prendi's baking. We wanna lick the bowl.' Mrs Prendergast, the Wallanders' long suffering housekeeper, did her best. Most of the time they were exasperating and troublesome, but her kind heart would take over and she'd indulge them. Certainly no one else in the household took an interest in them.

Tom, emulating his mother in one of her hectoring moods, said, 'No food till we've finished. If you won't help, I'll go and get the village kids. They'll sort you lot out.'

They were a ragged bunch, the Wallander children, condemned to live on the top floor of 'La Grande Maison'. No attempt was made to educate or teach them to read or write. They lived outdoors the greater part of the year. In the colder months they played cricket or football in the corridors and had been known to arrange obstacle and piggyback races; the winner claiming all the Fry's chocolate bars Mr Wallander bought on a Saturday night. Violet and Rose, at fourteen and twelve, supervised the younger children in the nursery. The old, discarded toys left by the previous incumbents of the house were their playthings together with poor old Dobbin, the rocking horse, who'd been ridden so hard one of his glass eyes had popped out. Mortimer, Hubert and Baby were a handful. Baby had never been given a proper name or christened as Mrs Wallander had lost interest after number nine. So Baby it remained.

KENSHŌ House of Secrets

Meals for the children were spasmodic and delivered to the upper floor by a fearful Maisie, who would deliver the trays and run.

Mr Wallander endeavoured to come home later and later extending his already long days at the Exchange. Maisie the tweeny and Mrs Prendergast ran the house between them, whilst a poor old soul called Maggie came in four times a week to do the scrubbing and polishing. Otherwise, Charlie the boot boy leaded grates, kept the range alight, cleaned boots and shoes, shone the silver and scoured pans. Laundry was sent out. Once a week a gardener came to tend the garden, or what remained of it after the children had rampaged through it.

Months went by. Mrs Wallander began to assemble her salon, ignoring her children's existence. Her days were occupied planning soirées and dinner parties with the help of Letitia, a superior and rather snooty, upstairs maid. On this particular day Mrs Wallander announced, 'Letty, everything must be extra special tonight. The Chancellor of the University is coming. This is a distinct honour. He's a Marquess. All must be perfect. I'll have no truck with anything else. The children must be put to bed early and their part of the house locked. I don't want any crying infants spoiling my debut into Oxford society.'

No sooner had Mr Wallander arrived home than he was chivvied into his dress coat and white waistcoat and told to behave. Protesting weakly, he said, 'Not another night of entertaining, Eunice. Can't we have a night off and be on our own?' His wife took little notice as Letty struggled to lace her mistress into her corset. The fashionable hourglass figure of the decade had long eluded Mrs Wallander. Ten children and a hearty appetite had seen to that. However, she was determined to be the centre of attention, particularly with the gentlemen.

No sooner was she ready than Mrs Wallander bustled downstairs to check the dining room, her pride and joy. She was immensely satisfied with the dark red damask wallpaper and gold brocade

KENSHŌ   House of Secrets

high backed chairs but complained bitterly to her husband about the lack of pictures. 'Wallander, you'll have to scour the London auction rooms for family portraits.'

'But Eunice, we can't have other people's likenesses on our walls. Who will we say they are?'

'Don't be silly, husband. We'll make something up. I must have aristocratic forebears if I'm to be Oxford's leading hostess.'

Once the company arrived, drinks were served in the drawing room. After curtseying deeply to a rather world weary and elderly Chancellor, Mrs Wallander made the rounds determined to exhibit her innate style and social skills. The room's French windows looked out on the front of the house and were wide open on this temperate evening. Suddenly, without warning, there was an enormous clatter. To the guests' horror, a small boy plummeted from above. An alarmed Mr Wallander rushed out and bent over the recumbent figure. A bruised and bloodied Tom lay on the drive. Wringing his hands, Mr Wallander exclaimed, 'My poor boy, what on earth were you doing?' Unabashed Tom got up and coolly brushed himself down, grinning from ear to ear.

The Chancellor stepped out of the room and, looking down at Tom, addressed himself to the sheepish Mr Wallander, 'Your boy, Wallander, eh? He's got spirit. Where did you come from, boy?'

Tom pointed to the third floor where part of the drainpipe could be seen hanging loose from the building, 'We was locked in. I wanted summat to eat,' he said boldly.

The Chancellor frowned, 'This won't do, Wallander. Won't do at all. What are you running here – some sort of prison? If there's anything I can't abide it's to see children treated badly. Come in here, young man. We'll find you something to eat and, Wallander, I want to hear no more about locking children away, d'ya hear?'

KENSHŌ House of Secrets

That night a seething Mrs Wallander said, 'Well that's it. That child's trouble. He must be sent away to school. Find him a place, Wallander. Be sharp about it.'

Tom was packed off pronto to the Revd Humphrey Gibson's Academy for Boys in deepest Dartmoor. The Wallander children were distraught. Tom had been their leader and instigator. The young ones missed his energetic piggybacks and the older ones his unending ingenuity. Violet and Rose consoled them saying, 'Tom will be back for the holidays. Then there'll be more adventures.'

Tom's first term at the Academy started uneventfully enough. However, towards the end of that term, Mr Wallander received a note to say Tom was ill with fever. He was to be sent home by the next carrier. Mr Wallander, beside himself with worry, tried to attract his wife's attention, 'Eunice, the boy's ill. We must make arrangements – perhaps a nurse, what do you think?'

Tish-toshing, Mrs Wallander said, 'A fuss about nothing. The boy just wants an excuse to come home.'

A pale and sickly Tom arrived back. Violet and Rose tried their best to look after him, keeping him away from the other children, but they were all so excited to see him that even the youngest would sneak in behind their backs. Mr Wallander was all for calling in a doctor, 'Tom's not getting better, Eunice. In fact, he looks worse.'

But Mrs Wallander was adamant, 'I can't let it be known we've sickness in the house. I've a grand musical occasion planned for next month. There's a rumour that the King himself might make an appearance if I can persuade Mrs Keppel to come.'

As the days moved on, each of the children fell ill until there was only Violet and Baby who were healthy. Violet, at her wits' end,

KENSHŌ House of Secrets

went downstairs to plead with her mother, 'Please, please call a doctor, Mama. The little ones are sick now too.'

But Mrs Wallander was unmoved, 'If you need help, Violet, I'll lend you Letty. No doubt Mrs Prendergast can help out too. But you must stay in your part of the house. I don't want infection spread down here. The children are tough, they'll survive. I can't think about them now. I might have the King of England here soon.'

Lamentably for Mrs Wallander, events overtook her plans. One by one each of the children got sicker and started to fade away. Violet was distraught. She moved Baby down to Mrs Prendergast's quarters. Though she herself was mildly ill, the other eight children were showing alarming symptoms. When Mr Wallander finally did take control and a doctor was called, it was too late. 'My God, man,' he said to the quivering Mr Wallander, 'these children have scarlet fever. Why didn't you call me earlier? They must go into isolation immediately.' But it was no use. By the time the ambulance came, all eight children had breathed their last.

Mr Wallander, head in hands, wept copiously, 'Eunice, I can't believe I've been so weak. What have I done? There's only Violet and Baby left out of our ten beautiful children.'

'Oh, for goodness sake Wallander, rouse yourself. I can't have it known we're a house of death. You must arrange for the undertakers to come at night and collect the bodies. I'll get Maisie and Mrs Prendergast to fumigate the whole of the third floor. Nothing must prevent my entry into society now I'm becoming so well-known. Nothing. Do you hear, Wallander?'

Mr Wallander was broken, feeling every day of his fifty five years. He could barely bring himself to make the arrangements for a family vault and the funeral. Why couldn't he have stood up to his wife? A night service was organised surreptitiously at the local

KENSHŌ House of Secrets

church. No one except the family was to attend. Baby was left in Mrs Prendergast's care. An insouciant Mrs Wallander, garbed from head to foot in innumerable black veils so as not to be recognised, followed Violet and Mr Wallander up the aisle behind eight tiny white coffins. As they neared the altar, Violet started to sway. Mr Wallander caught her before she fell and carried her outside to the fresh air.

'What a fuss,' Mrs Wallander grumbled, 'I can't see why that girl is so worked up. Deaths happens every day, especially to children.'

It was years later when Mr Wallander's will was read after his premature death that Mrs Wallander found out what her husband had done. All his savings and his pension had been ploughed into building a grand mausoleum in the nearby cemetery for his dead children. It was there he himself was interred, surrounded by golden cherubim representing each of his eight dead children. Two life sized fiery angels guarded the entrance. There was no space left for his wife, only one for Violet and one for Baby's son, the grandson he was never to meet.

…by now Mika had come to the last sheet of handwritten script. The full force of the children's deaths hit her hard. Tears rolled down her cheeks and pooled on her dressing gown. Surprisingly, she realised she was no longer frightened of what she'd thought were the yūrei. All Mika felt was a deep sorrow. The ghosts of those long lost children must be left alone to play and run about the nursery at will. She was sad she and Tolly had got rid of their toys. Keen to make amends she went into the nursery. Taking the blanket off the old rocking horse's head, she said, 'Solly, Dobbin. Understand now. Please to forgive.'

KENSHŌ   House of Secrets

CHAPTER 40
Talk of the past

Mika was eager to see and talk to Jack. Over the past weeks their meetings had been sporadic, interspersed with so much work it was difficult to catch up. Jack's fact finding trip to London about his grandfather had not been particularly fruitful. He was now contemplating writing to his father, although they were hardly on the best of terms. When Mika and Jack finally met and sat down to eat in their favourite Italian restaurant, Jack said, 'Let's enjoy being together. I just want to look at you. I've missed you so much. I feel we're moving apart and I don't want that to happen. Tell me you feel the same.'

Mika smiled her enchanting smile, 'I miss too, Jack. So much happen. I want tell you about Kenshō House but hear your news too. We eat then talk,' she leant over and taking his free hand and holding it for a moment, turned it over and kissed his palm.

Jack blushed furiously, 'Mika, Mika. This is so unlike you. It's me who should be doing that, but I love you for it. Why don't you try some of my carbonara?' They sat grinning and feeding one another succulent parts of the dishes.

Once they'd finished and all the dishes were cleared away, they shared a tiramisu. Jack said, 'Now we can talk, though all I want to do is look at you in that beautiful cheongsam. You look so mysterious yet stunning, quite beyond my reach.'

It was Mika's turn to blush, 'Jack, I not know what to say. I yours. No beyond reach. Just ordinary Japanese girl. Not special.'

'You are to me though,' Jack murmured as he kissed her on the cheek. 'You are my oriental lotus.'

KENSHŌ   House of Secrets

Mika began to giggle, 'Now Jack, too far. I not exotic flower. Ordinary,' adding sternly, 'we talk serious. No flirt,' but she couldn't help smiling.

'Very well,' Jack said attempting to look contrite. 'I'm no further forward on my family. My London friend's search discovered my grandfather was a German Jew, a scientist in Berlin in the thirties. He fled after Kristallnacht in '38 taking his wife and my mother to London. Soon after that the family moved to America. Something to do with a government project. I need to talk to my father, but you know how difficult that is.'

'But why your mother not tell about her father?'

'I think there was something she was ashamed of. Once she went to university she cut off all contact with her parents. I never knew them. Anyway that's all there is. Let's talk about you instead.'

Mika shrugged, 'Hear nothing from grandfather. He write short letter in New Year but say little. Only want talk to me. Important but not say.' Jokingly she added, 'Perhaps he come visit,' she burst out laughing at the thought of it. 'Think not. He not travel much in Japan so not come here. But Jack, I read rest of story of Kenshō House. Here I bring photos.' She drew the dilapidated album, she'd found in the attic, out of her bag. 'Here Wallander family, last people to live in house before Colonel. Parents and ten children. Look at clothes. How women move in dress like that? Here Baby youngest, Violet eldest, Colonel's aunt, leave him house. She and sister look after children. Bad, bad story. Eight of children die scarlet fever. So sad, so young. Think maybe ghosts I hear at night – children playing, riding rocking horse.'

'What happened to the other two children?'

'Baby, run off with gardener – 15, pregnant – big scandal. Mr Wallander disown. Baby, Colonel's mother, die young. Violet

KENSHŌ   House of Secrets

look after Mrs Wallander who go mad, die in asylum. Violet stay in house till die in 1940s. Never leave ghost brothers and sisters.'

'What about you?' Jack asked, 'How do you feel about the ghosts now?'

Mika smiled, looking relieved, 'No problem. I happy at last, no fear, now know house story Not yūrei to do with me.'

'Will you tell the Colonel the story?'

'Not sure, Jack. He old and sick. Should he know? It sad. Also not know what happen his war diary. Did Sanshō give him?'

It was at that very moment back in Kenshō House that Sanshō felt his ears burning. Was someone somewhere talking about him? Maybe it was something to do with that diary. It had been a while since Mika had given it to him. Due to the Colonel's state of mind, he'd decided to put the wretched thing away not bothering to read it. He was as unwilling as the Colonel to relive old memories. His alter ego, Fred Wilkins from Brixton, had vanished long ago reinvented as Sanshō, guru and faithful servant. Going AWOL from the British Army in 1940 and ending up in an Indian jail was nothing to be proud of. So why would he want to be responsible for dredging up another man's painful memories, especially the Colonel's?

Since Christmas, the Colonel had fallen into yet another deep depression, unable to stir himself. One of the mornings, when they'd finished their meditation practice, the Colonel said, 'Sanshō, I don't think I've much longer. There's nothing for me here. Julian will be glad to see the back of me. My work no longer excites me. What's the point of going on?'

Sanshō didn't know what to say. Doing his best to console his old friend, he said, 'But, Colonel, you love your studies and your family showed how happy they were to see you at Christmas.

KENSHŌ House of Secrets

Why don't I encourage the children to come up on a visit? Youngsters always cheer one up.'

'No, Sanshō, not today. I couldn't cope with the noise. Except for Ptolemy they're too young to talk to. Even he's more than I can stand just now. Best leave me with Bakti. He and I understand one another. He'll keep me company. Take a break. Go home and sit in your garden. I'll be fine.'

Not used to free time, Sanshō wandered back to his house. There were times when he could cheerfully throttle the old man, however after all these years he was truly fond of him and was worried. Maybe it was time to look at that diary. There might be a clue to the Colonel's misery, or even some good memories he could share.

Retrieving the diary from its hiding place, Sanshō began to read. A couple of hours later he heaved an enormous sigh. Putting the diary down, he lay back. It had been a revelation. No wonder the Colonel had suffered all these years. He knew he himself was in no position to pass judgement; his own life was hardly spotless.

Later, returning to the big house, he found the Colonel sitting as he'd left him, staring into space. Laying a comforting hand on the Colonel's shoulder, the old man looked up making an effort to smile, 'There you are, old friend. I thought you'd gone off and left me. I deserve it the mood I'm in these days. Please don't go. I don't think I could bear that.'

'Never,' Sanshō said vehemently, 'I'll be here as long as you need me.'

KENSHŌ House of Secrets

CHAPTER 41
The seduction

Julian was pleasantly surprised when Daisy reported back on her meeting with Rhianna. At long last he was free, off the hook. Feeling inordinately grateful to Daisy, he said, 'I'd like to find a way to repay you. Perhaps a little gift. I'd be happy to buy something for you, maybe some jewellery.'

Daisy grinned, 'No need for that Prof. I'll certainly think of some sort of repayment though, you can be sure of that.'

Julian didn't think he liked the sound of that, it was positively threatening. However, feeling euphoric, he decided to ignore the insinuation. All he had to do now was get his and Phoebe's marriage back on track. That might be easier said than done as Phoebe had become more distant by the day. Any advances he made towards her were brushed off. It was as if his wife had morphed into a completely different person. The new clothes and haircut had started it. Talking to her now was like trying to hold on to handfuls of sand, no sooner did he get her attention than she was somewhere else, 'Phoebe, Phoebe are you listening? We need to have a serious discussion.'

'Really, Julian. What about?' Phoebe said dreamily.

'About the state of our marriage for one thing, and the fact that you are using our home as a lodging house. You're always on the go, out and about. Even the children never know where they are with you and when you're here you're in a world of your own. I don't know what's happening to you.'

'Nothing's happening to me, Julian. I'm busy like you. You're out at college all day and I'm here.'

KENSHŌ   House of Secrets

'Daisy says you're not though, and she's left to sort out the children. I want to know what you're doing. I have rights as your husband.'

'Don't be stuffy, Julian. I'm out and about. Do you expect me to be tied to the house? I used to be your domestic slave, but things have changed. I've vacated that role.'

Julian began to huff and puff, ' That was never my idea. I never wanted you to end up as my slave. Surely this is the other extreme. Perhaps we should consider marriage guidance.'

'Pouf to that,' Phoebe said scornfully. 'Lots of couples live like us. I'm not inclined to talk to some outsider about our marital problems. Honestly, I can't see we have any.'

Finding his efforts in vain, Julian gave up trying. Once the children were in bed and Phoebe was God knows where, he and Daisy resumed their cosy little dinners together. It was the only consolation Julian had these days. Bit by bit Daisy inveigled herself further into his life. She no longer called him Prof but Julian or even 'dear' or 'darling' when she forgot. Her repertoire of cordon bleu meals was expanding as was Julian's midriff. He would stand in front of the mirror attempting to hold in his growing paunch, bemoaning the loss of his once fine figure. The rich sauces and desserts had taken their toll. His former carnal appetites had been replaced by a passion for gourmet food and wine.

Daisy, awaiting her moment, built up the tension between them, hoping a well satiated Julian would fall into her clutches. Phoebe was forgotten and out of the running. The field was wide open. By now Daisy had built up an impressive portfolio of Julian's past misdemeanours. Seduction was imminent, with emotional blackmail as a backup if needed. Theirs was not going to be one of Julian's usual transitory affairs. This was for keeps. The night and the scene was set. Phoebe departed as usual. Daisy, decked

KENSHŌ House of Secrets

out in a low-cut dress under which was the sexiest of black underwear, served oysters, lobster thermidor, chocolate covered strawberries and champagne. A dazed Julian said, 'Some treat, Daisy! What did I do to deserve all this?'

'Oh I don't know,' Daisy said flirtatiously, 'perhaps you'll have to find a reason,' and then proceeded to pour generous amounts of champagne into his glass.

Julian had no trouble working his way through the sumptuous meal. After, as they sat in front of the drawing room fire nursing brandies, he said, 'This is the life, Daisy. I could live like this for ever.'

'And so you shall,' quipped Daisy.

'Whatever do you mean?'

'Well,' Daisy said moving closer and stretching out a wandering hand, 'maybe this is the life you deserve and should have had and I could be the one to give it to you.'

Taken aback, Julian recoiled, 'Look Daisy, I know I owe you for the Rhianna business but I'm married to Phoebe. I know she and I are barely jogging along at present, but we are content and there's the children.'

'What if I told you Phoebe might be having an affair? What would you think then?'

'I'd never believe it. Not Phoebe. She's too decent. Hardly the type to be unfaithful.' Deliberating for a second, he said thoughtfully, 'Though, of course, there's been that new look and her attitude towards me has changed radically. She's no longer the old subservient, worshipping Phoebe I married.'

KENSHŌ House of Secrets

By now Daisy's hand had reached Julian's groin, but he was too preoccupied to notice. Very quietly Daisy whispered in his ear, 'Shall we go upstairs? I can see something stirring down here,' as she stroked his crotch.

'I don't know, Daisy,' Julian made every effort to sound reluctant, but inside felt his juices beginning to flow. What harm could it do? It had been a long time since…Phoebe was never in the mood, had a headache or some such excuse. How could a little diversion with Daisy matter? Silently they ascended the stairs, Daisy careful to precede Julian, making him fully aware of her black underwear under the shortest of skirts. At the top Julian pulled her towards him, but she held her finger to his lips whispering, 'We mustn't wake the children,' and pushed him towards his and Phoebe's bedroom.

'Not there, Daisy,' Julian protested but to no avail. Daisy was determined it was the marital bed or nothing. Before he had a chance she was on him, kneeling astride and undressing them both with deft hands. Things became so frenzied that neither of them heard the click of the front door or the sound of feet running up the stairs. They were in a hot and hungry clinch when Phoebe threw open the bedroom door. Shocked, she backed on to the landing, 'Argh - Julian - in our home - in our bed. How could you?' Without another word she shot back down the stairs, racing out the front door and back to her car, and driving off as if all the demons in hell were pursuing her.

A bewildered Julian tried to disentangle himself from the bedsheets and Daisy, 'I must go after her, Daisy.'

'I don't think so, Prof,' Daisy said drily, reverting to her old name for him. 'You're with me now. You're mine. I know you inside out, know everything about you in fact. Over the last months I've made it my business to study you and your secrets.'

A stunned Julian said, 'For goodness sake why, and what secrets?'

KENSHŌ   House of Secrets

'First the 'what' - Lucy's premature death. So unexpected having a heart attack at her age.' Julian paled and stopped dragging on his clothes. 'Then there was the PhD thesis that, surprisingly, Lucy never submitted yet was the same topic as yours. Could that be the very one you presented when your original one had been referred? Next we come to Rhianna and the baby.' Teasingly she said, 'What would that churchy Dean say about that? Remember that last interview with him you told me about, when you promised to be a good little boy? And now the 'why'. Simple. I want us to be together for ever. Once Phoebe leaves for good, we can think about not just a relationship but marriage.'

A flustered frantic Julian began to stutter and stammer, 'Surely you don't think blackmail will provide a good basis for a relationship let alone a marriage?'

'Oh, but I do,' Daisy said triumphantly. 'I think Professor mine, that your career as well as your marriage is in my hands. Now just lay back. Let me help you relax; you look far too stressed. From now on I'm going to take exceptionally good care of you, my darling Professor, you can depend on that.'

This wasn't what Julian wanted to hear. How had he got into this fix? Panicking and terrified, he could feel his freedom being gradually snatched away from him. He was where he didn't want to be, under someone's power and control; a bird in a cage with no window to fly out of.

KENSHŌ House of Secrets

CHAPTER 42
Phoebe and Geoffrey's future

A tear stained Phoebe arrived at Geoffrey's cottage in nearby Wolvercote. He'd rented the place since the New Year to be nearer to her. In the past weeks this had been their rendezvous. Phoebe, still unsure of her feelings, would not let herself be carried away by anything more physical than kissing. Tonight, everything was different. All her previous misgivings and guilt about Geoffrey and her marriage had been blown apart. Banging and banging on the cottage door, it seemed forever before a dishevelled Geoffrey answered. Shocked at the state of her, he said, 'My darling girl, what's happened? Come here, let me hold you.'

Phoebe fell into his arms, babbling incomprehensibly, 'Julian, Julian...I know he flirted with the students particularly the first years. I never thought…in our bed of all places. I don't know what to do.' She wrung her hands.

After a lot of cajoling, Geoffrey pieced together the story. His face froze, 'That out and out bastard. I've a good mind to go round and give him a thrashing.'

'No, no,' Phoebe squeaked, barely able to talk. 'No, that's not what I want. Perhaps this is for the best, giving me the kick I need to leave. This last year I wasn't even sure Julian and I still had a marriage. It's the children I'm worried about, particularly Tolly.'

'But Tolly's not that close to his father, is he, and the other two are so young they won't know what's going on?'

'I can't go back there, Geoffrey. What am I to do? I can't pretend anymore.'

'There's no question of your going back. You'll stay here. In the morning we'll go over, pack your things, and collect the children. I've plenty of room for them.'

KENSHŌ   House of Secrets

Phoebe said uncertainly, 'It's so quick, so final. I've had no time to prepare the children, but I must make sure they're alright and settled tonight.' Recovering, she added sardonically, 'I don't suppose Julian or Daisy have checked on them.'

Geoffrey frowned, 'If you must go back, you must. I'll run you over and wait in the driveway.'

Kenshō House was in darkness when they arrived. Phoebe sped out of the car, quietly unlocking the front door. There was only a light in Julian's study. Phoebe crept up to the children's rooms. Sadilla was tucked up with her stuffed tiger, the one Geoffrey had bought her at Legoland. Kepha, as ever, had his thumb firmly attached to the roof of his mouth. In the other room curly haired Tolly was half awake, saying sleepily, 'Is you alright, Mum? You looks as if you's been crying?'

'I'm fine, Tolly. Go back to sleep. I think we're all going to be alright now.'

'Did you see Uncle Geoffrey 'gain?'

'I did. He's looking forward to going riding with you soon.'

'I likes horses, Mum, real ones not that old rocking horse.'

Phoebe laughed, 'You just might have a horse of your own someday, we'll see.'

'That's good. Night, Mum,' Tolly turned over and immediately fell asleep.

Reassured, Phoebe left, leaving the door slightly ajar and making every effort not to look across at hers and Julian's bedroom. Who knew what shenanigans she'd find in there? Her clothes could wait till morning. Retracing her steps, she'd just reached the bottom of the stairs, when she was confronted by Julian, 'You

KENSHŌ House of Secrets

don't have to creep around, Phoebe. This is your home after all.' He hung his head in a penitent manner, 'I'm truly sorry. I know it was a shock but I can assure you it was a one-off. Daisy's gone home. It won't happen again,' he lied unconvincingly.

'No, Julian, it won't. I'm leaving you. Tomorrow morning I'll be back for my things. The children will be coming with me.'

'But where will you go, surely not a hotel with the children? They'll be fine here with me and Daisy.'

At that, Phoebe's temper erupted, 'If you think I'm leaving my beautiful children with that scheming trollop you're very much mistaken. No, they're coming with me and staying at a friend's house.'

'What friend? I've never heard of you having friends before. Is this where you've been running off to every evening?'

'It's no good getting on your high horse, Julian. Think of your own situation. Anyway, the friend is someone you know, Geoffrey Eggleston. He's a Professor like you.'

'Not that halfwit you were dating before we met. I thought he'd decamped to America, leaving you high and dry. You were always moaning he never contacted you but just left. Why's he turned up all of a sudden?'

'It's not 'all of a sudden'. He's been a visiting Professor at college since the beginning of last term and looked me up as an old friend.'

'I bet it's more than an old friend he wants,' Julian sneered out of the corner of his mouth. 'No wonder you've been tarting yourself up recently and showing little interest in me or the children.'

KENSHŌ   House of Secrets

Stung by his remark, Phoebe gave as good as she got, 'I was hardly 'tarting' myself up, as you put it. I got up one day and realised I was only thirty, even if I do have three children. I'm still young - almost half your age, though you treat me like a pathetic middle aged woman without a brain. It's taken me ten years to stop worshipping at your feet and wake up to the realisation I don't love you anymore. I'm off. I'll be back in the morning.'

'Not for my children, you won't,' a peeved Julian bellowed. 'What's mine stays mine. You get off with lover boy, but the children stay with me. I don't know what Father will think.'

'Not much,' Phoebe spat out. 'He's never thought much of you as a son or a father. I should know. Haven't we been walking on eggshells around that old man for years because of the house. And as for the children, we'll see what the lawyers have to say about your history of flirtations and tonight's escapade. As for Daisy, I can't see her letting you go that easily. I expect she's already celebrating finding such a lucrative meal ticket, and don't imagine the Dean will be in your corner when the scandal breaks. Being High Church, he's hardly likely to approve of divorce or your affairs.'

With those parting words Phoebe closed the front door firmly, leaving a shattered Julian on the other side. He couldn't believe what had just happened. Had Phoebe suddenly grown a backbone after all these years? His mind was in turmoil. What should he do about Daisy? And what about his father? There was a time when he'd wanted the old man's approval, but now he would get short shrift. There'd be no sympathy from that quarter.

KENSHŌ   House of Secrets

CHAPTER 43
The aftermath

Early next morning the majority of the household was in ignorance about Phoebe's overnight absence. Once Daisy arrived she gathered the children together as usual in the kitchen, noticing Julian wandering into the dining room. He looked a hundred years old, listless and weary. 'What's happened?' she whispered, 'Did Phoebe come home?'

'Not now,' Julian said petulantly, 'not in front of the children...'

Busy boiling eggs for the children and making toast and coffee for Julian, Daisy congratulated herself. It looked as if Phoebe had fled the coop. But what of the children? Daisy didn't mind if Phoebe left the children. She was practically bringing them up anyway.

Mika arrived and asked, 'Where Phoebe?', looking round the kitchen. There was no reply. Sensing something untoward, Mika took a seat opposite Tolly and tried again, 'Where your mother, Tolly?'

'Dunno, she was here last night,' he said through a mouthful of egg and soldiers. 'We was talking about horses. She says I's might have one someday soon.'

Mika's eyebrows rose but she didn't say anything, 'Shall I take Professor san breakfast in, Daisy?'

'No thanks, Mika. I need a word with him.'

Trying to get any response from Julian was impossible. He just grunted when Daisy poured his coffee. She persevered, 'Do come along now, Prof. Tell all.'

'Later, Daisy, when we're on our own. I need to see Father after breakfast, then I've an early meeting at college.'

KENSHŌ House of Secrets

Daisy was not satisfied. Exactly what was going on? She needed to know where she stood. Her earlier good spirits faded. She scowled at the children when she returned to the kitchen, but they were too busy eating to notice. Only Mika detected the change of mood.

Up on the next floor of the house, the Colonel was also in a grouchy frame of mind. When his son appeared at the main door without warning, he ordered Sanshō not to let him in. 'But, Colonel, it must be important for him to come up here and so early in the morning. You know he never comes unless invited.'

'Oh very well, but impress on him to be brief. I'm not at my best and certainly not at this time of day.'

Julian came in and stood before his father's desk with a hangdog expression. 'So what is it this time, Julian? Hope it's not money as there's little enough to spare after paying the running costs of this house, which you note I pay for. Or have you been caught with one of your floozies again?'

'Something like that, Father. It's Phoebe. She's left me.'

'...and what did you do to make a good girl like Phoebe leave? Granted, she's a dithery creature, but she's honest and truthful which is more than I can say about you, boy.'

Mumbling, with his head down like a naughty boy in the headmaster's study, Julian said, 'She found me in bed with Daisy last night. It was a momentary aberration, but she's gone off with this chap, says she's taking the children.'

'What's that, boy? Speak up. I can barely hear you.'

Sweating, squirming and growing more uncomfortable by the minute, Julian repeated the sad story.

KENSHŌ House of Secrets

'What did you expect?' the Colonel growled. 'Phoebe's an attractive young woman. I noticed at Christmas how pretty she was looking, not quite as drab as she used to be. Why you couldn't see that beats me. I certainly never had this trouble with women. My wife and I had a rock solid marriage until she died. No flirting about like you do.' Becoming more and more irritable, the old man said, 'Goodness, you're a middle aged man. What are you doing falling into bed with little bits of skirt like that Daisy? She's barely twenty.'

'Twenty five,' Julian said sulkily, 'and quite old enough to know what she was doing.'

'So were you, boy,' the old man said snappishly. 'Now what's going to happen? I hope there's not going to be a scandal. Won't do my name or yours any good, that is, if you've any reputation left.'

'Phoebe's coming today to collect the children. I want them to stay with me but she's adamant threatening me with the courts, the Dean and God knows what.'

'The children should be with their mother, there's no doubt about that,' the old man said in a severe tone. 'They can't stay here with you and your fancy woman. I don't approve either but you're welcome to your paramour as long as you both stay in your part of the house. And what about sweet little Mika? What are you going to do about her? She can't be exposed to all this sordid bed-hopping.'

'Really, Father, it's not like that. Mika has to stay till the end of next term. There are weeks to go yet unless I send her home early. I don't want to do that. It wouldn't look good having promised the college she could stay the year.'

The Colonel shook his head as if he were at the end of his tether, 'That's all I can stand to hear now. Be off now, boy. Take your

KENSHŌ House of Secrets

complicated love life and leave me in peace with Sanshō. Let me know what's been decided. I'd like to see that Tolly before the children leave with their mother. He's a good head on his shoulders, a sensible lad. Took a fancy to him at Christmas. Speaks his mind. More people could do with following his example.' The Colonel looked pointedly at his son.

Julian shambled off. He and his father never seemed to hit it off. Sometimes he was relieved his father had Sanshō. At other times he hated the superior way the two of them treated him as if he were the village idiot. They were so smug in their studies of ancient sacred wisdoms and daily Zen meditations, making him feel like an outsider.

As soon as Julian departed for college, Phoebe arrived to collect the children who'd been kept home from school. Daisy made herself scarce, so Phoebe asked Mika to join them in the kitchen. Sitting close together, the three children sat hunched round the table as if expecting bad news. Kepha, not happy in his chair, made his way to Mika's lap, sucking on the habitual thumb. Unsure of how to start Phoebe took a deep breath, and launched into, 'Daddy and I have not been getting on well lately. We need a break. Uncle Geoffrey has invited us all to stay at his cottage. It's only a mile away, so you'll go to school as usual. Mika will stay here (looking reassuringly at Mika) until she goes home to Japan at the end of next term. You'll still see Daddy, just not as much. It'll be a real adventure at Uncle Geoffrey's. His cottage is a lot smaller than Kenshō House but you'll be able to take some of your prized possessions. What do you think?'

Tolly's face lit up, 'Sounds fun Mum, but I's miss Mika. Can I come and see her?'

'Of course,' Phoebe said relieved her eldest was in favour. This meant the two youngest would follow his lead. Sadilla piped up, 'Can I take my dollies and teddy?' followed by Kepha, not wanting to be left out, 'Wot 'bout my trucks?'

KENSHŌ   House of Secrets

'Don't worry, my darlings. You can take what you want.'

A confused Mika asked, 'Phoebe, possible to stay here without you? What Professor san say? What about Daisy?'

'Julian's fine with you being here, though you may have to make your own food and clean your part of the house. Not sure about Daisy, that's up to Julian. But you'll be welcome at Geoffrey's if someone can bring you over, maybe your boyfriend?' Phoebe said encouragingly.

Mika smiled, 'Will ask Jack. So solly Phoebe about you and Professor san. Hope become better.' It was difficult to say more in front of the children.

Tolly, always one to seize on an opportunity, said, 'Maybe a horse now, Mum?'

Phoebe laughed at his cheek, 'Afraid not Tolly, you'll have to wait. Geoffrey only has a tiny garden. But am sure he'll take you riding.' As they went off to pack, Phoebe took Tolly to one side and said, 'Your grandfather would like to see you. I think he took a liking to you at Christmas. Can you pop up and see him before we go?'

Grousing, Tolly said, 'Does I have to, Mum? OK - will if Mika come too. I don't likes that Sanshō.'

The pair climbed the stairs to the heavy door and knocked. Sanshō, in his munificence, greeted them warmly for a change, 'Come in. The Colonel's expecting you.'

For once, the Colonel was all smiles, holding out a hand to a sulky Tolly, 'Hear you're leaving today young man?'

'Yes, we's going to Mum's friend, Uncle Geoffrey.'

KENSHŌ   House of Secrets

The old man winced. This was the first he'd heard of Uncle Geoffrey, but he continued, 'Very good. Come and see me when you can and teach me more of your magic tricks.' Noticing Mika lurking uncertainly on the threshold, he beckoned her forward, 'Mika, my dear, please come and join us. You never did tell me what you found in the attics. Any skeletons or buried treasure, heh?'

Uneasily, Mika said, 'No, Colonel san. Only old paper.' She could see Tolly was just about to mention the diary and shook her head warningly. He made a sign 'my lips are sealed' behind the Colonel's back, who was occupied with calling to Sanshō, 'Bring tea and chocolate biscuits, there's a good man. Can't you see this boy needs his victuals? He's a growing lad.'

Later that day, when the Blenkinsop children had been loaded into the car with all their treasures, Mika said to Phoebe, 'Hope life better with friend. Please to keep in touch.'

Phoebe hugged Mika tightly, something she'd never done before. 'I will, Mika. I will. I don't know our plans as yet. Cheerily, she added, 'We may go back to America with Geoffrey in the summer, if he's not had enough of us by then and is willing to take the four of us on.'

Left reeling, a shocked Mika was astounded by the turn of events. Everything had happened so fast. She'd barely had a moment to take a breath since Phoebe's announcement. How could a family split up like that? Why hadn't she noticed? Clearly, her English was still not good enough. It was mystifying!

KENSHŌ   House of Secrets

CHAPTER 44
Family affairs

Life at Geoffrey's became routine for the children as they adapted to their change of circumstance, although they missed the space they'd had at Kenshō House and their dogs who'd been left with Julian. Phoebe was amused to see Geoffrey's behaviour with the children. It was if he'd become one of them. The greatest surprise was Tolly. In the past, Phoebe had always worried about her eldest. He tended to be a loner, although bright and intelligent, but was better with adults than his peers. Now he and Geoffrey were inseparable. It was a pleasure to see two blonde heads in cahoots over a board game or trialling one of Tolly's innumerable magic tricks. Intuitively, they behaved like father and son. Phoebe had never been sure of Tolly's parentage. Now it seemed obvious. Her fears were assuaged at last but how could she bring herself to tell either of them? What would their reactions be after years of being kept apart? They might end up resenting her.

As it turned out, Julian was to be the catalyst. Arriving one Saturday afternoon in a steaming rage, he found Tolly and Geoffrey building some sort of edifice in the garden. Sadilla and Kepha, up to their armpits in mud, were pulling at stones and rocks to add to the structure. Phoebe was nowhere to be seen. As Julian drove up he was confronted with a familial scene of togetherness. Grinding his brakes, he skidded to a halt, and, banging the driver's door with unnecessary force, strode up the path towards the gathering, yelling, 'What do you think you're doing with **my** wife and **my** children?'

Geoffrey, taken aback by Julian's fury, calmly stepped forward and, taking him by the arm, led him into the house. 'Get a grip, man. Do you want to frighten your children? Come into the kitchen and we can talk.'

A furious Julian shook Geoffrey off and strutted into the kitchen, 'I remember you only too well from all those years ago. You were

KENSHŌ House of Secrets

no good for Phoebe then and you're certainly no good for her now. She needs to pull herself together, be sensible and come home.'

Taking no notice, Geoffrey put the kettle on, 'Tea, coffee or something stronger?'

But there was no calming Julian. He embarked on yet another tirade, 'I don't know why Phoebe up and left like that. It was a momentary slip on my part...and to take the children as well. I can't think what's got into her. She would never have dreamed of behaving like this a year ago.'

Geoffrey carefully poured out the tea and, as an afterthought, retrieved a bottle of brandy from the cupboard and placed it next to Julian. Patiently, as if talking to a recalcitrant child, he said, 'I think, Julian, your so-called 'momentary slip' was the last straw. Phoebe had had enough. From what I gather, you've a less than spotless reputation but to bring an affair right into yours and Phoebe's home and bed was the end. Goodness, man, have you no self-control? Phoebe is such a lovely, attractive, generous woman, why did you even look elsewhere?' All of this was delivered in quiet measured tones. Julian, taken aback by such directness, cowered down and drank his tea, after splashing it with a liberal amount of brandy.

Attempting to take back the initiative, he said almost in a whine, 'Where is Phoebe? It's her I want to talk to.'

'She'll be back in a minute,' Geoffrey said passively. 'You're welcome to wait but I must get back to the kids. 'We're right in the middle of things.'

'**My** kids, you mean,' Julian said forcefully, attempting to muster his previous aggression, 'they're **my** kids.'

KENSHŌ House of Secrets

'Of course they are,' Geoffrey replied amiably. 'Well, I'm going to carry on helping **your** kids. See you later,' and disappeared out the door.

Julian was left licking his wounds, seething and brooding. It was a good half hour before Phoebe drove up. By then Julian had managed to work himself up again into his earlier state of fury, 'Where on earth have you been, Phoebe? Why are you leaving our children with that man and floating round the town?'

Phoebe sighed but didn't respond. Plonking the shopping down hard on the kitchen table, she said, 'We live here now, Julian. Geoffrey is excellent with our children. He makes a far better father than you ever did.'

Julian began more ranting and raving, 'He's not their father though, I am. I want you and them back home where you belong, do you hear me?'

'I hear you alright, but neither I nor the children are coming back to live at Kenshō House. I want a divorce. I've plenty of grounds if you want to make it a dirty fight. We may be returning with Geoffrey to America when he leaves at the end of the summer term.'

'What about you then, living here with your lover? It'll be tit for tat.'

'Hardly,' Phoebe said coolly. 'I've been making some enquiries since we left. Janice was extremely helpful particularly about Rhianna and 'a possible baby'.'

Humiliated, Julian began to bluster, 'It's a lie. Nothing to it. A hysterical first year claiming she was pregnant. It was a schoolgirl crush embellished into a romantic fantasy. She's left college now, thank goodness.'

KENSHŌ House of Secrets

'And did it reach the Dean's ears?' Phoebe enquired in a mock innocent tone.

The choleric colour Julian was exhibiting drained from his face. His voice shook as he said, 'Of course not, it was nonsense. A stupid little girl who was infatuated with me because I paid her attention.'

Phoebe scoffed, 'But there were so many of these so called incidents. I suppose when you seduced me on the couch in your study I was just one in a long line up, though of course I really did fall pregnant, unlike poor Rhianna. I expect that's why you married me. I don't suppose you loved me, but it wouldn't have looked good if you'd abandoned me just when your career was on the ascendant. Back then I was young and naive enough to think you loved me as much as I loved you.'

Julian was silent, staring down at the table. Attempting to collect himself, he spluttered, 'I did love you then. You were a sweet pliant little thing. I wanted to protect you. A waif, pregnant with Tolly, with no family to support you. I can't think what's happened to you since. Why have you become so tough and unfeeling?'

'I grew up,' Phoebe said flatly. 'It took me a while but I'm my own person now. That's how I want our children to see me, not some quivering wreck waiting for her bullying master to come home.'

Feeling he was losing ground, Julian retorted, 'And what about the children? I don't want my son and heir, and the young ones, growing up in America. Tolly will eventually inherit Kenshō House. He should be brought up like a proper English gentleman, go to the right schools and learn to speak properly. Boarding school will soon knock him into shape. It made me the man I am today.'

KENSHŌ   House of Secrets

Phoebe shuddered, 'And look what sort of man that is. No, Tolly, Sadilla and Kepha go with me wherever I end up. They can come and stay with you during the long summer vac if they're so inclined.'

Determined to have the last word, Julian said brusquely, 'That won't do. I'll see my solicitor tomorrow and start court proceedings. You're certainly not taking my eldest out of the country.'

Phoebe held herself back from a quick retort. Was this the moment? What would be the consequences if she told him now? She needn't have been apprehensive. It was already teetering on the edge of her tongue and popped out quite naturally, 'Tolly's not your son.'

'Whatever do you mean?' Julian was bemused. 'Of course he's mine. I remember when you were pregnant. I was even at the birth.'

Without saying anything further, Phoebe beckoned him to the window, where two heads could be seen bending over a rough sketch map. 'See, there's his father. I was never sure. Every day with Geoffrey it becomes clearer. I never really did know which of you it was.'

Speechless, Julian stood and stared at the two heads. All he managed was, 'You tricked me. I can't believe you deceived me all these years. I want a DNA test. All this time…and you cheated your way into a marriage with me.' Too stunned to say more, he pushed past Phoebe. Storming down the garden path to his car, he practically ran over Geoffrey who was coming towards him. 'You, of all people,' he grunted, 'well good luck to you. You're welcome to that lying bitch.'

Taken aback, Geoffrey rushed into the house, 'Phoebe darling, what's happened? Is it all over with him?'

KENSHŌ House of Secrets

'It's over alright,' Phoebe said with relish, 'it's definitely over. Julian's suffering from hurt pride. Apparently,' she added wryly, 'I seem to have got the last laugh, if you can call it that. But, Geoffrey, there's something important I have to tell you. I don't know how you're going to take it. It'll be a shock and a surprise, hopefully a good one. After that, we both have to speak to Tolly.'

Puzzled, Geoffrey put his arms round her, 'Whatever it is, Phoebe, I'm up for it. We're all so happy, nothing can spoil that. I had no idea how much I wanted a family. It's been a revelation to me.' Phoebe breathed a sigh of relief and relaxed in his arms. She'd made the right decision this time. At last she and the children could find the happiness they deserved.

KENSHŌ House of Secrets

CHAPTER 45
The proposal

On the day Phoebe and the children left Kenshō House, Mika felt deserted. Everything had happened so fast. How could a ten year marriage break down without warning? She was sad she and Tolly hadn't spent more time together, and she'd only just begun to know Phoebe too. The pang she felt in her heart was similar to the one she'd felt when she'd left her grandfather's house and moved to Tokyo and then London. It was a fear of being alone and abandoned. What should she do? Could she stay on at Kenshō House with everything that had happened? Desperate for support, she rang Jack, 'I not know what to do,' she sobbed softly. Jack had never heard Mika cry before. She was always calm and composed.

'Please don't upset yourself, Mika. I'll be right over. Whatever it is, we'll tackle it together. Make tea, it'll soothe you.' Speeding through Oxford on his motor bike and spinning his wheels on the gravel driveway, Jack arrived. Ignoring the door knocker, he barged straight in and marched through the house to find a desolate Mika in the kitchen. Pulling her towards him he breathed into her neck, 'No need to worry. I'm here now. We'll work things out.'

'Phoebe and children gone,' she reiterated in a disconsolate tone.

'Where?' an astounded Jack asked.

'To live with Phoebe's friend. Weeks ago Tolly tell me of uncle but take no notice. This Geoffrey. Friend from America.'

'A relative?'

'No. Good friend of Phoebe but not sure else. What to do, Jack?'

KENSHŌ House of Secrets

'I think we need to talk to the Prof. I'll wait till he comes home. What about Daisy? Where is she?'

'Not know. Gone out. Not tell anything at breakfast.'

Julian arrived late afternoon. By then, Mika was feeling better, reassured by Jack's presence. When Julian entered the kitchen his eyebrows shot up questioningly, seeing Mika holding a strange young man's hand. Jack wasted no time, 'Sir, I'm Jack. Mika's friend. She's upset about Phoebe and the children leaving so unexpectedly this morning and asked me to come over. Will you have some tea? I've made a fresh pot.'

A worn looking Julian sat down heavily, 'I'm sorry, Mika, this must have come as a terrible blow. As you probably know by now, Phoebe and I have parted. She's taken the children with her. But I don't want this to affect you in any way. You are welcome to stay. I promised the college and your grandfather you would have a home here till June and that's how it will be. Does that reassure you?'

'Arigatō Professor san but grandfather may not like.'

'I don't think your grandfather will mind too much. Daisy will be in and out doing most of the housekeeping. The Colonel and Sanshō are here if you need them. I won't be around much as I'll be preparing for exams, as will you. Perhaps, (looking questioningly at Jack) your young man could keep you company if you feel you're on your own?'

An embarrassed Mika bowed her head, 'Arigatō Professor san, Jack busy. I OK on own.'

Intervening, Jack said, 'Sir, if it's alright I'll pick Mika up every day, take her to college or the library and drop her back in the evening.'

KENSHŌ House of Secrets

Pleased to be off the hook, Julian said hastily, 'Certainly, whatever's convenient. Mika has the run of the house except for the Colonel's floor. Daisy will be on hand to make breakfast and an evening meal. Now, sorry both, I have to get on with some work. Help yourself to whatever food there is. I'll see you later.' Mika nodded uneasily but squeezed Jack's hand hard under the table.

'What is it?' he asked when Julian disappeared.

'Not sure grandfather approve,' she whispered. 'Not how he think English family behave.'

Jack laughed lightly, 'Seriously Mika, all families have problems, even Japanese ones. Why don't we get out of here and head for town and something to eat? You'll feel better then. There's something I want to talk to you about.'

Mika climbed on the back of the bike and they set out for Oxford. Later, as they ate, Jack said, 'I know this isn't the best timing or even the most romantic but I....' He produced something from his breast pocket, dropped to one knee in the middle of the restaurant and asked, 'Will you marry me?' adding, 'not immediately, of course, but after a long engagement?' offering Mika a sparkling diamond and emerald ring. 'Sorry it's not new. It was left to me by my mother. I know she would want you to have it.'

A self-conscious Mika, with tears in her eyes, struggled to pull Jack to his feet whilst the diners clapped and cheered. Speaking so that only he could hear, she said, 'I want marry you, Jack, but first need write grandfather for permission. He important to me. Must agree.'

'Please, please take the ring. Wear it once you hear from your grandfather. I love you. That's all that matters. I'll wait for you as long as it takes.' Not concerned about the audience, he kissed Mika thoroughly despite her protests and they both sat back

KENSHŌ House of Secrets

smiling foolishly at one another. By now the restaurant was in an uproar. Before they could calm down, a waiter was standing at their table with a bottle of champagne. As they drank, everyone stood, raised their glasses and shouted, 'Good luck. Good on you. Congratulations.'

Mika was overcome. Trembling and shaking, she stared and stared at the beautiful ring. So much had happened in the last twelve hours, it was hard to take it all in. What would her grandfather say? She knew she loved Jack, but it was complicated. How could they be together from such different countries and cultures?

Jack, seeing her panic, tried to soothe her, 'Don't worry, Mika, my darling. It will work out for us.' Inwardly, Mika smiled. This was what she loved about Jack. He was an incurable optimist. Her young life in Japan had often been grey and forbidding, whereas Jack sailed through life spreading sunshine, laughter and joy.

A week or two later in Wajima, a shaken and horrified Takeshi read Mika's letter for the second time. This couldn't be. An engagement, with marriage to follow, to an American of all people. The nation who'd murdered his beloved wife and her family and left Mika's father - his son - suffering and dying from the effects of the bomb. There was nothing for it. He must go to England and sort this out. Mika was young and ingenuous. Falling in love for the first time had probably overwhelmed her. It was a mere flight of fancy in a strange country. He would book a flight, talk some sense into his granddaughter and bring her back to the peace and quiet of their home. She would soon get over this boy and settle down happily with one of her own countrymen.

KENSHŌ House of Secrets

CHAPTER 46
Trinity Term
Takeshi reacts

Easter came and went. Mika, dreading hearing from her grandfather, consoled herself that 'no news was good news'. Deciding to ignore her concerns, she concentrated on her studies. With the prelims on the horizon, she and Jack spent most of their days at tutorials, in the library, or sitting in Kenshō House's kitchen drinking gallons of tea and testing one another. The house was abnormally quiet now the dogs, Dot and Dash, had decamped to Geoffrey's cottage. The only sound to be heard was the drone of the Colonel's lift as it moved up and down. There was the odd sighting of Daisy but they'd become infrequent since Julian had withdrawn to the college. She'd long stopped producing any meals, leaving Mika to cater for herself. Privately, Mika was of the opinion that Julian might be doing his best to avoid Daisy but had no idea why.

Phoebe, Geoffrey, the children and the dogs were now all happily tucked up in his tiny cottage and in no particular need of visitors. Mika had ventured there on a couple of occasions but, finding the place a frenzy of noise and activity, had retired to the comparative peace of Kenshō House. Tolly had wholly adopted Geoffrey as his new friend, having little interest in Mika. It was sad, but only to be expected, and Mika was happy for him. He deserved a father figure.

Late one chilly April afternoon, the doorbell at Kenshō House rang, followed by a loud rapping. Mika and Jack, huddling round the kitchen range as usual, were toasting crumpets and discussing their assignments. Mika, alarmed by the knocking, said, 'Must be Julian. He forget keys.' She raced to the door and, opening it, nearly fainted with shock. An ill-tempered, dishevelled Takeshi Kato stood on the threshold, shivering with cold. He scowled at Mika, 'You invite in? Freezing.'

KENSHŌ   House of Secrets

Mika bowed low, 'Of course, Ojii-sama, most honourable grandfather. Welcome to Kenshō House. Please to enter.' Not knowing what to do she took hold of his ancient satchel, helping him off with his shoes and his hantan, his only winter jacket. Trying to catch her breath Mika gasped, 'Not believe you really here, Ojii-sama. Such long way. Plees to come to kitchen. Warm there.' As she showed him down the passage to the kitchen, she remembered Jack. What would her grandfather think? At the kitchen door she paused saying, 'Honourable grandfather. Jack here too. He like meet you.' Or so she hoped.

Jack looked up as they entered, taken aback to see Mika accompanying a small, wizened, old Japanese man. Mika bustled her grandfather close to the range, 'Warm here. I make tea.'

Jack jumped to his feet and bowed, presuming this was Mika's grandfather, 'Welcome, sir. I'm Jack Sylvester. You must be exhausted after your journey. Please take my seat.'

Takeshi, not appeased, announced formidably, 'Young man. I Mika's grandfather.' Continuing grouchily he said, 'Not come far today, London. Yesterday long, long flight from Tokyo.' He took Jack's chair, holding his aged hands towards the heat. Trying to conceal her anxiety, Mika busied herself making tea. Eventually she presented a bowl of green tea to her grandfather, who wrapped both hands round it but said nothing.

Nervously Mika said, 'You receive letter, Ojii-sama?'

'Yes,' was the curt reply.

A desperate stillness descended. Jack tried to catch Mika's eye but she was sitting, head bowed, looking down at her clasped hands in her lap.

'Engaged!' Takeshi finally spat out the word. 'Not ask but tell honourable grandfather. Is this modern way?'

KENSHŌ   House of Secrets

Mika, beside herself with shame, seemed unaware that Takeshi's spoken English was practically fluent. Apologetically she said humbly, 'Engagement not official till you say. See wear ring on necklace.' She bent forward and drew the ring out from under her sweater.

'And you?' Takeshi asked as if he'd only just noticed Jack.

Biting his lip, Jack said, 'Sir, I realise this was a surprise. I love your granddaughter and want her to become my wife,' adding as an afterthought, 'with your blessing of course.'

'You both students,' Takeshi said sternly. 'How you afford wife?'

Disconcerted, Jack said, 'We thought a long engagement till we finish our studies. I have a scholarship here for the year and money from my mother's inheritance. Mika could go back to Boston with me in June and continue her studies at the university there.' Mika looked up in astonishment. They'd both been so carried away, with being together and almost engaged, there'd been no talk of their future or where they'd live. She'd half thought Jack would come back to Japan with her or they would both stay on in England.

Takeshi was appalled, 'Not possible, not possible. No question. Mika return with me this week. She marry nice Japanese boy not gaijin. It no good, no good at all. Upset ancestors. Shame upon family.'

Mika said nothing. Jack, looking to her for support, reached across and touched her hand but she sat still as a statue, head bent. When at last she did look up, her eyes were full of tears, 'Jack, you go. I talk with grandfather. I phone later.' Once she'd spoken, Jack had no choice but to pack up his books and leave. As he passed he leaned down and gently kissed the top of her head. Bowing low to Takeshi, he gave Mika one last anguished glance as he left the

KENSHŌ   House of Secrets

room. Takeshi made the semblance of a bow in return, though continued to sit, his hands gripped tightly round his bowl of tea.

Tentatively, Mika said, 'Pleased you here, Ojii-sama but must speak with Colonel. His house, he must welcome guests.'

Takeshi nodded, 'That correct. I honoured to meet Colonel. You arrange. I lot to talk about with you but meet Colonel first.'

Mika left him in the kitchen and made for the stairs, glad to have something to do. Knocking on the heavy wooden door, she haltingly explained to Sanshō who led her in to see the Colonel who was, as ever, sitting at his desk, Bakti at his feet. Surprised at the intrusion, he raised an eyebrow but, seeing Mika's distraught state, asked her to sit. Too distressed, Mika remained standing shifting from foot to foot, as she poured out the story of her grandfather's surprise visit and the controversy over her engagement. Finishing, she said, 'I not know what to do,' and burst into tears.

Sanshō and the Colonel, completely thrown off balance, began to fuss round her, 'Do please sit down here, Mika my dear. Sanshō make tea or perhaps a little brandy. Seems as if our little Japanese friend has had a bad fright.' Sanshō produced a thimble full of brandy which Mika obediently drank, coughing and spluttering as she did so.

'Don't worry,' the Colonel said reassuringly. 'Sanshō and I will take care of your grandfather. Bring him up. We'll have a talk, one old man to another. Am sure there's a way to sort all this out.' He smiled at Mika, but over her head he frowned at Sanshō as if to say, 'so much for a quiet day of study.' Half an hour later, Takeshi was installed in the Colonel's quarters and they were chatting like old friends. Leaving them together, Mika started thinking how strange it was that her grandfather's English was so good, yet he'd always said he didn't understand or speak much of the language.

KENSHŌ   House of Secrets

Expecting to interpret, Mika had been brusquely dismissed. Back in the kitchen, she tried to console herself while she waited.

Two hours went by, then Takeshi reappeared. He was like a different man, smiling and saying blithely, 'Colonel san invite to stay few days. Better than London hotel. Now have plenty time to talk to you properly, granddaughter.' Mika, hoping this was a good omen, began to feel reassured.

Takeshi continued, 'Colonel and Sanshō prepare meal for us this evening. Must find time to talk with you – very important. Engagement not good. Not at all happy. I think you return to Japan with me.' Hoping the meal might moderate Takeshi's attitude, Mika kept her own counsel. What was the important thing he had to tell her? Of course, her grandfather was an old man now. Hopefully, it wasn't anything to do with his health. The last thing she wanted was to go back to Japan, though she might not have any choice.

Later that evening, after an excellent meal of sushi, chicken katsu and sake, the Colonel and Takeshi withdrew to admire the Colonel's katana collection. The sake must have had the desired effect. By the time the Colonel got to the magnificent Muramasa sword Mika had given him, Takeshi was all for demonstrating his Samurai skills. Jumping high in the air he brandished the sword as his ancestors would have done. The Colonel looked on admiring the old man's agility, 'I wish I was that sprightly, yet we're nearly of an age. Look at me, a bag of bones tied to a wheelchair.'

Sympathetically, Takeshi said, 'It sad, Colonel san. But begin to feel age too now. Tired. We talk more tomorrow, yes?'

The Colonel gestured to Sanshō to show Takeshi to one of the spare bedrooms on their floor, apologising, 'The bed may be too soft for you, Kato san. Feel free to move the mattress to the floor if that suits you better.'

KENSHŌ House of Secrets

Takeshi bowed deeply, then turned and kissed his granddaughter on the forehead, 'Goodnight granddaughter. We talk tomorrow.' Mika was completely disconcerted. The gesture was so out of character for her grandfather. In all their years together there'd been no physical demonstrations of affection ever. Perhaps it was the sake, or the Colonel's influence.

Thanking the Colonel and Sanshō, Mika made her way to her own floor, hoping the morning would provide an amicable compromise to the matter of her engagement. Last thing at night, removing her ring from her necklace, she kissed it, placed it on the third finger of her left hand and turned over to sleep. Her dreams were full of marriage to Jack and life in one of Boston's colonial houses, surrounded by beautiful blonde, almond-eyed children.

KENSHŌ   House of Secrets
CHAPTER 47
The Colonel and Takeshi recollect the war

The next morning Takeshi and the Colonel sat down to one of Sanshō's special breakfasts. Sanshō looked on in amazement at the unusual camaraderie between the two old men. It was as if the suffering the Colonel had experienced at the hands of the Japanese all those years ago had been completely erased. After breakfast, the Colonel brought up the subject of Mika's proposed engagement to the American student. Takeshi frowned, 'Not possible Colonel san. Circumstances against it. Not in favour.' Aware of Mika's distress and not a person to give up easily, the Colonel persevered. Finally, Takeshi politely replied, 'I explain. You understand because of shared experience in war.'

Sanshō was intrigued. Perhaps this was the very moment the Colonel would confide his own harrowing story. Leaving the two men together, Sanshō removed himself to the kitchen, unobtrusive but within earshot.

Takeshi began, '1943, I engineering student Tokyo Imperial University but drafted into war. Marry childhood friend Sakura just before.' Wistfully, he added, 'Most beautiful, fragile delicate blossom.' The Colonel nodded encouragingly. Takeshi continued, '1944, we have son Riki. I speak good English,' he faltered, 'sent to train as interrogator.' Looking directly at the Colonel he said harshly, 'No choice, Colonel san. I one of Emperor's army 'single life mean less than a feather'. We not think like you in West. No room for individual, only collective. That way lies strength. Before I good simple boy after cruel, callous man.'

A single tear ran down the Colonel's face as he listened.

Takeshi carried on, his voice shaking, 'Terrible things. Cannot speak of. Torture, punishments, suffering beyond death. British, American prisoners dishonoured because of surrender. Men's spirits broken. Carry shame now, Colonel san. Guilt with me all

KENSHŌ   House of Secrets

times. Haunted by yūrei of dead young men. Disgrace to ancestors. Must pay,' Takeshi's whole body started to shudder. His hands shook. The Colonel bent towards him, taking the old Japanese's hands in his twisted arthritic ones. They sat for a long time. A concerned Sanshō wondered if he should take them brandy but he was frozen to the spot holding his breath, unable to move.

The silence continued. Finally Takeshi shook himself, straightened his back, removed his hands from the Colonel's grasp, 'Spring 1945, I granted leave. Tokyo bombing bad. Send Sakura and Riki to parents' home.' He stopped again, his face grey, his body convulsed with paroxysms of soundless grief.

An anguished Colonel asked in a voice barely audible, 'Where was that, my friend?'

'Nagasaki,' came the bald reply.

The Colonel compressed his lips, shaking his head in disbelief, not wanting or knowing how to break the moment. Eventually he asked, 'What happened?'

'American bomb kill Sakura and parents. I save Riki. He my life but always sick with radiation, die soon after his marriage. Mariko, his wife, die too after Mika birth. Left to bring up baby on own. See, now not ever possible for Mika and American. No good come of it. I not tell Mika about bomb or parents but must.' Takeshi's voice cracked and broke. He bent his head and wept as he'd never done in the past forty years. The Colonel reached over from his wheelchair and touched the shoulder of the grieving man, 'Take comfort, my friend. Mika is a lovely girl. A credit to you. She'll cope and understand, knowing how much you love her and were trying to protect her.'
'But I betray her...not tell of parents or grandmother. What to do? My Mika marry American...cannot bear...too much pain. Went to Nagasaki in New Year...first time since bomb...but too many

KENSHŌ   House of Secrets

memories. Not forgive Americans. How can granddaughter marry one?'

The Colonel sat back and said quietly, 'You and I, Kato san, are the past. These two young people are the future. We must let the past go.' Regretfully, the Colonel added, 'I too have spent my life living in the past. My part in the war wasn't as heroic as people thought. I never deserved my rank or my medals,' and added in a harsh whisper, 'instead betrayed a friend and have had to live with that since. There's no hope of redemption from my ancestors either. You've been open and honest with me. I want to do the same. To my shame, I've never told my story to another living soul. I once wrote it in my diary but that's been lost in the mists of time.'

Takeshi sat motionless as if carved out of stone but Sanshō pricked up his ears. He couldn't believe the Colonel was at last going to tell a complete stranger everything, a Japanese at that. All these years he'd waited on the old man hand and foot, yet the Colonel had never breathed a word to him. If Sanshō hadn't read the diary he wouldn't have been any the wiser. So much for loyalty. However, he was impatient to hear it all now. The diary had skimmed over much of the detail. It was hard to believe he'd actually been in the camp while it was all happening yet knew nothing of it.

The Colonel cleared his throat nervously, and Sanshō moved his chair closer to get a better view of the two old men. As the Colonel began to talk, it was as if the years fell away and the crippled old man vanished, to be replaced by the fit active Colonel Blenkinsop of 1942. Sanshō could almost feel and smell the dust, the heat and the humidity of Singapore. Memories flooded back as the Colonel continued. The noises of the jungle, the buzzing of cicadas, monkey shrieks, the chirping of frogs, bird calls and the smell of decaying vegetation seemed to engulf the three of them as they were transported back to those dark days.

KENSHŌ   House of Secrets

CHAPTER 48
The Colonel relives Singapore, February 1942

'Sgt. Baines, where's Private Wilkins? He's never here when he's wanted. I don't know why I ever took him on as my driver. He spent too much time in those ashrams. Probably thinks he's in the Indian army rather than the British one. All that meditation and incense burning he does, what good is it doing him? He'll never be anything but a private. Anyway, I need him quickly. I've got to get to headquarters. There's a flap on.' The Colonel was half talking to himself as he acted out the scene. Sanshō felt strange hearing himself referred to as Private Wilkins, as if he were a character in a book he'd once read. But he moved closer as the Colonel continued.

'When Wilkins and I arrived at HQ it was chaos. Orders were being given, then overridden. Many of the middle ranks had been injured or killed. Often there were only sergeants and corporals in command. The strategy from above had been based on the Japanese attacking from the sea. At one time the powers that be had had a reserve plan, called Operation Matador based in Malaya, but that'd long been abandoned. So the Japanese army caught us on the hop, attacking through the backdoor of Malaya and Thailand.

On the eighth of February, the Japanese crossed the straits, landing on Singapore Island. We were forced to retreat. As the month passed the Japanese took hold, thirty thousand of them routed Singapore. The city was shrouded in black smoke from the Pulau Bukum oil tanks and the Naval Base. Leaderless men wandered round making for the docks. Constant bombing made the city inaccessible with hundreds of unburied bodies and wrecked cars blocking the streets. My men and I did our best but were forced back to the suburbs. As we retreated, some Australian troops joined us. They were a ragged looking bunch, weapon-less,

KENSHŌ House of Secrets

and exhausted from fighting up country. Food and water supplies were low; we shared what we had. The resident Malays had no time for us, spitting as we passed, considering us cowards for being defeated. Once the water pipes were cut it was all over. On the fifteenth of February, the order came from General Percival. We were to surrender, lay down our weapons. I was ashamed to pass on such an order. Men cried as they laid down their guns and waited for the enemy.'

At this point the Colonel suddenly became aware of Takeshi, sitting, head bowed, listening intently. The Colonel sighed heavily, 'At three o'clock that afternoon, in the heat of the day, the Japanese slipped out from trees and bushes and surrounded us. A tiny officer stepped forward carrying an enormous two-handed sword and addressed me, 'You Percival? Number one man?'

'No, I'm Colonel Gerald Mortimer Blenkinsop of the 18th Infantry Division.'

The little officer tut-tutted and motioned for us to line up and leave our packs and belongings. We were herded into a nearby stadium, packed in like cattle. It was grim, especially not knowing if we were going to be shot or not. Days went by. There was no sign of movement from the Japanese. Small amounts of rice were given to us. But, with no latrines and men crammed on top of one another, the rains soon turned the place into a stinking sewer.'

The Colonel shuddered at the memory. Takeshi sat stony-faced, saying nothing.

'After about a week, we were marched out of the stadium, relieved not to have been killed but dreading what was to come. It turned out we were on our way to Changi. One of the guards told us we were headed for the area near the old civilian prison twenty miles away. I tried to keep my men's spirits up as best I could. We took turns with the stretchers for the injured, boosting morale by telling jokes against our captors. The Australians were

KENSHŌ   House of Secrets

still with us. I fell in with their Major, a man called Bruce Devereaux from Melbourne. He was the same age, a professional soldier like me, with a wife and son back in Oz. Having something in common we struck up a friendship, as you do in those circumstances. His strength of mind and daredevil skills impressed me. I'd always been a cautious, careful man. Bruce, however, would wind up the guards unmercifully, receiving beating after beating. Through it all he remained cheerfully unscathed as if thrashings were commonplace. Jokingly he would say, 'You should see some of those roughnecks in the outback pubs. A scrap or two gives them a thirst.' Gradually I found out more about him. It was the strangest of coincidences that his family originated from my part of the world in Oxfordshire.' The Colonel smiled at the memory.

'Those early days at Changi were not so bad. We had a certain amount of freedom. There was nowhere to escape to. Living in palm leaf huts left by workers from the nearby rubber estate gave us a degree of comfort. The diet was negligible, boiled rice with curry every meal. You could hardly call it curry. It was mainly hard lumps floating in water with a bit of beef flavouring. Occasionally we acquired a little bread and fruit from the locals, but the fruit, often rotten, gave us the gripe. At the time the men had more energy, so fights would erupt over any scraps of food that were available. We knew we were destined for slave labour but didn't know where. It was months later we found ourselves en route to build the Thailand/Burma railway.

The old man swallowed painfully, 'Being a senior officer and a leader meant keeping oneself apart from one's men, something I'd always done. But I had no one to talk to. By now, Wilkins, my driver, had fallen in with his old mates so I barely saw him. Bruce, being a Major, should have followed my example and remained remote from his men. However, he was an extrovert, a natural leader. His persuasive charm and bonhomie meant he could always get his men to do what he wanted. I think he felt sorry for

KENSHŌ House of Secrets

me and my 'stiff upper lip'. Of an evening, he would sit and join me for a smoke, with cigs we'd blag from the guards.

It was on one of those evenings he told me about his grandmother, Letty, who preferred to be called Letitia. Of all things, she'd been a maid to the Wallanders, relatives on my mother's side. The Wallander family had moved into 'La Grande Maison' at Wolvercote at the turn of the century. Letty was some sort of superior maid to Mrs Wallander, sorting out her social events and acting as her dresser. I could hardly believe it. I stammered, 'But that's where my mother was brought up. My Aunt Violet Wallander still lives there though I know little of that side of the family.'

Bruce said, 'My grandmother used to tell about a terrible tragedy that happened to that family, but I don't remember the details.' Once he mentioned it I started to be intrigued about the house, having no inkling then I was to inherit it later.'

Pulling himself back to the present with his mind still wandering, the Colonel mused, 'I never did find out what the tragedy was. Your Mika seemed to believe there were 'yūrei' on the nursery floor but, despite poking around the house, came up with nothing.' The word 'yūrei' unsettled Takeshi. Could the ancestors be haunting Mika? He must get her away from this place, then realising the Colonel was still unburdening himself he bent forward again to listen.

'We left Changi by train in June of '42, arriving at Ban Pong in Thailand. The journey was horrendous. Thirty of us piled in metal box cars like cattle. The heat was exhausting. At Ban Pong there were barracks to sleep in with each man allowed two foot of space. I can't bring myself to describe the living hell of the work. Within a short time even the fittest amongst us were felled by malaria, beriberi, dysentery and tropical ulcers, as well as the daily beatings. We turned into barely breathing skeletons. I did my best to stand up for my men but usually spent long periods in

KENSHŌ House of Secrets

the cage for my pains. Wilkins, went down with dysentery and was out of it for weeks, blabbing on about Buddhist monks and singing bowls. We did our best, feeding him watery soup and morsels of bread, to keep his strength up.

Bruce, being the entrepreneur he was, started an arrangement with the locals to supply us with fruit and odds and ends of food. There was a place outside the fence where they would dig a hole and leave us a bag of goodies. He or I would collect it, and share out the mangos, bananas or duck eggs to the weakest or the sick. This one particular day, I'd gone to collect the booty but got caught by one of the guards. Dragging me back to the camp by my hair, he called the commander. Everyone was put on parade. I was beaten within an inch of my life and thrown into one of the cages in the blazing sun. I was told if I didn't say who in the camp or the village had helped me, I was to be executed.

I had no idea how long I was out there. Night and day were all one. When the sun went down my men would bring me handfuls of rice or part of a mango. Eventually I was dragged in front of the commander. As I didn't answer, they began pouring water down my throat. Once I was full to bursting they took it in turns stamping on my stomach. That's when I did it. I betrayed Bruce, blurting out his name. The water torture stopped. I was thrown back in the cage in front of the paraded men.

Bruce was dragged out. They struck his body and head repeatedly with wooden clubs. Finally, the commander emerged from his hut, carrying what I now know as a Muramasa sword. Bruce was forced to kneel with his neck outstretched. As he did so, he looked straight across at me, winked wickedly giving a thumbs up and saying, 'Good on ya' cobber'. I couldn't bear to watch but knew I must. The commander raised the sword above his head then brought it down in a powerful arc. The curved blade scythed through the air, glittering in the sun. Time stood still. There was a faint hissing sound. Bruce's head rolled across the ground in front of his crumpled body. The silence was deadly. Everyone held

KENSHŌ House of Secrets

their breath. Then the gasp came, the disbelief, the shock. Several men fainted and had to be dragged back to the barracks by their comrades. No one looked at me. After that the men sent me to Coventry. I survived the cage and was finally let out. But I was now truly alone. Wilkins, when he recovered, kept me going. Of course, he knew nothing, and the other men never talked. One day I tried to cut my throat with a rusty knife and it was Wilkins who found me and bandaged me up.

The Colonel gulped back a sob, 'I never meant to betray Bruce. I'm not sure I knew what I was doing. That's no excuse. I've had to live with his death every day of my life. I just hope my own death is close, but what is there for me on the other side?'

'You solly,' Takeshi said carefully, 'that what matter. Man can only take so much. My people use practice of bushidō during war as excuse for cruelty, some more than most. We both sad old men. I think we ask redemption from ancestors.' The two old men sat closely together, heads bowed, hands clasped. It was as if they carried the sins of both nations on their backs. Not knowing whether to intrude, Sanshō brought in a decanter of whiskey, poured them both drinks but didn't speak. Everything that had to be said had been said.

KENSHŌ   House of Secrets

CHAPTER 49
Takeshi and Mika

Takeshi was in a subdued mood the day after he and the Colonel had talked. They ate their breakfast in silence as Sanshō disappeared into the galley kitchen. Finally, Takeshi said, 'Colonel san, I speak to Mika. After you and I talk, urgent I now tell her about family. Left too long. She must know. I leave, see her. Then we return to Japan.'

'Thank you for listening, Kato san. I'm grateful. You've helped ease my burden. Do what you think is best. Am sure Mika will understand and forgive you. Neither of us has long, perhaps she will go back home with you. I wish you farewell and Godspeed, my friend. We shall never meet again in this life.'

Takeshi bowed deeply, 'I wish well, Colonel san too. We experience more than most men. Not easy forgive or forget, but we must try do both.' Before leaving he thanked Sanshō, lurking in the kitchen, 'Take good care Colonel san. He not well today. Much agony and torment yesterday. Need watch,' he said warningly.

Sanshō nodded and, bowing deeply, pointed him in the direction of Mika's floor, 'Great honour, Kato san,' he murmured.

Mika was on her way downstairs when she bumped into her grandfather. She beamed with pleasure and bowed, 'Ohayou gozaimasu, Ojii-sama. How was talk with Colonel san?'

'Draining,' was the only reply she got. 'Mika, I need talk to you. Can we sit?'

'Please to come to kitchen, Ojii-sama. Most comfortable and warm. Professor Julian left for day.' They sat across the table from one another. Takeshi took a deep breath and embarked on his tale. Mika, concerned about the pain she saw etched on his face, tried

KENSHŌ   House of Secrets

to interrupt but he stopped her with a raised hand, 'Must tell all, granddaughter. Important you understand.'

When he was finished, Mika was speechless. All these years and she'd known nothing about her parents, or her grandmother, and now this. What was she to think? No doubt it had all come to the surface due to her engagement. Would her grandfather have told her otherwise? From her grandfather's point of view she could see why the engagement was impossible, but she loved Jack. Nevertheless, she couldn't abandon her grandfather either. He was an old man and needed her. At this moment he looked exhausted and every year of his age. She'd no choice. There was no possibility now of marrying an American or moving to America. It was odd she'd never thought of Jack like that – an American – he was just 'Jack' to her.

Japan it would have to be. She couldn't stop thinking how her mother and father must have suffered after the bomb, all that pain, all those operations. It was a miracle she'd been born. Yet she was fit and healthy and owed her life to her grandfather. From his point of view there was dishonour in a first generation child of 'hibakusha' (survivors of the bomb) marrying the enemy.

Takeshi took Mika's hand and kissed it tenderly. She could feel the warmth of a tear as it dropped on her skin, 'I solly, Mika, saiai no magomusume. We must return to Japan.'

Mika nodded. Her grandfather had never shown such a sign of love for her before. His had always been the 'bushidō' way – following the Samurai virtues. Yet Mika could sense a gentleness in her grandfather she'd never seen before. She couldn't abandon him after all he'd gone through. Stoically, she said, 'I pack, Ojii-sama. We leave. Must see Professor san, as polite. Must say goodbye.'

'Of course,' Takeshi said. 'I wait here. Tired. Must rest before journey.'

KENSHŌ   House of Secrets

Mika was alarmed as the old man laid his head on the table and closed his eyes. The journey and his talks with the Colonel had worn him to the bone. Later, as Mika returned downstairs dragging her overladen bags, the front door opened and Julian appeared, 'My dear, where are you going? Are you leaving? I hope it's not because of our family drama.'

'No, Professor san. My grandfather arrive yesterday from Japan. He talk long with Colonel and stay night, but now want me return Japan with him. I must. He very old man. Maybe sick.'

'Naturally, my dear, I understand. Should I meet him, do you suppose, or would that be too much for him?'

'He honour meet you, Professor san. He in kitchen resting.'

Julian entered the kitchen and saw an ancient Japanese fast asleep on the table. 'I won't wake him,' he whispered. 'What can I do to help, Mika? I would run you both to London but, as you know, my car can only take two people. Shall I arrange a taxi to the station?'

'That velly kind, Professor san. I collect grandfather's bag and then wake him. But need ticket London/Tokyo.'

'Don't worry, my dear. I'll arrange everything. Give me the details. I'll have the ticket waiting for you at the airport. Perhaps you should stay in London tonight as the journey may be too much for your grandfather?'

'Grandfather have hotel. We stay overnight there I think.'

Julian hesitated, 'What about your boyfriend? Jack, isn't it? Do you want me to tell him what's happened?'

'Plees, I cannot face Professor san. Big pain, sadness for me.' A huge wave of emotion shook Mika's tiny frame. 'Plees to give him

KENSHŌ House of Secrets

this.' She took the engagement ring from the chain round her neck and handed it to Julian.

Julian was shocked, 'I didn't realise you were that serious, and engaged. Why break it off? You looked so happy together when I saw you last.'

'Not possible to explain,' Mika said, struggling with her feelings. 'I not marry American – wrong. Grandfather right. Big mistake. I solly but no good.'

Julian shook his head, 'Certainly, I will pass the message on, but it would be better coming from you. Your young man's going to be distraught. Surely you should see him to explain and, at the very least, say goodbye.'

'No,' Mika said adamantly. 'Plees Professor, I know big trouble for you but not see Jack. Break heart. Must return home with grandfather. I wake him now.'

Within the hour Mika and Takeshi were on a train hurtling to London. Doing her best not to cry, Mika buried herself in a book. Her grandfather, still all-in, leant against the seat rest and slept. Mika was full of recriminations and guilt, finding it hard to come to terms with what she'd done to her beloved Jack? Self-reproach and shame drummed away in her head, pulsating in time with the train, as they sped further and further away from Oxford.

KENSHŌ   House of Secrets
CHAPTER 50
Julian deals with bad news

Once Takeshi and Mika had left for Japan, Julian racked his brains wondering how to find Jack. Imparting bad news was not something he normally did, leaving it to others to cope with any messes. However, he needn't have worried. That evening, as he was attempting to throw together a basic meal of bread and cheese, the phone rang. An agitated Jack asked for Mika. Caught off balance, Julian took a large gulp of whiskey and soda and said apologetically, 'Sorry, old chap. Mika's returned to Japan with her grandfather. She asked me to tell you. I was going to contact you tomorrow at college.'

Jack was horrified, barely able to speak, 'But she…I…We're engaged or as good as. We're…going to marry. Why didn't she speak to me? Did she leave a letter?'

'No letter,' Julian said. 'I'm so sorry. It all happened in a rush. Mika was very upset. I don't know what went on between her and her grandfather, but the old man spent some time with my father, the Colonel. Afterwards, her grandfather told Mika something which affected her deeply. She kept saying she could never marry an American but must return to Japan, that her grandfather was unwell and needed her. I wish I could tell you more. She left her engagement ring with me. What should I do with it?' There was no response from the other end of the line, just the sound of a receiver being dropped. Hearing the engaged tone, Julian hung up.

The poor boy, Julian thought, feeling unusually compassionate. But his sympathy didn't last long. No sooner had he sat down to demolish his cheese sandwich and drink more whiskey than he began to feel sorrier for himself instead, saying out loud, 'Poor me, I've been left high and dry too.' The day before, he'd received divorce papers from Phoebe. She'd not wasted any time he thought resentfully. Ten years of marriage and three children -

KENSHŌ House of Secrets

well two that were actually his - down the drain. He knew he should go up and break the news to his father, but their encounters only made him feel inadequate, so, perhaps it was best to postpone till he was feeling stronger. Settling down in his study, Julian dimmed the lights and put on his favourite Beethoven. Keeping the decanter close at hand, he decided to get blind drunk and blot out the last month.

A faint knocking at the front door shook him out of his stupor. There was the sound of a key in the lock. His spirits rose. Perhaps Phoebe had had a change of mind. However, the study door was flung open, to reveal a recalcitrant Daisy, hands on hips and with an even shorter skirt than usual. He registered something different about her, but in his drunken haze couldn't think what. 'Where've you been Julian? I've tried to contact you for weeks. Every time I came round, there was only Mika and that boyfriend of hers. I left messages all over, even with snooty Janice. Didn't you get them? What's going on?'

Wincing at her forcefulness, Julian grovelled, 'Sorry, my dear. It's exams. I've a lot on my plate since Phoebe and the children left.'

'That's no excuse. They made little difference to your life when they were here. Am sure they barely count now they've decamped to Phoebe's boyfriend's.'

'What's so urgent?' Julian asked mildly. 'I took it for granted you were still coming every day to provide meals for Mika and keep on top of the housework.'

'That finished weeks ago,' Daisy said shortly, 'as you very well know. Mika was quite capable of sorting herself out. I didn't see much point in coming round when you weren't here. Have you been purposely avoiding me?'

KENSHŌ   House of Secrets

'Of course not,' Julian said emphatically, trying to sound believable. 'You know how much I think of you. The family would have been lost without you.'

'That's alright then,' Daisy said, somewhat appeased, 'as I've wonderful news for you.'

'What would that be?' Julian asked vaguely. Perhaps at long last Daisy had met someone and was going to get married.

'You'll be pleased,' Daisy announced confidently. 'We're pregnant.'

At first, Julian had no idea what she meant, 'What '**we**' do you mean?'

'Why you and me, silly Billy. Who else did you think?'

Julian began to splutter and choke. Daisy strode over and banged him hard between the shoulder blades. Whilst he struggled for breath, she continued, 'It's the shock. I knew you'd be thrilled. Another little Blenkinsop on the way. We're going to be such a happy little family.'

All Julian could do was stutter, 'But…there was only that one occasion…I don't remember much about it…When Phoebe…'

'It only takes one,' Daisy said with a smirk. 'Just shows what a stud you are. First there was Phoebe, then Rhianna and now me. Pretty good going for fifty plus. What a guy!'

Weakly, Julian protested, 'Phoebe's my wife, well at least she was then, and Rhianna was never pregnant. That was only a fantasy in her head.' Trying to collect his thoughts, he asked, 'How many months?'

KENSHŌ House of Secrets

'Nearly two,' Daisy said proudly. 'I felt sure the night we did 'it'. Now I'm going to be a mother. You're going to be a father again. How lucky are we? This is what I've always wanted. By the way, I've brought my stuff. It's in the hall. Now Phoebe's out of the picture, there's nothing to stop us shacking up together.'

Julian was horrified. To think earlier that evening he'd been sitting feeling sorry for himself. Now he longed to be alone and away from this fiasco. Rallying, he said, 'That won't do, Daisy. I've a position to keep up. You certainly can't move in or 'shack up' with me as you so delicately put it. It's not possible. The college and the Dean wouldn't approve. I'm prepared to support the child if you decide to have it, or even pay for an abortion, but that's it.'

A mutinous Daisy sat down on one of the leather chairs opposite, her jaw set, 'There'll be no abortion, do you hear? I want your baby. I intend us to marry as soon as your divorce comes through. Don't forget all those sordid little details I know about your past. You wouldn't want them to become public, now would you? Let's say for appearance's sake that I'm your 'live-in' housekeeper. That will shut the gossips up. After all, you share the house with your father and that peculiar monk fellow. The Dean and the college won't know that I'm not here to look after them as they're so old, as well as you.'

In a more persuasive and seductive tone, she added, 'Let's take a trip upstairs. I'll pick a bedroom just for the look of it. Then I'll get down to cooking you one of my special meals.' Looking disdainfully at his plate, she remarked, 'Bread and cheese isn't at all suitable for a grown man, let alone one who is shortly to become a father.'

Appraising him carefully, Daisy continued, 'You've become much too thin for my liking. You need feeding up. Don't worry my darling, I'll soon have you just as I like you, my big boy with a bit of flesh on your bones.'

KENSHŌ   House of Secrets

It was no use. Julian groaned. He was a beaten man, back in captivity, a turkey being fattened up for Christmas. Surrendering, he allowed Daisy to take charge and found himself manoeuvred up the stairs to the master bedroom.

'Come on, my dear old darling,' Daisy cajoled. 'I've missed you so much. Let me make it up to you. I'll cook us something tasty later. We'll soon have you back to your delightful curvy self, won't we, my own dear Professor?'

KENSHŌ   House of Secrets

CHAPTER 51
The Colonel departs

After Takeshi's exit, the Colonel went downhill fast. Sanshō was worried, wondering if he should tell Mr Julian. Finally, when he did pluck up the courage to venture downstairs, there was such a kerfuffle in the kitchen, he retreated. It was obvious Daisy had returned. Now was definitely not a good time to talk to Mr Julian. He decided to wait a few days to see if the old man improved. All the talking and confessing of the last few days had probably taken its toll on the Colonel. He just needed rest and quiet to help him recover.

During one of the Colonel's better days the old man said, 'Sanshō my friend, I need to tell you about my past.'

'No need, Colonel, I know everything I need to know. The past is the past. As it's such a lovely Spring afternoon, why I don't wheel you down to the Japanese garden. We can sit awhile.'

'That would be pleasant, Sanshō, but I think not. I feel I must stay close to the house today. It's as if the ancestors are calling me. It won't be long now, my friend. Thank you for your devoted service to me. I will never be able to repay you as I would wish.'

'I've been happy to do it, Colonel. But I think you're mistaken, you've plenty of time yet. You're just feeling low today. It'll pass. I'll leave you with Bakti and go shopping. I think the poor old boy's feeling his age too.' He bent over and stroked the dog's ears fondly but there was little response.

Returning hours later, Sanshō was relieved to find the Colonel still in the same position in his wheelchair. Both he and Bakti were snoring loudly. By now it was late. Sanshō wondered if he should move the Colonel to the day bed but it seemed a shame to wake him, and instead covered him with a tartan rug. Not wanting to disturb the sleeping pair and feeling his own age, Sanshō tiptoed

KENSHŌ   House of Secrets

out and made for the coach house. He could come back later and see to the Colonel. Badly in need of a rest, Sanshō lay down and stretched out, missing the comfort of Bakti. He must have slept hours longer than he realised because it was the dawn light shining through the shutters that woke him. In a blind panic and worried sick about the Colonel, Sanshō stumbled his way back to the house. The house was quiet, not a movement from anywhere.

On the Colonel's floor there was an eerie stillness. It was as if the house was waiting. Calling to the Colonel as he opened the big oak door, Sanshō received no response or welcome bark from Bakti. Fearful, Sanshō rushed in. It was evident the Colonel had died in his sleep and probably sometime ago. His head was slumped on his chest and his lips were a blueish purple. Astonishingly, he must have had the strength to get the Muramasa sword out of its case because he was holding it, the point of the blade directed at his stomach. His hands, outstretched to the hilt, were already stiff in rigor mortis. It made Sanshō think of 'seppuku' – the honour killing the Japanese carried out on themselves although the Colonel had obviously died before he could complete the ritual. Bakti lay at the Colonel's feet, also dead. It was if they'd arranged their own ceremonial deaths.

Overcome with shock, Sanshō sat down and cried and cried. He didn't even know whether he was grieving for the old man, Bakti or himself. There'd been many a time when he wished he and the Colonel had never met, but now he was consumed with sorrow thinking of all the years they'd spent together. It had been longer than many marriages. What was he to do now? How was he to go on without the Colonel? What sort of future could he look forward to at his age? If he returned to India, would his old ashram welcome him? That's where he wanted to die but how could he afford the fare? Over the years the Colonel had paid him a pittance but never enough to allow for savings. Of course, he'd had the run of the house, the garden and food provided, but little actual money. Now, Mr Julian would probably sell up and throw Sanshō out on the street with nothing.

KENSHŌ House of Secrets

Composing himself, Sanshō knew he must tell Mr Julian. The Colonel mustn't be seen like this in his wheelchair. Struggling, he pushed and pulled the Colonel's body on to the nearby daybed, but try as he might he couldn't loosen the Colonel's hands from the sword. Gently he picked up Bakti and lay him at the old man's feet. It was like looking at the tableau of a Crusader. The old man only needed a suit of armour and it would be perfect. What a time to find humour. Chuckling at the thought, Sanshō pulled the Colonel's old dress uniform from the wardrobe. He managed to wrap the jacket with all its medals round the Colonel's upper body under the sword and lay the trousers over his legs. It was a magnificent sight. If only he had a camera. He was satisfied. The old man now had the dignity in death that he'd had in life. The upright sword gave him the look of a victorious conqueror.

Loath to leave his two old friends, Sanshō knew he must face Mr Julian. The old lift clanked down to the ground floor just as Julian was about to leave for work. Sanshō realised hours must have gone by since he'd discovered the Colonel's body, yet it seemed like seconds.

'Your father,' Sanshō mouthed painfully.

'What about him? Has he heard about Daisy being here? I suppose he wants to give me another of his lectures?'

'No, he's dead,' Sanshō said flatly.

'Good grief, I thought he'd go on for ever. What happened?'

'Just old age,' Sanshō said miserably. 'He died in his sleep. Do you want to come up and see him? I don't know what arrangements you want me to make.'

'I'll do all that,' Julian said hurriedly. 'Don't you bother. I suppose I ought to see the old boy one last time. At least he can't tell me off anymore.'

KENSHŌ   House of Secrets

However, for once Julian was lost for words when he viewed the scene in the Colonel's apartment. Mouth agape, he stood and stared. Finally, he said, 'What's the sword all about? Did you put it there?'

'No,' Sanshō said apologetically. 'It was in his hands when I came this morning. I couldn't pull it away. I think he must have died not long after I went home, so it must have been hours…I overslept you see…'his words dwindled away.

Julian swallowed hard, 'I don't know what the undertaker will make of it. Perhaps it will have to go in the coffin with him and Bakti. Leave it with me.'

For once he looked across at the pale, shaking Sanshō with compassion, 'It must have been a terrible shock for you. You look all in. Why don't you go home? I'll come across later and talk through the arrangements.'

Sanshō was only too willing to agree. A terrible wave of exhaustion had suddenly engulfed him. Barely able to make it home, he lit an incense burner for his old friend and for Bakti. Sitar music drifted through the house as he sat in the Japanese garden, for probably the last time, looking out at the view the Colonel had loved so much.

KENSHŌ House of Secrets

CHAPTER 52
A Funeral and endings

On the day of the Colonel's funeral, Julian was astounded to see what an eclectic bunch of people had turned up especially as the old man was a virtual recluse. There were academics, professors from all the colleges, local dignitaries, including the Lord Mayor of Oxford and a phalanx of Buddhist monks.

Following the Colonel's instructions, Julian had had the old Wallander mausoleum in the local cemetery opened up. It hadn't been in use since his Great Aunt Violet had died in the forties. Apparently the Colonel knew a space had been left for him, being Baby's son. Julian thought this odd considering his own mother, the Colonel's wife who'd been killed in the London bombing, had been buried elsewhere. At the time he'd been a young child, so his mother's family had taken charge, sending him to public school as soon as he was old enough. No wonder he and his father had always been estranged. The Colonel was not the fatherly type. Once he'd taken up residence in Kenshō House after the war, he paid only sporadic visits to Julian's school. During the holidays, Julian was expected to stay with friends. It was Sanshō who fulfilled the role of the Colonel's confidant and lifelong companion. No wonder Julian was jealous. Anyway, at long last the Colonel was out of his life for good, he was glad of it, and would make damn sure that Sanshō was soon ejected as well.

The service was to take place in the drawing room at Kenshō House. The Colonel's open coffin, surrounded by white and yellow chrysanthemums, was on display in the adjoining dining room. The Colonel, resplendent in his uniform, lay there looking proud and distinguished. After a lot of manoeuvring, the undertaker had managed to release the sword from the Colonel's iron grip and place it beside him. Bakti lay at the Colonel's feet.

KENSHŌ House of Secrets

On first glance, Phoebe, who'd arrived with the children and Geoffrey, whispered in his ear, 'How macabre. Don't let the children wander in there, they'll have nightmares for weeks.'

True to form, a curious Tolly managed to wend his way in and, looking down at the Colonel, said in his inimitable way, 'Gee, Grandfather, you looks like one of King Arthur's knights.' By now, Tolly's quaint speech patterns were even more bizarre, interspersed as they were with Americanisms. Julian, who was standing close by, cringed. Goodness knows what that child's speech would be like once he got to America. He consoled himself with the fact that Tolly wasn't his son after all. Perhaps he'd have more say in the upbringing of his and Daisy's child, though he doubted it. She would probably be the one calling the shots.

Taking another look at the coffin, as a bevy of white clad monks clustered round it, bowing, chanting 'om' and tinkling Tibetan bells, Julian glowered. What a showman his father was! Even to the last. It was plain embarrassing. All the Oxford luminaries sat resolutely in their seats in the drawing room. Dressed in conventional black, they didn't stir to either view the coffin or the antics of the monks in the next room. These were his sort of people, Julian thought. English, proper, reserved and poker backed. He'd been loath to set up this type of spectacle for his father's departure, but it was the honourable thing to do as his son. The Colonel's last wishes on this earth, he supposed, must be respected.

Sanshō had been delegated to act as celebrant. Dressed in an ostentatious white robe, he came over to Julian, 'I think we should start now, Mr Julian.' The monks moved round to stand at the back of the room whilst Sanshō intoned the ritual introduction, reciting the names of the ten Buddhas. The majority of the congregation looked bemused, particularly when they were invited to sing 'The Litany of the Great Compassionate One.' There was uneasy tittering whilst Sanshō led the monks in singing the Scripture. Glances were exchanged between members of the

KENSHŌ   House of Secrets

congregation whilst the Lord Mayor fiddled with his chain. Only Tolly was transfixed by it all, looking on with a sense of wonder that belied his years. It was an excessively long service with Sanshō's reciting and the monks' chanting.

Finally, Sanshō said quietly but authoritatively, 'Colonel Gerald Mortimer Blenkinsop V.C. has finished his appointed time on this earth. Let him go on his way to join his ancestors in Nirvana.' This was followed by the pure tones of the singing bowls and the tolling of a single bell. Once the ceremony ended, the whole place emitted a collective sigh of relief, relishing the thought of the refreshments to follow. The enterrement at the mausoleum was to be done privately later that day. In the meantime Julian had arranged with Daisy to provide drinks and vegetarian snacks on the terrace, as it was such a fine day, and there was a stampede when he opened the French doors.

It was Julian's first encounter with Phoebe since receiving the divorce papers. She came up to him and said sympathetically, 'I'm sorry about the Colonel. I know you two didn't have an easy relationship, but you've done him proud today.'

'Thank you, my dear. I'm pleased you brought the children. Just a pity Geoffrey's here but I suppose we have to be civil for their sake.'

'Let's at least try,' Phoebe said assertively. 'I need to tell you that at the end of the month we're returning to America with Geoffrey. He's got a tenured position at Harvard. You are welcome to visit of course, and when the children are older they can spend summers with you here.'

Taking a large slurp of whiskey, Julian scowled, 'I'm not sure about that. I'll be selling the house as soon as.' Biting his lip he added, 'Daisy is pregnant. She and I will be setting up home together, probably somewhere close to the college.'

KENSHŌ   House of Secrets

Phoebe burst out laughing, and, in a tone tinged with irony and sarcasm, said, 'Goodness, Julian, you really are going to be living out a middle aged man's wet dream with your young floozie. Though am not too sure about the pregnancy bit. Hope you're prepared for wet nappies and sleepless nights. You certainly weren't when we had those three - nodding towards Tolly, Sadilla and Kepha. If I remember rightly, that was all down to me in those days. How will you manage at your age?'

Sulkily, Julian said, 'I expect I'll cope whilst you live it up in the groves of academe with the intelligentsia. All those cocktail parties…how will **you** manage?'

'Oh, with pleasure,' Phoebe said airily. 'I've rediscovered my lost youth. Geoffrey has sorted out good schools for the children. No doubt, we'll have an au pair or a housekeeper and I'm going back to my Egyptology studies full-time to finally get my degree. So I'll be a student again.'

Trying to conceal his envy and exasperation, Julian said, 'Before you go, there's father's will. He specifically asked for you and the children to be present.' By now, most of the guests including the monks had left.

Sanshō, Phoebe, the children and Julian congregated in his study. The Colonel's attorney arrived and after formalities explained: *'The Colonel's manuscripts are to go to the Bodleian Library. The militaria collection is to be on loan to Julian's Nissan Institute. Kenshō House is to be sold. From the proceeds, Sanshō will receive a life pension and twenty percent of the sale'*. Julian gave a screech of disbelief, but worse was to come. *'Tolly as the eldest grandchild is to receive ten per cent of the sale, Sadilla and Kepha five percent each, to be held in trust by their mother until they come of age at twenty one. The remainder of the monies and the contents of the house is left to Julian.'*

Shocked to the core, Julian was dumbfounded. At this rate, he and Daisy would be lucky to rent a small apartment in central Oxford

KENSHŌ   House of Secrets

let alone buy the townhouse she'd set her heart on. Phoebe, surprised at the Colonel's final wishes, attempted to console Julian but seeing he was stupefied and too dazed for sympathy she said, 'I think we should go now, children. Say goodbye to Daddy. You'll see him before we leave for America.' Julian sat motionless, frozen, making no attempt to hug them.

Once he and Sanshō were alone, Sanshō brought over the decanter of whiskey, 'Have a drink, Mr Julian. You'll feel better soon. I can't believe the Colonel looked after me like that. I thought I'd be kicked out without a penny to my name.'

Julian, desperate to explode with rage and venom, wanted to say that's exactly what should have happened. That evil old man! Julian had always anticipated his father would manage to stick the knife in somehow. He had to have the last word. Now what on earth would life with Daisy be like? There'd be no chance of escape. In a carefully controlled tone and attempting to be civil, Julian turned to Sanshō and asked, 'What will you do now the house is to be sold?'

'I'll go back to my old ashram in India,' Sanshō said equably. 'My guru and teacher is ancient but still alive and will welcome me back. With your permission, I would like to be present at the enterrement.'

'Very well,' Julian said in a subdued and defeated voice. 'The undertaker should have done his stuff by now and prepared the Colonel's tomb. You can drive over to the cemetery with me.'

No one could possibly miss the Wallander mausoleum at the cemetery. The massive Victorian stone edifice, adorned with life size angels, was the centrepiece of the graveyard. The undertaker took out a rusty set of keys and unlocked the colossal oak doors. The unoiled hinges squeaked and ground as they were forced open again. Clouds of dust and the stench of years of detritus swamped them. Coughing and sneezing, the company stood,

KENSHŌ House of Secrets

heads bent, as the Colonel and Bakti's coffin was carried in. The undertaker asked, 'Would you like to say a few parting words, sir?'

Julian shook his head, anxious to get out of this melancholic place, 'No, I think my father has had plenty to go on with from today's service.'

'What about the sword? Shall I retrieve it, sir?'

In unison, Sanshō and Julian said, 'No'.

'Let the old boy have it,' Julian said bitterly. 'It probably meant more to him than I ever did.' Looking round, Julian said, 'It'll suit the old man, this dingy, dreary place, just like his old parchments. Mind you, there seems to be an excess of cherubim to keep him company. I wonder what that's all about. Why so many? The Wallander family's dead children, I suppose. Babies and the young rarely lived into adult hood in those days.' Julian gave one last contemptuous look behind him and curled his lip, as the great oak doors were closed and locked for the last time.

As the party sped off, Julian and Sanshō in Julian's red Ferrari and the undertakers in their hearse, eight ghost children emerged from the shadows of the mausoleum. They knelt beside the Colonel's tomb claiming him as their own. Tom Wallander said to his older sister, Violet, 'He's arrived. Baby's son. One of us. He's come home to his family at last. We'll take good care of him from now on won't we, kids?'

KENSHŌ   House of Secrets

CHAPTER 53
Jack's family history

Jack was still reeling from Mika's swift departure. He couldn't believe she'd leave like that without a word. Once he'd got over the initial shock he'd tried ringing her, but her number was no longer in service. Then he'd tried writing to her grandfather's address. Again, no reply.

The exams were now upon him. Jack was forced to put his anguish to one side and concentrate on work. The next weeks of June were busy with study and revision but always in the background were the sharp pains and pangs of loss and desolation. On the last day of his exams, not knowing what to do, Jack decided to return to Boston being he and his father were on better terms. In fact, Mr Sylvester had written his son many generous letters, begging him to come back so they could talk honestly.

Saying goodbye to Oxford was depressing, especially when Jack realised he'd made few friends there in the last nine months. His life had been bound up with Mika. Now what did he have to show for it? However, it meant there was nothing to leave behind. He must carve out a new future for himself without her, though that was easier said than done. So many of his plans had centred on Mika: their marriage, her entry into the Undergrad-Programme at Boston, his transfer to a journalism degree. Now Mika was thousands of miles away. He was heartbroken and couldn't bear the thought that he'd never see that sweet face again.

Back home in Boston, Jack's father set out to be as affable and co-operative as possible. There was no talk of Jack joining the firm or even outings to the stuffy country club. One evening Mr Sylvester said, 'Jack, you're my only son. I would have liked you in the firm. However, since Christmas I've done some tough soul searching, and realise I don't want to lose you because of my stubborn pride.

KENSHŌ   House of Secrets

We only have each other. If you intend being a writer so be it. I'm prepared to finance you till you see if you can make it.'

Jack was pleasantly surprised, 'That's very fair of you, Father, but I won't need your money. I'm transferring my scholarship to a journalism degree. Eventually I'll be able to earn my living as a journalist and hone my writing skills at the same time. I'm grateful for the offer though.'

Relieved they'd managed to overcome one hurdle, Mr Sylvester bit his lip, wondering how to bring up the next touchy subject. Cautiously he asked, 'What's happened about your Japanese girlfriend?'

'It's over,' Jack said brusquely. 'She went back to Japan with her grandfather. I've not heard from her since.'

'I'm sorry, son. I know she meant a lot to you. Perhaps it's for the best.'

'How can you say that and why 'for the best'?'

Mr Sylvester gritted his teeth, 'It's complicated, to do with past history rather than the present. I never wanted to talk about this, but maybe now you're old enough to understand...I suppose I can't put it off any longer.'

Upset and irritated, Jack said, 'Whatever it is, tell me. I've had enough of mysteries and being kept in the dark. Just spit it out.'

Swallowing nervously, Mr Sylvester said, 'It's about your grandfather. Your mother's father.'

'What about him? I tried to find out about him in London. What's the big secret? Was he a murderer or something?'

KENSHŌ House of Secrets

The colour drained from his father's face, 'Not exactly, not in the way you mean.'

'Well what?' Jack demanded, getting more and more exasperated. 'If there are skeletons in the family closet, I might as well know about them.'

'Your grandfather was a brilliant physicist, a Professor at a German university, and a Jew. His wife, your grandmother, however, was Aryan and they had a child, your mother. Once the Nazis came to power, all Jews and anyone with Jewish heritage were under threat. Your grandfather was in constant fear of losing his job and his home, maybe even his life. Kristallnacht in '38 brought things to a head. Nazi mobs torched synagogues, Jewish homes, and businesses. Your grandfather knew he had to get his family out.'

'What was grandfather's name?'

'Jakob Stein. He later anglicised it to Jack Stone.'

'No wonder, I couldn't find any records of him in London.'

'There was another reason for that,' Mr Sylvester continued. 'Jakob and his family were smuggled into England with nothing except the clothes they stood up in. They went through tough times. Jakob even worked as a cleaner in a factory, however, he did have contacts from his university days. After a few years, through them, was able to find a job in scientific research at Aldermaston.' Mr Sylvester hesitated, 'I'm not sure it's a good idea raking up the past, Jack, now you and your girl have broken up.'

'But you can't stop now,' Jack was adamant. 'I need to know what it is you're keeping from me. What it has to do with mine and Mika's relationship?'

KENSHŌ   House of Secrets

Mr Sylvester grimaced, 'Very well, here's the rest. It was whilst Jakob was doing scientific research for the government that he was transferred to Tube Alloys.'

Jack looked mystified, 'What on earth was that? It sounds pretty innocuous.'

'That was the point, it was meant to be. It was the codename for the manufacture of the British atomic bomb.'

'What has that to do with Mika? I don't understand.'

'You will,' Mr Sylvester said bleakly. 'Be patient. After Pearl Harbour, we became allies of the British. As both countries were working on atomic bombs, it was decided to collaborate. Twenty British scientists relocated to Los Alamos in '43 to work on a joint venture. Jakob was one of those scientists.'

Jack began to get a bad feeling, not sure he wanted to hear the rest. But Pandora's box was open now. He gestured for his father to go on.

Mr Sylvester exhaled, 'Your grandfather worked directly under J. R. Oppenheimer. You might know the name. Your grandfather's team worked on the second atomic bomb called 'Fat Man' – the one that destroyed Nagasaki, killing thousands of Japanese. Now do you see how difficult it would be for you to marry your Japanese girl?'

'I still don't get it. What happened after the war? Why did Mom keep this quiet? Was she ashamed of her father?'

'You've got to understand Jack, the climate in America after the war was very different. Of course, the two bombs brought about the Japanese surrender, but there was a lot of controversy about the necessity for them and the devastation and loss of lives they'd caused. In fact, a considerable amount of guilt began to surface.

KENSHŌ House of Secrets

Even Oppenheimer himself had regrets later. He always quoted the Hindu Bhagawad Gira, 'Now I am become Death, the destroyer of worlds.'

'But what about Mom? Why did she hide this from me?'

Crossly, Mr Sylvester said, 'You're not listening, Jack. Opinions were divided in 50s and 60s America. Jakob Stein, now Jack Stone, applied to stay on in America with his family. Your mother was brought up all American, having little time for her German/Jewish roots or her father's role in the war.

At university she became a pacifist. After long violent arguments with your grandfather, she became alienated from him once her mother died. By '61 she was a full time activist, taking part in the 'Women Strike for Peace' march. That was when I met her. I was also in the peace movement. In the late seventies we married, settled down and had different priorities. Career and family became more important. Unfortunately, having rap sheets and reputations as political agitators forced us to change our names and start afresh. Otherwise, I wouldn't be the respectable lawyer and pillar of society you see before you today.'

Jack was bemused, 'But why give it all up if you felt that strongly?'

His father laughed, 'Pragmatism, I suppose. Your mother and I were young and swept along by ideals and passions. There came a time when we had to grow up and find peace and normality.'

Looking sad and rather wistful, Mr Sylvester said, 'Everything comes to an end, even youthful fervour. Now Jack, I'm afraid there's more. I have to tell you something far more personal.'

'What else can there be? Haven't there been enough revelations for today?'

KENSHŌ   House of Secrets

'Unfortunately, no. When your mother and I established ourselves in Boston, we were in our forties and found we couldn't have children. Something we both wanted badly.' Mr Sylvester swallowed, 'Of course you're our, or my, son now and always will be. But in truth we adopted you. We'd given up hope of children. An old activist friend of your mother's came along. Finding herself pregnant, and being seriously ill, she begged your mother to take you when you were born. Sadly, Suzie died giving birth to you, so, shortly after, we adopted you officially.'

This was such a bolt from the blue, Jack didn't know whether to be upset or relieved. Maybe this was why he'd always felt so unconnected to his parents. At last there was a good reason for it. They'd given him everything materially but they were like stereotypes rather than live, breathing, caring people. There was little affection or even love. Now he understood why. By reconstructing themselves they'd left their true natures and passions behind. There was no substance to them.

Mr Sylvester, seeing the range of emotions flitting across Jack's face, felt a tremendous surge of empathy and compassion for his son. Never in the past having demonstrated any signs of tenderness, he placed his hand on Jack's shoulder and patted him fondly. Jack, too lost in thought hardly noticed, but kept asking himself where should he go from here? What next? The answer was unmistakable - he was not going to give up on Mika, he needed her more than ever, and was going to raise heaven and earth to get her back despite all the obstacles. Japan was his next stop.

KENSHŌ   House of Secrets

CHAPTER 54
Reconciliations, meetings and marriage
Wajima, Japan, June 2001

The following week Jack felt totally committed as he set off for the airport and his flight to Tokyo. He owed his father nothing. There was duty, of course, but he was going to choose his own life. Despite all his father had told him about his grandfather's part in the atomic bomb, he felt optimistic he and Mika could build a life together. The main thing was did she still love him? This he must find out. Surely love was stronger than their complicated family histories.

After a fifteen hour flight to Tokyo, Jack decided to stay in the city for a couple of nights to explore and acclimatise himself. He didn't want to arrive at Mika's home exhausted and travel worn; after all there was a confrontation with her grandfather to face. Later that week, taking the bullet train from Tokyo to Kanazawe, he found it relatively easy to get a connection to Wajima. Wajima was teeming with people, all buying fresh fish and vegetables at the morning market. No one spoke English. At last, Jack found a Tourist Office where the assistant spoke perfect English but had no idea of the whereabouts of Takeshi Kato's address, saying, 'Must be out of town. Difficult find. Taxi best.'

After making a lot of enquiries, the taxi driver finally pulled up in front of an isolated minka. Without checking if it was the right place, he dropped Jack off and sped away, leaving him stranded. Receiving no answer at the minka, Jack panicked. Pulling himself together, he reconnoitred the back of the house. Here a miniature Japanese garden had been constructed with a tiny pagoda, a bridge and a waterfall. Captivated, Jack wandered through the garden and found a paved path to a building at the far end. Perhaps this was Takeshi Kato's dōjō, the one Mika had told him about. Sliding the door open cautiously, he was stunned to come face to face with the old man he'd seen in Oxford. To his

KENSHŌ   House of Secrets

consternation, Takeshi was leaping high in the air like a man quarter of his age, whirling a katana sword from right to left. Jack cowered back. What if the old man attacked him? Trying hard to remember the Kendō moves he'd been taught, he reached for one of the wooden staves. Hearing a noise behind him, Takeshi turned sharply and thrust out his sword. In a split second, he realised the tall blonde young man in front of him was not an enemy and dropped the katana. However, he was quick to notice the young man's stubborn chin, unwavering look and defensive posture with the stave. Imagine this gaijin thinking he could fight him - he, Kato Takeshi, with his Samurai ancestry. Jack bowed deeply and deferentially and replaced the stave on the wall.

Once they'd exchanged formal greetings, Takeshi asked, 'You fight? Martial arts maybe?' trying to contain his amusement and disdain.

'I'm learning Kendō,' Jack replied, 'but merely a novice.' He stood and waited, wondering what was to follow. He hoped it wouldn't be a challenge to fight. Despite Takeshi's great age, Jack knew he didn't stand a chance.

Takeshi scowled. How dare this boy have the insolence to follow Mika all the way here, although his indignation was tinged with a grudging respect. Perhaps there was more to this relationship than he'd at first thought, 'Come to house. Will make tea.'

Outside the minka, Takeshi motioned Jack to remove his shoes before entering, then invited him to sit cross-legged on the tatami mat. Nothing was spoken as Takeshi went through the ritual of the tea ceremony. The tea bowl, whisk and tea scoop were cleansed. Once the preparation of the utensils was complete, Takeshi prepared a bowl of thick tea and handed it to his guest. Jack, used to the formality of the tea ceremony, followed the instructions Mika had given him on previous occasions.

KENSHŌ   House of Secrets

Neither men spoke, so Jack decided to take the lead, 'I've come to see Mika, Kato san. We were engaged to be married. I need to hear from her if she no longer wants that.'

Disturbingly and in complete contrast to the calm and gentleness of the tea ceremony, Takeshi reacted with barely controlled violence, 'Mika never marry American. Americans kill wife, parents, make my son and wife, Mika's parents, sick and die.'

Shocked but not deterred, Jack fought back, 'But that's history, Kato san. Mika and I are the future. Surely now our two nations are at peace, we must heal and reconcile.'

'Not right,' Takeshi spat out. 'Not right your people bomb Nagasaki. Nothing left, thousands die, innocent people and children.'

'But Mika and I should be pointing the way forward,' Jack argued and finally realising the discussion was going nowhere, wondered where Mika was. Perhaps she could act as mediator. Desperate, he muttered, 'Where is Mika?' hoping and praying she wasn't far away.

'She visit graves honourable parents. Home soon.'

Neither had anything more to say and sat glaring at one another. The silence was finally broken by the sound of Mika's geta on the path and the opening of the sliding door. As she stood in the doorway, Jack was overawed. There was his beautiful Mika, in her everyday kimono, looking like an exquisite porcelain figurine. But neither he nor Takeshi were prepared for Mika's fierce reaction when she spotted Jack.

Her grave little face lit up and broke into a thousand smiles like exploding firecrackers. She began to laugh and talk at the same time. Rushing towards Jack, she ignored all the formalities due her grandfather and held out both hands, 'Oh Jack, how I long see

KENSHŌ House of Secrets

you. So solly leave like that.' Enormous tears welled up out of her dark almond eyes and she began to sob uncontrollably.

Neither Jack nor Takeshi knew what to do. One minute she'd been delirious with happiness, now she was crying as if her heart would break, 'Jack, I not able to marry. Solly, I love so much.'

Takeshi was stunned. He'd never seen his beloved granddaughter behave like this. She was always so reserved and composed. To his chagrin, she'd actually ignored him as if he didn't exist. This was definitely the influence of the 'yūrei'. They'd come back to lay claim to his granddaughter and force him to let her go. Fleetingly, he remembered the tiny baby he'd found in Nagasaki all those years ago. He'd been so sure the baby was his son, Riki. Perhaps he'd been wrong. What if he'd stolen someone else's baby and now was condemned to pay the price? It was the one secret he must never tell his beloved Mika, the one he must take to his grave. Bowing deeply, he left the room a troubled man, leaving the young lovers to themselves.

'Darling Mika,' Jack said, wiping away her tears, 'I can't live without you whatever your grandfather says.' After she calmed down, he sat and told her about his own grandfather. 'I know, Mika, we must honour our families but they must also respect us and our choices. I can't make up for what my grandfather did. Neither can you, yours. What we can do is build a better life and future for our children. So will you take a chance and marry me?' Delving into his pocket he brought out the diamond and emerald ring, 'Will you accept this now?'

'Yes,' Mika said with defiance, 'must be together always.'

When Takeshi returned he'd come to a decision, hard as it was. Making an immense effort, he said, 'We go to dōjō, you show what learn at Kendō,' looking directly at Jack, who sat holding hands with Mika as she gazed in rapture at the ring on her finger. Realising he was well and truly thwarted, Takeshi added, 'After

KENSHŌ   House of Secrets

we plan wedding.' If this was how it was to be, it must be done properly following the Kato family traditions.

Taken aback, Mika exclaimed, 'Here? Now?'

'Yes,' Takeshi said sternly and brusquely. 'Must be as ancestors want. Sylvester san you sleep in dōjō. I arrange tatami and mattress for you.'

Within days, the wedding was organised as Takeshi demanded - a traditional Shinto ceremony at a local shrine. Mika wore a white wedding kimono and uchikake (white headdress) with a red parasol. Takeshi had made sure Jack was dressed in a traditional black kimono, though it had been hard to find one long enough and broad enough. A large 'S' was embroidered on the back to represent the Sylvester family. Jack had half hoped his father would drop everything and fly to Japan for the ceremony but there'd been no reply to his cable.

On the actual wedding day, they were a tight knit group: Mika, Jack, Takeshi and a Shinto priest. Just as the priest was about to offer up a prayer to the gods, a black limousine drew up and out stepped Mr Sylvester. Jack was dumbstruck. Forgetting the formality of the affair and his former feelings about his father, he ran over and, to Mr Sylvester's astonishment, threw his arms around him, 'I'm so glad you've come. It means everything to us.'

Mr Sylvester, blushing with embarrassment, gestured for Jack to return to the ceremony, bowing deeply first to Takeshi, then Mika and then the priest. After the oaths were taken, the couple shared three nuptial cups of sake (san-san-ku do). Rings were exchanged and final offerings made to the gods.

Takeshi had arranged a celebratory meal at the minka. Whilst Jack and Mika changed into less formal clothes, he welcomed Jack's father reluctantly but formally, 'Honourable Sylvester san, welcome to my house. Pleased to meet honourable father-in-law.'

KENSHŌ   House of Secrets

Mr Sylvester bowed in response, 'The honour is mine, Kato san. I couldn't let you know I was coming. It was a rush. I was eager to meet Mika.'

Once the meal was underway, the outer doors of the minka were slid back. Pervading scents of jasmine, hydrangea and iris flooded the room. Mr Sylvester, struggling to bend his long legs into the correct seiza position for sitting, leant over and spoke softly to his new daughter-in-law, 'Mika, I am glad about yours and Jack's marriage, despite my initial concerns, and want my son to be happy. From now on my home in Boston is your home. You and Jack are young and have your whole future before you. I want to help in any way I can. If you and Jack decide to come back with me to America, I'll convert part of the house so you can have your own space and privacy.'

'Arigatō, Sylvester san,' Mika said humbly. 'I like to come but worry about grandfather.'

'Please call me 'Father'. Don't worry about your grandfather. I'm sure he will make his own decisions and want what's best for you. I can see he and I have a lot in common, but we're not as tough as we seem, and will do anything for the people we love,'(he looked fondly across at his son who was struggling with chopsticks, whilst attempting a serious conversation with Takeshi).

Delighted that Jack and his father were on good terms again, Mika just hoped her new father-in-law was right about her grandfather. Family was everything to her especially since she'd discovered her own ancestry. She desperately wanted to go to America with Jack and continue her studies yet how could she leave Ojii-sama? Later that day, Takeshi, only too conscious of Mika's state of mind, said, 'Granddaughter, your place is with husband and father-in-law in America now. They look after you, my job is done.' Pressing a large envelope into her hand he said, 'I save money since you were baby. Dowry. You make me proud in America.'

KENSHŌ House of Secrets

Mika could not hold back her tears and clung to the old man, though he was as rigid as ever. He unbent enough to say, 'You write. Tell me of America. Maybe visit Boston next year.' Mika could hardly believe her ears. First Nagasaki, then Oxford and now Boston. What had happened to the grandfather who'd never travelled further than Tokyo?

After their conversation, everything happened at speed. Takeshi, not a man to prolong goodbyes, hurried the arrangements along. He knew it would be hard for both he and Mika to part but if this was what the ancestors had ordained, who was he to go against them? The newlyweds were to fly home with Mr Sylvester on a direct flight from Tokyo to Boston. Takeshi refused to see them off or even travel as far as Tokyo but hugged and held his granddaughter as he'd never done before. Mika was crying so hard she thought her heart would burst, 'You will come next year, Ojii-sama, promise.'

Takeshi nodded, 'If ancestors allow my granddaughter.'

On the flight Jack held Mika's hand tightly, wiping away the odd tear that ran down her cheek, saying 'This isn't 'goodbye' for ever, my darling. Your grandfather will visit. We can come back at any time.' Trying to take her mind off her sadness, he added, 'I can't understand how we won them both over.' He squeezed her hand, 'Can you believe it, my father was as inflexible and unyielding as your grandfather at the beginning? What happened to them both?'

Showing the hint of a smile at last, Mika said smugly, 'Ancestors arrange. Yūrei not all bad. Maybe work on our behalf.'

'You and your yūrei,' Jack shuddered mockingly and laughed, just make sure they don't come home with us. Can we please leave them in Japan?'

KENSHŌ   House of Secrets

Adopting an inscrutable expression, Mika whispered in a hushed, otherworldly tone, 'Maybe, who knows, wait and see...'

'Now you really have given me the jitters,' Jack replied, 'but as long as I have you, I'm sure the ancestors and their ghosts will leave us alone.' Heads together, they sat and giggled.

Back in Wajima, Takeshi was thoughtful. He knew his time was running out. The ancestors were watching and waiting for him, just as they had for the Colonel. But Takeshi wasn't ready yet. He was waiting too. Next year in Boston, a Japanese American baby would be born - a boy who would need his great grandfather to teach him the meaning of 'bushidō' - the way of the Samurai.

There was no time to lose; practice needed to begin. The dōjō was calling, he must go. Back in the dōjō, as if in a trance, Takeshi picked up the Cherry Blossom bowl, tracing the liquid gold in the cracks with his finger, and thinking about Sakura. She would have loved to see her great grandson when he was born. But it was no use daydreaming; the purity of the discipline and the ancestors must be obeyed.

That day, his sap was rising, as Takeshi began to move - the katana flying with greater and greater speed and swiftness. Its blade shimmering as it skimmed, slashed and scythed the golden motes of dust floating through the window.

Takeshi felt lighter and lighter, free from guilt at last, jumping higher and higher, exalted and transcendent in the early morning light, at one with the universe.

KENSHŌ House of Secrets

POSTSCRIPT

Kenshō House is empty and abandoned now, a 'For Sale' notice propped against one of its trees. All the occupants have departed for other climes.

Phoebe is married to Geoffrey and together with the children and the dogs, Dot and Dash, reside in Cambridge, Massachusetts. In the summers they retreat to their ranch in Texas, where Tolly fulfils his aspirations to be a cowboy.

Sanshō has retired to his former ashram in Benares, tending to his ancient mentor and guru as they bathe in the Ganges every day. He always remembers the Colonel in his meditations placing offerings to the Buddha for his old friend's redemption.

Julian and Daisy, also married, struggle on with their screaming baby in a miniscule apartment in Oxford. These days Julian is home in time for baby's bath and forbidden to work late as there's so much to do at home. His girth has increased out of all proportion. If asked, he emphatically maintains he's contented despite the loss of Kenshō House, his red Ferrari and of course, his freedom.

Silence has finally descended on Kenshō House giving it the peace and quiet it desires, enabling it to breathe again. No people, children or dogs disturb the calm. The only sounds are on the third floor. Faint echoes of laughter and merriment reverberate in the nursery, whilst the corridors vibrate with the pitter patter of tiny feet running, jumping and hopping. In the background the thump, thump, thump of an ancient one eyed rocking horse, being ridden for dear life, is all-conquering.

ABOUT THE AUTHOR

Rosemary Hamer comes from Aberystwyth, Wales, has travelled extensively and followed three different career paths. She has now retired to the Wirral and concentrates on writing.

'Kenshō…House of Secrets' – is her fourth novel.

Her first novel 'The Christmas House'(2015) was a dramatized version of her mother's early life.

'The Shadow Shaper'(2018) was about twenty year old Eleanor who gets drawn into the murky world of spying during the Cold War.

'Portrait of a Death'(2019) follows the journey of a painting of a mysterious lady as it passes through the decades and hands of four sets of characters from Paris via London ending up in New York.

Printed in Great Britain
by Amazon